ROGUE AGENTS

BOOK FIVE IN THE JUSTIN HALL SERIES

ETHAN JONES

Thank you

for purchasing this novel
from the best-selling Justin Hall series.

To my parents

This work would have not been possible without the great support of my wife and son. I would also like to thank Claude Dancourt, Ty Hutchinson and Kenneth Teicher for their helpful suggestions.

PROLOGUE

Islamabad, Pakistan
April 6, 7:25 p.m.

I f Peng had trusted his gut instinct and not left the safety of his bulletproof Mercedes SUV, the mission might have taken a different turn. But he could not afford to return to Shanghai empty-handed and in shame. His boss—Jaw-long, a high-ranking, powerful leader of the Communist Party of China Political Bureau—considered any failure or mistake on the part of his people a personal embarrassment. And he took draconian measures against all who dishonored his name, coming down upon them with wrath and fury. He lived up to his name, which meant "like a dragon."

So Peng disregarded the clear signs the plan was going sideways. The first sign was that the weapons-grade uranium smugglers had changed the time and location of their meeting at the last moment. They were supposed to meet at six o'clock, but a phone call postponed their meeting to seven thirty. Last-moment changes in their trade meant trouble, usually for the party that had to be subjected to the change of plans.

The original venue had been an upscale neighborhood in the northeast part of the city, near the Diplomatic Enclave—also known as the Red Zone—which housed embassies, foreign missions, and official residences. The security presence surrounding the

Diplomatic Enclave included local uniformed and plainclothes police, private security guards, and military contractors. The new location was a warehouse in a run-down section on the opposite side of the city, known as a den of all sorts of immoral, corrupt, and illegal activities. The six bodyguards Peng was bringing for protection would be insufficient, as his men would be utterly outnumbered and outgunned as they stood in the middle of the smugglers' backyard.

His three-car convoy reached the first checkpoint—two cement barricades joined by barbed-wire coils placed at the mouth of a dark, narrow back alley. Four men in white robes and swinging AK assault rifles flanked their SUVs. Peng ignored the second sign of trouble: the apparent ambush into which the smugglers were dragging them. He stifled the premonition boiling in the pit of his stomach, the hunch that told him it was time to turn around and flee before the beginning of the bullets' hailstorm. He grinned at two bearded guards who shone flashlights in their faces and checked their passports, but not their SUVs. They gave directions to Peng's driver on how to get to the warehouse, then they gestured to the other guards to pull away the barbed-wire coils.

Peng rolled up his window but the putrid smell of raw sewage had already filled the Mercedes. He told his driver, Shan, to slow down as they entered the pothole-ridden alley littered with garbage. A group of men were selling vegetables heaped on two long tables on the other side of the alley, under a dim light bulb hanging on a small stake fastened to a wall. The two-story blockhouses were decrepit, and looked even more seedy and ghostly in the darkness swallowing most of the neighborhood. The area had no streetlights but for the occasional dim glow coming from a window. If it were not for the Mercedes' headlights, they would have had serious trouble finding their way in the pitch-black night.

The back alley grew wider as they made a left turn and came to the warehouse entrance. A large military-looking truck and a small Toyota sedan were parked to the left side, by the gray metal door that was showing signs of rust at the bottom. A white truck and a black Jeep were on the right side.

Two gunmen were waiting for Peng and his crew next to the Jeep. They gestured with their AKs for the drivers to stop by the Toyota, then they called on Peng and his driver alone to come out of the Mercedes.

The third sign, Peng thought. *Divide and conquer.*

He reconsidered his decision to step into the snake pit but at this point it was already too late. Peng had no other choice but to face the smugglers, complete the exchange, and deliver the uranium to his boss the next day. He picked up the radio and told his men that he and Shan were going in to complete the exchange.

Peng sighed and took a deep breath. He ran his hands through his combed-back black hair and, against his better judgment, opened the door and stepped outside.

One of the gunmen—a young man with a three-inch-long beard, tiny gray eyes, and a menacing grin—gestured to Peng and his driver to follow him.

Peng nodded and did as ordered. Shan came after him, carrying a leather briefcase in his left hand.

The second gunman stayed back and kept them in the sight of his AK. A third man appeared from the Jeep and joined the second gunman. The third man had no weapons in his hands, but he was a large, muscular man.

Maybe he doesn't believe he needs one, Peng thought, and suppressed a small smile. He carried a Glock 19 pistol in a hip holster and another one in an ankle holster. Shan was armed with a Beretta pistol in his shoulder holster and another Beretta was concealed in a false bottom inside the briefcase, underneath the stacks of cash. The gunmen had not searched them, believing they themselves had the upper hand because of their assault rifles. Peng grinned. *It's not always about the size of the gun . . .*

The first gunman pushed open the warehouse door. It rolled with a loud metallic screech, and they all walked in with a quick pace. The cement floor was dirty, and Peng felt grains of sand underneath his expensive Italian leather shoes. The warehouse was well lit by powerful halogen lamps hanging from the vaulted ceiling. A white, windowless van was parked against the barren cinderblock wall on the left side, with its rear facing the warehouse door. Three rows of wide shelves—loaded with wooden crates, barrels, and sacks—took up most of the space at the center. On the far end of the warehouse and to the right—about fifty yards away—there was an olive green Land Rover, and the small light inside the Rover's cabin was on. Two silhouettes were visible: two people sitting in the driver's and the front passenger seats.

The first gunman shouted at Peng to stop after he had taken about a dozen steps inside the warehouse. Peng looked around just as the man without any weapons rolled back the warehouse door.

"There's the boss," Shan said in a low voice in Chinese.

Peng did not recognize the clean-shaven face of the man in a white *salwar kameez*—the long shirt and baggy pants commonly worn by men in Pakistan—and a white prayer cap. Two guards were walking two steps behind him, carrying AKs in relaxed low ready position, the muzzles of their rifles pointing down. The man walked with a proud gait, trying to conceal a slight limp in his right foot. He stopped about six feet away from Peng and examined Peng's face with his small black eyes. A moment later, he said, "Welcome to my country and my home." His English had a thick Pakistani accent.

Peng gave him a small nod but kept his face unsmiling. "Where is Wajid?" he asked in a stark tone that conveyed more than curiosity and that demanded an explanation.

"My name is Mehmood," the man replied in a booming voice that matched Peng's tone and filled the entire warehouse. He took a step forward, spread out his arms, and added, "I am in charge now."

Peng said nothing. His eyes focused on Mehmood's guards. They had raised their weapons a few inches, in response to their master's growl. Peng took a deep breath and thought carefully about his next words.

"We have the money," he said in a calm voice as he pointed at Shan, who lifted up his briefcase.

A million dollars was inside the briefcase. The rest of the agreed-upon payment of ten million was in two extra-large duffel bags in the second and the third Mercedes. Peng was not going to bring all the money along before he had seen and confirmed the uranium was in the warehouse.

"And we have the merchandise." Mehmood cocked his head toward the van. His voice had lost some of the earlier thunder.

Peng nodded and walked toward the van.

Mehmood led the way, but he kept a close eye on Peng. Both men distrusted each other. Mehmood's guards had formed somewhat of a circle around Mehmood and Peng. Shan was staying three steps behind Peng.

"Here's a sample of what you requested." Mehmood turned a latch and opened the van's rear doors. "Two pounds of U-235, highly enriched uranium, straight from the Khan research lab."

Peng stared at the silver metallic briefcase that had a large yellow stain on the side. It was about two feet long and one foot wide, with four wheels and a retractable handle. He thought about one of Mehmood's words: sample.

"I didn't come all the way here for a sample," he said slowly but firmly, with a stern headshake. "Wajid promised me fifteen pounds of uranium, not two."

Mehmood's face remained calm. "There were some complications. The nuclear physicists helping us from inside the lab are asking for more money, so they can bribe guards and other facilitators in this trade. There will be a delay, but this should be enough to prove to you our abilities to deliver on our promises."

"Check it out," Peng told Shan.

Shan reached slowly for his left side pocket and pulled out a Geiger counter. It was a small yellow device slightly larger than a smartphone. He walked toward the van and pointed the device in the direction of the suitcase. A crackling sound came from the device. The sound grew louder and the counter's clicking became faster the closer Shan got to the suitcase. He read the numbers on the LCD display of the device and gave everyone a quick nod. "We're still good," he said in English. "Radiation, but in low levels."

Mehmood nodded and gave Peng a triumphant grin.

Shan popped open the suitcase and continued his inspection.

Peng pondered his options. He could complete the exchange and return home with the two pounds, but he doubted Jaw-long would be pleased with that result. Even if he did, Peng would have to come back to Pakistan in a matter of days or weeks, when it would be even hotter and muggier than now. He hated this place, its hot weather that made him sweat constantly, its dirt and sand—and the flies, the flies that were everywhere, attracted by the garbage that was also everywhere. No, he could not go back without the entire shipment. *Maybe he's lying. Maybe he wants all the money and also wants to keep the uranium and sell it to another buyer.* Peng knew there were other players in the black market interested in a shipment of that size, which was sufficient to make a one-kiloton nuclear bomb with the explosive energy of 1,000 tons of TNT. It would be about five times more powerful than the two jets that had brought down the two towers of the World Trade Center.

Shan completed his inspection but did not close the suitcase. He stepped away from the van and returned to his position.

"Where is the rest of the uranium?" Peng asked.

Mehmood's eyes narrowed as he fixed Peng with an angry gaze. "This is all we have. I explained we have had complications—"

Peng cut him off with a swift draw of his Glock. He kept his pistols loaded with a round in the chamber, and he pointed his Glock at Mehmood's head.

"Give me *all* the goods or I'll blow your brains out." Peng spat his words.

Mehmood's guards were caught by surprise. They scrambled to raise and cock their AKs. More gun shuffling came from behind Peng, along with the familiar sounds of hammers cocked and weapons readying to fire. Peng did not blink or turn his head to the sides. Shan should have pulled out his Beretta and had his back. And as long as he held the master of this ragtag group at gunpoint, the guards were not going to shoot without his order.

"Calm down . . . everybody calm down," Mehmood said in a wavering tone. His eyes bounced around as he seemed to assess the situation and make a decision. "No need for guns or shooting in here."

Peng kept his stretched hand steady, holding the pistol about two feet away from Mehmood's head. "I want *all* the uranium," he said slowly, stressing each word as if Mehmood barely understood English. "*All* of it."

Mehmood offered a shrug. "This is the entire package, our shipment. We have nothing else to give but our lives."

It was Peng's turn to make a decision. He kept his eyes glued to Mehmood's face and tried to read the Pakistani. He found no visible clues that the man was lying. But it was not enough.

"We will search the warehouse," Peng said. "Order your men to stand down."

Mehmood shook his head. "You're calling me a liar? You come to my home and you think you can treat me like this, like a piece of garbage?"

Someone slid their feet on the rough cement right behind Peng. Then came a metallic click, not a hammer cocking but a hollow sound, as if an AK steel buttstock was banging against another metallic object, like a pistol or a magazine. Peng's eyes veered off Mehmood's face for a fraction of a second.

It was a fraction of a second too long.

Mehmood threw his hands and body against Peng's right hand holding the pistol. A round went off. It echoed like a cannon in the tense air of the silent warehouse.

The attack caught Peng by surprise. He felt a blow to the left side of his face as Mehmood hit him with a mean right fist. Peng's Glock was still in his hand, but Mehmood's vicious grip had taken hold of his wrist. The Pakistani's fingernails were cutting deep into his skin, as Mehmood was trying to pry the pistol from Peng's hand.

They fought over the Glock for a few moments, pushing and shoving each other. Then Mehmood jammed an elbow into Peng's ribs and Peng struggled for breath. Mehmood was larger and heavier than he. Peng's fingers were still around the pistol, so he pulled the trigger. The bullet struck somewhere in the warehouse's ceiling.

A short rifle burst came from behind them, followed almost instantaneously by two pistol shots. Then three loud thumps like heavy sacks falling to the ground.

Peng assumed a guard and Shan had exchanged fire.

"Shan, Shan," he shouted.

No answer.

There were no more gunshots, but he heard some shuffling of feet very close to him.

The guards won't shoot me as long as we're still fighting.

Mehmood threw another fist, but Peng ducked. He let go of the Glock and slipped his hand away from Mehmood's grasp. He twisted his small body behind Mehmood and hooked his right arm around Mehmood's neck. Peng placed his left hand at the top of Mehmood's neck and put him in a chokehold.

"Stay back, stay back or I'll kill him," Peng shouted at a guard who was just two feet away.

The guard nodded and did not take another step. Peng kept his hold around Mehmood's head, but did not press tight against the man's carotid arteries. He was not trying to cut off the blood flow and incapacitate the man. He just wanted to use Mehmood as a human shield and get his guards to drop their weapons.

Mehmood tried to shake him off. Peng pulled him toward the van, trying to hide behind Mehmood as much as he could, to make himself a smaller target. Two of Mehmood's guards still had their AKs pointed at him. A third guard was sidestepping to Peng's left, looking for the right moment to jump at Peng. And Shan was lying on his stomach with his left arm twisted underneath him and a pool of blood around his head.

"Stay back," Peng shouted.

Mehmood let out a heavy groan and moved his head slightly to the right. His jaws snapped as he tried to bite Peng's forearm. His attempt failed, but he succeeded in relieving some of the pressure. Peng felt his solid grip loosen up. Mehmood raised his shoulders and reached back swiftly with his left hand. He went for Peng's left-hand fingers and began to peel them off his head.

Peng realized Mehmood would slip out of his hold in a matter of seconds. Peng looked around for a weapon, anything he could use before it was too late. His eyes caught a glimpse of the suitcase and the two cylinders inside it. *Yes, that's it.*

He pulled hard with his right arm, tightening the crook of his elbow on Mehmood's throat, who let go of Peng's left hand. Peng used that exact moment to reach for a cylinder.

As he turned slightly, he heard a gunshot and at the same instant he felt a piercing pain in his lower back. The bullet knocked him to his knees. Peng fell against the back of the van, his head slamming on the dirty floor of the van next to the suitcase.

He heard Mehmood's huffing and puffing behind him. Peng raised his eyes slowly, feeling all his strength slowly leaving his body. He saw the cylinders still in the suitcase, just a few inches away from his bleeding face.

"You tried to kill me . . . me . . . you worthless scum." Mehmood's words exploded as he gasped, trying to catch his breath. "Now I'll show you what happens to those who dare to touch me."

Peng took a shallow breath and moved his right hand toward the cylinder. It felt cold against his fingers and heavier than he had thought, considering its size of about eight inches. He winced as he brought up his other hand onto the van's floor and began to unscrew the cylinder's cap.

"I will cut you up and feed you to the dogs," Mehmood howled. "You will beg me to end your miserable life."

Peng winced and ignored the pain shooting up through his body. He grinned as the cap came loose. He twisted it once again. And once more.

He heard heavy footsteps and knew it was time.

"Now you will pay, you son of—"

"No, *you* will," Peng said.

He turned his head and looked at Mehmood's dark, rage-filled eyes. Peng mustered all the strength left in him and threw a handful of the cylinder's contents into Mehmood's face.

"Ah." Mehmood shrieked in pain. "Help, help me!"

He lifted his hands to his eyes as he tried to scrub away the burning radioactive powder.

"Now *you* will have a painful death," Peng said in a low voice but loud enough for Mehmood to hear his words.

One of the guards raised his AK.

Peng looked straight at the gun's barrel pointed at him.

A moment later, the guard fired a long barrage. Peng felt a bullet strike him in the chest. Then another bullet hit lower, closer to the right side. When the third bullet struck against his head, Peng was already dead.

Beijing, China
April 6, 11:45 p.m.

Jaw-long stared at the two BlackBerry smartphones on his office desk, then at the fixed-line phone handset a few inches further, next to his laptop and a cold, half-drunk cup of tea with a saucer. Over an hour had passed since the time when the exchange should have taken place, but Peng had not checked in. Jaw-long had received no news. No news meant bad news, which in Jaw-long's situation meant terrible news.

His first attempt to obtain the uranium from a Chinese facility had failed, and his men were almost caught in the act. If Plan B had now gone south, he would be forced to move on to Plan C. It was the option he disliked the most and which he hoped he would not have to use, even as a last resort. Plan C was dangerous and, if it backfired, Jaw-long might as well have signed his own death sentence. But he was in bed with a Saudi prince known for his ruthless ambition throughout the Middle East. Jaw-long had found himself between a rock and a hard place.

He swiveled in his chair and threw a quick glance at the photo hanging on the wall right above his head. It was a portrait of the Communist Party General Secretary and the President of China, Zhao Zheng. Once a mentor and a dear friend, Zheng had locked horns with Jaw-long over the economic direction of the new comprehensive reform in the country over the last few months. Recently, the bitter conflict had escalated into open attacks and character assassination, and Zheng had outmaneuvered Jaw-long at the last National Congress of the Communist Party, gathering sufficient support to be elected the party's General Secretary. Still reeling from the crushing defeat, Jaw-long was forced to seek unconventional methods of regrouping, reinforcing, and regaining the lost support. A tried and true way of winning over the opposition was to shower them with lavish gifts, entice them with promises of position and power, and reward them with cold hard cash. American dollars in offshore bank accounts, beyond the authority of the all-controlling Communist state. Millions of dollars. Millions of dollars that were little more than spare change to a billionaire Saudi prince.

Jaw-long let out a deep, long sigh and thought of his family. If his deal with the Saudis was discovered, he would be killed or thrown in jail. Such fates Zheng had forced upon other opposition members, accusing them of bribery and abuse of power. Jaw-long's son and wife would also be dragged in the mud over the charges, accused as collaborators and stripped of all privileges and powers that came with Jaw-long's important position. Even in the best-case scenario his son would never be allowed to complete his university studies or find a decent job. His wife would have to quit teaching and move back to her family's remote village at the foot of the rugged Qilian Mountains. No, Jaw-long had to make the deal with the Saudis work. He would have to set into motion the dreaded Plan C and go with the Canadian connection.

The sharp ring of one of the BlackBerry smartphones broke his train of thought. Jaw-long reached for the closest handset, before realizing it was the other one that was ringing. He frowned and carefully picked it up, as if it was going to burn his hand. He looked at the ID, shook his head, and drew back his lips. It was not Peng, but Enlai, the man Jaw-long had sent to investigate Peng's disappearance and his silence. Enlai was already in Islamabad, serving as a shadow operative on behalf of Jaw-long, keeping an eye from a distance on Peng's operation. Jaw-long had been trained in the ways of the secret intelligence and had served in the Ministry of State Security—China's foreign intelligence agency—climbing to the top position in the Bureau of Counterintelligence, also known as the Sixth Bureau. Enlai had been one of his top operatives before he crossed over to become a private security contractor. Redundancy was entrenched deep into Jaw-long's survival system.

"This is Jaw-long," he said in a cold voice. "Tell me you've found Peng?"

A moment of silence, then Enlai said, "Negative, boss. Peng has gone off the grid."

Jaw-long cursed under his breath. "Report," he barked into the phone.

"The location of Peng's meeting was in a hostile area, almost impenetrable. About twenty gunmen were guarding the warehouse. Still, I was able to follow Peng's convoy. He entered the warehouse along with one of his men, leaving the other bodyguards outside. Shortly after that, gunfire erupted from inside the warehouse. Then the gunmen opened up on Peng's bodyguards, killing everyone," Enlai said in a cold, detached voice.

Jaw-long cursed again. He slammed his fist on the desk and kicked his feet furiously underneath it. The wastebasket flew across the room and the desk rattled as his feet smacked against its underside. He did not care about the death of his men. They were expendable and easily replaceable. The loss of the ten million dollars was a heavy blow. His situation was going from worse to unsalvageable.

Jaw-long tried to take a deep breath but he wheezed, his lungs seizing up. He coughed to clear his throat and paused to clear his mind. Finally he said, "Go on."

"Two cars rushed from the warehouse to a local medical center. Before I proceeded to follow them, I saw a few bodies lying on the floor of the warehouse but I cannot confirm if one of them was Peng's.

"At the medical center, one of the nurses told me a local man was admitted because of radioactive exposure. The doctors at the medical center are getting some help from experts from a hospital with decontamination procedures and the further treatment of this patient."

Jaw-long frowned and felt the burning pain of a severe headache. *Oh, this stress is going to kill me before Zheng or the Saudi prince lay their hands on me.*

Enlai said, "Soon this will be all over the national media . . ."

"And then the international hyenas will dispatch their high-paid reporters." Jaw-long's voice dripped with scorn. *And soon the Saudis will hear all about it. What a mess.*

"What are my orders?" Enlai asked.

His voice had a rushed feel, and it echoed Jaw-long's sentiment. They needed to do something very soon, before the Pakistani authorities discovered the radiation source and connected the dots.

"Erase all traces of our involvement," Jaw-long said in a hurried voice. He pushed back his chair and jumped up to his feet. "Get rid of the dead bodies. Pay off and use any methods to cut off any ties of those men to us, to me. And find Peng."

"Understood."

"I want updates every hour."

"Yes. Anything else?"

"No."

Jaw-long ended the call and clutched his fingers around the smartphone. He wanted to throw it against the wall or perhaps aim it at Zheng's photo and knock the smile off his pale face. But that would not resolve anything, and he would still be sinking deep in his quagmire. He needed to make good on his promise to the Saudis and deliver the shipment of uranium. Peng's disappearance had made such delivery impossible. Jaw-long could ask for and most likely would receive more time, but he still needed to obtain the weapons-grade uranium. And without any money and running out of time, his only option was Plan C.

He hovered over his desk for a few moments, then reached for the other smartphone. He held it in his hand but hesitated to dial the number. He put it down, cursed under his breath, and paced in his office. He felt like a lion confined to a small cage, the wrath and the rage sizzling in his soul. Finally, he scooped up the smartphone with a swift gesture and tapped the keys before he could change his mind.

A woman's voice on the other end of the call answered in a soft, sexy purr. "Hello, Jaw-long. How can I be of assistance?"

She put the emphasis on the last word, and Jaw-long felt a tingle run down his spine. He swallowed hard, then stumbled over his words. "The plan . . . we have to go with . . . Plan C. Engage the Canadians."

CHAPTER ONE

Al-Sukkari District, Southeast Aleppo, Syria
April 23, 10:15 a.m.

Justin Hall could hardly believe the gruesome spectacle unfolding in front of his eyes. Three blindfolded men in desert camouflage fatigues were being dragged through the reddish dirt road like lambs to the slaughter. The cheering crowd of armed men, a few women, and many children was welcoming the beheadings.

Justin had spent the last week in northern Syria with his Canadian Intelligence Service partners Carrie O'Connor and Nathan Smyth and three local operatives. Their initial mission was to intercept a large shipment of surface-to-air missiles intended for rebels of the Islamic Freedom Brigade fighting against the army troops loyal to the new transitional government. Peace talks about amnesty for the remaining extremist rebels had broken off two months ago and fierce fighting had erupted all over the country.

A powerful Turkish arms dealer had been funneling SA-7s and S-24s—powerful Russian-made missiles looted from Libya's stockpile after the former Libyan leader Moammar Gaddafi was overthrown in a violent uprising—to radical rebel groups similar in ideology to al-Qaeda, operating mostly in and around Aleppo. The city had been the scene of some of the most brutal battles over the last few days, and the missiles had been one of the major factors in turning the tide in favor of the rebels.

With the government preparing a large offensive, a new shipment of missiles could mean its humiliating defeat, which would throw the volatile country and the unstable region deeper into chaos. The jihadist fighters among the extremist rebels came from Afghanistan, Chechnya, and Yemen, and their ultimate goal was a Sharia state, based upon Islamic teachings, not just a new secular democratic government. The scenario of such rebels coming to power and exporting their influence beyond Syria's borders was to be avoided at all costs.

So the CIS's agents' original mission was redrawn to include the gathering of intelligence on one of the rebel group's strongholds and some of its most powerful leaders, while another team was dispatched to intercept and destroy the missiles. After confirming the current position of the rebel leaders and the absence of any potential for collateral damage, the agents were to call in a drone strike. A barrage of Hellfire missiles fired from a MQ-9 Reaper drone was going to take care of the rest.

And here they were, in southeast Aleppo, hot on the trail of two masterminds of the Islamic Freedom Brigade. Justin and Carrie had posed as foreign journalists from Egypt and Ireland, covering recent developments in the country. Justin spoke Arabic like a native and his Mediterranean complexion—dark olive skin, wavy raven hair, big black eyes, and a large, thick nose he had inherited from his Italian mother—allowed him to fit easily among the local population. He dressed in a kaftan, a long brown robe, and wore a white keffiyeh, a headdress, to protect his head and his neck from the scorching Syrian sun. Carrie's black burka hid her white face, her shoulder-length auburn hair, and a SIG P228 pistol. Nathan and the local operatives pretended to be the journalists' driver and security detail.

Earlier that morning, Justin had spotted one of their targets, Omar Ghani, an Afghani in his fifties who had fought with the Taliban insurgency against American forces during the Afghanistan War. Ghani was leaving a safe house and was about to get into a white Jeep, when a group of about twenty armed men arrived in a five-car convoy. They spread out around Ghani and his guards and brought three blindfolded men before him. A short exchange took place between Ghani and two men who seemed to be the leaders of the ragtag militia. Then joyful shouting broke out. Some gunmen fired their AKs in the air in celebration. Soon after, the entire neighborhood poured out onto the streets and headed toward a square with a perimeter of about four hundred yards, surrounded by houses and a small mosque—following Ghani and the gunmen who were dragging their captives—to enjoy the barbaric acts of beheadings.

Justin, Nathan, and one of the local agents stayed atop a low wall, near the back of the crowd, which was moving back and forth like a stormy sea. Some men were shouting slurs at the three blindfolded captives who had been forced down to their knees in front of the crowd. About four steps behind the captives, six gunmen were lined up, proudly displaying their AKs and bandoliers hanging across their chests.

Ghani and one of his men—a trusted guard who was always by his side—stepped forward, followed by one of the militia's leaders. The crowd roared with thundering shouts, mostly thanking Allah for this day of victory. Ghani raised his hands, but the cries continued for a few seconds, until the crowd settled for muted whispers.

Ghani gave a short, emotional speech, full of religious tones. He explained to the crowd why they fought the government, and glorified fellow fighters who had become martyrs for their cause. Then he pointed at the captives and identified them as members of a rival fighting faction, who had been accused of massacring women and children and collaborating with the government. Ghani said they had been tried and found guilty in a religious court. He concluded that now the time had come for them to die for their crimes.

The crowd erupted in another wave of jeers and shouts.

Justin looked to his right. His eyes found Carrie, who stood about twenty steps away, at the other side of the crowd. The other two local operatives were flanking her.

"It's really happening," he said in a low voice into his throat mike covered by his headdress.

"Yes, what a disgrace," Carrie replied into her mike and turned her head in his direction.

Her voice came clearly through his earpiece. "At least we've confirmed Ghani's location."

"Yes, it's the only good thing about this horror show. I've seen enough. Let's keep an eye on Ghani from a distance."

Justin peered as a tall, well-built man came from the left side and stood right behind the captives. He was dressed in a black robe, and a red-and-white checkered headdress was wrapped around his face. Only his eyes were visible. He held a long machete in his left hand and a curved-bladed sword in his right hand. The executioner.

"Wait," Justin said. "His eyes."

"I don't have the stomach for this, Justin," Carrie said in a stern voice.

"Neither do I, but I think . . . he might be our man."

"Who? Our other target, al-Nouaymi?"

"Yes."

Justin swung his camera from his shoulder, rearranged his rucksack on his back, and stepped forward.

"Where are you going?" Nathan asked via his throat mike. His voice was full of concern.

"To confirm his identity. Stay back."

Justin elbowed his way through the bellowing crowd, then stopped when he was near the front. He raised his camera and began to take photos. The scorching sun was behind Justin and was lighting up the surreal scene quite well.

The executioner's eyes were dark but calm. He gazed at the faces in the crowd, but his look was distant and devoid of emotion.

Justin slid back behind a large man to his right. No one in this area was supposed to know his identity, but he was not absolutely sure. And he did not want to be singled out by the executioner or one of the rebels' leaders. He needed to keep a low profile.

The executioner turned toward the first blindfolded captive. The man was on his knees with his hands tied behind his back. He was completely resigned to his doomed fate. The executioner lined up his sword's blade with the captive's neck, practicing his macabre move.

The captive must have felt the razor-sharp metal resting against his bloodied skin, because he shook his head and shrugged, trying to move away from the instrument of death. He muttered a few inaudible words, which quickly turned to shouts for mercy.

The executioner remained stone-faced, untouched by the pleas. He raised his sword and hacked down in a swift, powerful slash.

Time slowed down as the crowd turned silent.

The head rolled on the sandy ground. Blood gushed out of it and from the butchered body.

The executioner dropped his machete to the ground, picked up the head by its hair, and lifted it up. Blood spurted out of the head, spraying the executioner's face and chest. He showed the head to the howling mob, let out a loud shout of triumph, and dumped it next to the body.

Justin had seen people die: dear friends shot and killed by enemies, and many enemy combatants he had sent to the afterlife.

But it had never been like this. The beheading. The calmness of the executioner. The approval of the bloodthirsty mob. There was a true devaluation of human life in such a grisly public display.

The executioner waved his sword in the air while he shouted praises to Allah. The crowd cheered him on. His eyes had lost their initial calmness. They were now full of rage and hate, dripping with the lust for more blood and revenge.

He took a few slow, heavy steps toward the second captive. The executioner grabbed the captive brutally by the scruff of his neck and began to drag him forward. The captive let out a short, high-pitched squeak, which made Justin's flesh creep. The captive was a young boy, tall and muscular, but still no more than eleven or twelve years old.

Justin took a step forward. His hand instinctively hovered over the SIG P228 pistol in his waistband holster. His brown kaftan hid it well at his right thigh.

"Nathan, diversion," Justin whispered into his mike.

"What? Justin, you're going in?" Nathan replied in an incredulous tone.

"This is suicide, Justin." Carrie's voice rang in his ear. "Don't do it."

"Can't let this happen in front of my eyes," Justin said, taking another step forward.

He sidestepped around a woman holding a toddler in her arms, who was playing with a toy gun. Justin was now right behind two old men, in the third line, at the right-side edge of the crowd. He put his camera away in his rucksack without making too much noise or drawing too much attention.

The executioner lined up his sword with the boy's neck amid jubilant shouts from the ecstatic people. The boy's small body, kneeling underneath the blood-dripping blade, began to tremble as he sensed he was at death's door.

"Now, Nathan," Justin said, a bit louder than he intended.

His voice went unheard by the people around him, but Justin was sure Nathan had heard his order.

A long moment followed, then the executioner raised his sword.

A loud explosion stopped his arm in midair.

The blast came from one of the trucks at the right side of the square, near the mosque. It was about forty feet behind the line of the gunmen surrounding Ghani. Shrapnel from the smoldering truck rained over the gunmen, who turned their attention in that direction. Nathan had opted to fire a rocket-propelled grenade as a distraction.

Before they had a chance to rush toward the truck or fire their weapons, a long barrage of gunfire erupted from the left side. Justin recognized the rattle of the Steyr AUG assault rifle. One of his men—most likely Nizar, who was always fast on the trigger.

The stampeding crowd had already broken into small groups, and people were scampering in all directions. Two gunmen covered Ghani and began to withdraw toward their vehicles by the burning truck. The rest turned their weapons toward the source of the gunshots.

Justin moved out of the way of a couple of young men and pulled his pistol. He fired a quick round that hit the executioner in the head. He was dead before he hit the ground, next to the headless captive.

The gunmen were caught by surprise. One of them raised his AK, but Justin planted a bullet in the man's chest, then shot a second gunman who pointed a rifle at him. As the gunman fell to his death, his fingers twitched and squeezed the AK's trigger, sending a volley of bullets through the crowd.

Justin rolled on the ground, hiding behind the bodies of two men who had just been cut down by the dead man's barrage. He fired two more rounds, which hit another gunman in his chest and head.

The Steyr rumbled again, followed by the familiar staccato of AKs. Bullets kicked sand near his arms and struck the dead bodies. Their blood sprayed Justin's face, and he cocked his head to his right, away from the spatter.

A short pause followed and Justin seized the moment. He peeked over one of the bodies and fired a hurried shot at a gunman reloading his AK. Then Justin's eyes took in the entire square.

The crowd had all but vanished. The bodies of five dead gunmen were strewn about on the ground. A sixth wounded gunman let out a groan and tried to reach for a pistol next to his right hand. Justin fired a round and the gunman's hand lay still.

"Left side's clear," Justin said in his throat mike.

"Right side too." Carrie's voice came in his earpiece.

Justin heard distant gunfire and the rattle of car engines. A white Jeep disappeared in a cloud of dust, followed by another black truck.

"Nathan, don't let them go," Justin said.

"Got it, chief," Nathan replied. "Khaled and I are on their heels."

"Hareeb, cover us," Justin ordered one of his local operatives. "Carrie, let's mop up the place."

"I have your back, man," Hareeb said in a low voice with a thick accent.

Justin got to his feet and stepped cautiously around the bodies. He picked up an AK from one of the dead gunmen, cocked it, and fired off a round in the air. The gun worked well, and the previous owner had duct-taped two extra clips to the one latched to the rifle. This made it easier and faster to change the clips, by just pulling and flipping the magazines joined together.

The two captives were lying on the ground, tied up, but they were still breathing. Justin sidestepped the pools of blood that had caked the ground and knelt next to the boy. He whimpered like a frightened puppy.

"It's all right," Justin whispered in his ear in Arabic in a soft voice. "They're all dead. I will remove your blindfold and untie your hands now. Nod if you understand."

The boy's body went limp for a moment, then his bruised, bloodied head moved ever so slightly. "I understand you," he said in a low voice. "Thank you."

"You're welcome."

Justin lifted the blindfold and used the executioner's machete to cut the ropes tying the boy's hands. Then he helped the boy to his feet.

A long barrage came from Carrie's position, about ten yards to Justin's left. Two gunmen fell from atop a roof on the other side of the square.

"We have to go," Justin said and began to usher the boy away, toward Carrie. "I'll untie the other man."

The boy remained silent. His eyes had found the body of the beheaded captive. The boy fell to his knees and let out a sharp shriek as he picked up the head. Tears began to flow down the boy's face and he began to shake, while his hollering grew louder.

Justin stood silent. He had no words to comfort the boy for his loss.

The boy wiped his eyes with the backs of his hands and got to his feet. He marched toward the executioner and picked up the sword that had fallen on the ground. The boy raised the sword and lurched forward at the executioner. He began to hack at the dead body, slashing and ripping through it. Then he moved on to the other dead gunmen, swinging his blood-dripping sword with his small hands.

"That's enough," Justin shouted at him. "They're already dead, and nothing will bring back your father."

Rapid gunfire came from the left and the right. A couple of bullets whizzed past Justin's head and he dropped to the ground.

Hareeb's Steyr assault rifle cracked in a long, loud volley and the other gunfire ceased.

"Go, go, go," Justin said to the boy and pointed at Carrie, who had taken position next to the wall of a house further away to his left, about fifty yards away.

The boy listened this time. He grabbed one of the AKs on the ground and ran toward Carrie while keeping his head low. He made it to the wall and stood next to Carrie, with his gun ready for fire.

Justin moved to the next captive, removed his blindfold, and untied him. A couple of shots came from the right, but they were off target, kicking up dirt yards away from Justin. Hareeb and Nizar— who was covering Carrie's advance—fired short, calculated two- and three-round bursts against the shooters in that direction.

"Can you walk?" Justin asked the freed man, who was thin, with scruffy hair and a small beard. He looked weak and his left arm was dangling from his shoulder like a broken branch from a tree.

"Yes, yes, I can . . . walk." The man got to his knees with a wince and a sigh, then looked around. "Which way are we going?"

"This way." Justin pointed to the right, behind them. "We get to the house, then slide along to those vehicles." He moved his hand to indicate the objective, two gray trucks and a blue Jeep.

"All right," the man said.

Justin took a moment to lift the red-and-white checkered headdress of the dead executioner's face. He was right. It was their target, Mohammed al-Nouaymi.

"Follow me," Justin said.

He broke into a rush, keeping his head low but his eyes wide open, taking in every detail of the scene in front of him. A gunman appeared out of a second-story window and fired an AK at them. Bullets hit in front of Justin's feet, and he dove into the ground and rolled to his left, out of the volley.

The man Justin had freed was one second too late to move out of the barrage. Bullets caught him in the chest and legs. He fell face first on the ground and lay there motionless.

Justin tried to figure out if the man was still alive, but more bullets followed, boring holes in the sand all around him. Two rounds exploded very close to his feet, but he was able to crawl his way to the nearest house, and fell behind a corner.

A slug chipped away concrete chunks from the wall, but Justin was out of immediate danger, at least from the gunfire pouring forth from that direction. He looked at Carrie across the square.

"You okay?" Justin heard her voice in his earpiece.

"Yeah, but we lost the man I just released."

"Sorry, Justin."

He nodded. "Advancing to the vehicles to pursue Ghani."

"Roger that," said Carrie.

"Hareeb? Nizar?" Justin said.

Both men confirmed they had received the order loud and clear.

Justin slithered near the wall, paying particular attention to the windows, the doors, and the roofs of the houses. The entire neighborhood was hostile, and by now the rebels and their supporters in the area would have recovered from the initial shock of the ambush. Justin expected a counterattack from pretty much anyone who was old enough to point and shoot a weapon. The volatile situation pressed the urgency of their escape from the hot zone.

He came to a brown metal gate and peered through it. There was no one in the backyard. Justin quickened his pace, lowering his head as he came to a couple of windows. He listened for noises coming from the other side of the wall. Then an outburst of gunfire rang out from the door of the adjacent house.

Justin threw his body against the wall. Thankfully the gunman was a poor marksman, and his volley raised sand four feet away from Justin. He fired back and dropped the gunman with a double tap to his chest.

Justin secured another position away from the windows and near the door of the house, just underneath the place from which the gunman had taken his shots. His entire attention was focused upwards, expecting more gunmen to appear on the rooftop.

A quick burst came from above, but it was not directed at him. Justin stole a peek, but did not see the shooters. He threw his gaze to the other side of the square, but his eyes did not find Carrie. Hareeb was on his feet between two houses, firing his rifle toward the house behind Justin.

"Carrie, where are you?" Justin said in his throat mike.

"Behind the white sedan, at your two o'clock," she replied. "I'm okay."

"Good," Justin said.

He looked at the white car—a battered model that looked like a Nissan—then his eyes returned to Hareeb's position. The man was gone, and Justin's gaze caught a shooter on the roof of the house. He was holding a large weapon on his shoulders, a rocket-propelled grenade launcher, pointed at Justin.

Before Justin even had the time to think, the shooter fired his RPG. Justin dove to the ground, his only option. A second later, the screeching warhead cut through the air but there was no explosion behind him—or on any side, for that matter.

He looked up and saw a thick cloud of gray smoke over the position of the RPG shooter. *It must have misfired,* Justin thought, and let out a sigh of relief. Syrian rebels sometimes turned to homemade bombs to make up for a shortage in heavy weapons.

A moment later, an explosion came from his right. The stray RPG warhead had hit a house or another building. Justin broke into a fast sprint, taking advantage of a break in the gunfire. He covered about fifty yards before bullets stitched up the sand to his left, a couple of feet away from him.

Justin fired toward the gunmen who were shooting from a first-story window straight ahead. He emptied his entire magazine, then flipped the clip with a swift move and latched it back to his AK. He fired a few more rounds into the window, then resumed his dash toward the vehicles.

Carrie had already climbed aboard the blue Jeep. Hareeb was by the Jeep's rear wheels, laying a heavy curtain of suppressive fire to help Justin's advance. On the other side of the Jeep, Nizar was firing off his Steyr in the other direction, clearing up a path for them. Next to him, the boy Justin had saved from execution was also squeezing round after round from his AK, which looked way too big for his small hands.

Justin redoubled his efforts and rushed through the last few yards. He got to the Jeep and climbed in through the front passenger door.

"Let's get out of here," Carrie said and revved the engine.

Hareeb fired a few more rounds, then slid into the Jeep as a couple of bullets thudded against the back door. Nizar blasted a parting shot, then he got inside one of the gray trucks. The boy followed closely behind him.

"Everyone's okay?" Justin asked as Carrie hit the gas.

"I'm good," Hareeb replied.

The Jeep jerked forward and slid on the sand. Carrie turned the steering wheel and they rounded a sharp curve, barely missing the wall of a house to their right.

"We're doing good," Nizar's strong voice boomed over the airwaves.

"And the boy?" asked Justin.

A moment of pause, then Nizar said, "He's good too. Not wounded—well, other than what we all saw earlier."

Justin nodded and was glad the boy had been blindfolded during the execution of his father. It had spared him at least some of the horrors, but Justin was sure those horrors were going to haunt the boy for the rest of his life.

Justin said into his mike. "Nathan, come in."

There was some static, then Nathan's distant voice came in with interruptions. "Justin . . . we're . . . next . . . east from the square."

"Nathan, repeat your last," Justin said. "What's your position?"

Loud static was the only reply.

"Nathan, come in. Where are you?"

No answer, just the sharp static tone stabbing Justin's ear. Then complete silence.

"They have turned east, east," Justin said to Carrie.

"Got it," she replied and turned the steering wheel as a back alley came into her view up ahead.

The Jeep skidded on the sand and almost hit the corner of one of the houses. Carrie eased up on the gas pedal, hit the brakes, and regained control of the vehicle. She straightened the wheels and the Jeep picked up speed as they drove into the narrow alley. Nizar's gray truck followed about twenty yards behind them.

Gunshots rang from behind and a few bullets clanged against the back of the Jeep. One shattered the back window glass.

"Do something about it," Justin said in an edgy tone.

Hareeb cleared the remaining pieces from the window with the barrel of his Steyr assault rifle, then began to fire at will. He let off a long barrage, then switched to two-round bursts, to save his ammunition.

Two gunmen appeared atop the roof of one of the houses in the distance. The first gunman opened up with a burst of automatic fire. The rifle bounced in his hands and no bullets hit the Jeep.

The second gunman raised his RPG over the roof's parapet and pointed it in their direction.

Justin leaned out the window and began to fire his AK. His bullets struck the second gunman, but not before he fired off his RPG. The projectile ripped through the sky and flew over the left side of the Jeep, missing the hood by a few feet. It smashed into the wall behind, sprayed the Jeep with shrapnel and debris, and lifted a thin curtain of dust.

Hareeb moaned, then cursed the shooter. Some shrapnel had torn through his arms and he was bleeding from the right side of his face.

"Hareeb, can you see?" Justin asked.

Hareeb let out an annoyed grunt. "Yes, I'm good. Scratches. But I can't use the rifle."

"Let us take care of it," Nizar said from the second vehicle behind them.

"Take this." Justin tossed Hareeb a small first aid kit he had fished out of his rucksack by his feet.

Carrie hit the gas and the Jeep flew over dips and holes on the dusty road. Rapid, loud gunshots rang out from all directions. Two RPGs erupted up ahead, but too far away to cause any damage to the truck.

Justin aimed at three gunmen shooting from the rooftops of the next two houses, and laid a heavy barrage. One of the gunmen fell over the edge and came crashing down on the middle of the road. Carrie had no time to brake or swerve so she just drove over the gunman's body.

Justin reloaded his AK with the last clip. "I'm almost out," he said and began to fire two-round bursts.

"Here you go." Hareeb passed his Steyr to Justin. "The mag's full."

Carrie eased up on the brakes and the Jeep rounded another corner. The road grew wider and the houses were further apart.

They were now almost out of the rebels' neighborhood but still not out of danger.

"Trucks up ahead," Carrie said.

Justin looked in that direction just as a powerful explosion tore through the two-story house to their left, about fifty yards in front of the Jeep. Another blast razed to the ground the entire house across the road.

"Mortar fire," Justin said. "The jerks want to kill us even if they blow up the whole area."

He shot the last of his AK rounds, then switched to the Steyr. He fired a quick burst at two men who appeared to his right, but not before they sprayed the Jeep with their bullets. A couple of rounds struck the door. Another one skipped across the hood, and two others pierced holes in the windshield.

Carrie swore and flinched. A couple of glass fragments hit her face.

Justin squeezed his trigger. The gunmen fell backwards, their bodies hit by several bullets.

Two mortar rounds exploded in the distance behind them.

"How're they doing?" Justin asked without looking back as he reloaded his Steyr.

Hareeb took a long moment to reply. Justin turned his head. The gray truck appeared through a cloud of dust and smoke.

"They're still behind us," said Hareeb.

"And you? How are you doing?" asked Carrie.

"Eh, what will happen to me? They can't kill me."

A couple of rounds slammed the back of the Jeep as if to prove him wrong.

Carrie pressed harder on the gas, as the road ahead of them had less debris and potholes. They were now about two hundred yards from a cluster of vehicles parked to the side of the road, near a large three-story house. Half of the house was destroyed and the whitewashed walls of the other half were covered in black graffiti with anti-government slurs.

An RPG whooshed to the left side of the Jeep, smashing into a house wall a few yards away. Cinderblocks and other debris rolled onto the road. Carrie hit the brakes, then turned the steering wheel. She slowed even further, and Justin noticed Nathan and Khaled lying behind a couple of light machine guns set up among the vehicles.

Carrie parked their Jeep on the far end near a bullet-ridden black truck. The bodies of three gunmen were strewn about on the ground around it. Another white Jeep was further away, turned on its right side.

"How is everyone?" Justin asked Nathan and Khaled.

"We're okay. Flesh wounds and bruises. Nothing a little R and R will not fix," Nathan replied.

"What *he* said." Khaled flashed Justin his big, bright teeth.

"Ghani's back there in the Jeep," said Nathan. "Got a bullet in his head and two in his chest."

Justin frowned.

"There was no other way, man." Nathan noticed the frown even though he was mostly gazing through the iron sight of his RPK machine gun. "We wanted him alive, but they fought back."

Nizar pulled up his truck next to the Jeep, a thin cloud of dust trailing behind him.

"Ready?" Khaled asked Nathan.

"Give them a second," Nathan replied.

A truck appeared through the cloud and a man fired his rifle from the front passenger window.

Nathan and Khaled began to thunder their machine guns, their volleys aimed at the moving target. Their rounds began to riddle the hood and the windshield of the truck. A moment later, the driver— by now probably dead or gravely wounded—lost control of the truck, veered off the road, and crashed into the metal gate of a house. Nathan kept firing at the truck, while Khaled waited to see if more targets were going to appear in his sights.

Nathan eased his finger on the machine gun trigger. A tense silence reigned for a few moments, then a mortar shell exploded up ahead right in the middle of the road, perhaps fifty yards away from them.

"Their mortar fire's getting more accurate," Nathan said.

"It's time to say goodbye to Aleppo and Syria," Justin said.

Nathan and Khaled picked up their machine guns and put them in the back of their truck, a rusty, bullet-ridden Nissan.

Justin walked over to Nizar, who was having a hard time controlling the boy. "What's the matter?" Justin asked.

"He wants to go back and avenge his father."

"Yes, they all must die, those cowards, die like dogs," the boy cried in a high-pitched voice.

His small hand held up his AK and he gestured toward the neighborhood.

Justin crouched to be at eye level with the boy, whose eyes were dark with anger. "What's your name?" he asked the boy.

"Ayoub," the boy replied in a quick voice. "What are we waiting for? We should go back and fight. Kill them all like lambs."

"We will fight them another day. Another time, when we have more people, more guns, when you and others like—"

Ayoub tried to run back but Justin grabbed him. "No, no, you can't."

"But I . . . my father . . . I should."

Justin held Ayoub against his chest in a tight embrace. "You will avenge your father and everyone you've lost. It's only the right thing to do."

Ayoub nodded and began to cry silently. Justin felt the boy's warm tears and held Ayoub even tighter.

34

Two mortar rounds landed very near, splitting the air with their thunderous blasts.

"We have to go, right now," he whispered to Ayoub.

"Where are we going?" Ayoub asked as he followed Justin to the blue Jeep.

"Away. Far from here. Somewhere safe," Justin replied.

He climbed into the front passenger seat as another mortar shell exploded about a hundred yards ahead among the houses, lifting a plume of gray dust. Ayoub sat next to Hareeb, who gave the boy a warm smile.

Carrie stepped slowly on the gas and began to head their three-vehicle convoy. Nizar followed behind in his gray truck, and Nathan and Khaled brought up the rear.

"Down near the highway, then up north?" Carrie asked.

Justin nodded. "Let's pass Sheikh Saeed District, then make our way through the outskirts."

"Got it," Carrie said.

Justin nodded. He took a deep breath, then heaved a sigh of relief. His hand still held the Steyr assault rifle. He knew they would not be safe until they had crossed the border with Turkey, about thirty miles north. Most of the area was controlled by the government, with the occasional pockets of resistance in rebels' hands. He laid his head back against the seat's headrest, closed his eyes for a moment, and offered a silent prayer for safety of travel and victory in their next battle.

CHAPTER TWO

Gatineau, Canada
April 24, 10:35 p.m.

James McClain drove his red Mercedes-Benz 450SL hard and fast through Boulevard de Lucerne. It was a cool evening, with the temperature hovering around fifty degrees, and he had raised up the hardtop. The corner of his eye scanned the edge of the grove bordering the Ottawa River for any deer or other animals about to scurry across the street. The roadster glided on the wet asphalt while the engine roared through the quiet night.

He was the original owner of the Mercedes, which he had bought when he was stationed in West Berlin during the long, treacherous years of the Cold War. He was a field agent, just fresh off The Plant—the Canadian Intelligence Service training facility. He had discovered his love for German cars and German women and brought back home a unique specimen of each category, the roadster and his future wife, Martha.

The Mercedes was very dear to his heart, as it had saved his life on more than one occasion. Once, counterintelligence officers from the Ministry for State Security of East Germany—Stasi, as it was more commonly known—hunted McClain through the streets of East Berlin as he was helping with the defection of a KGB agent. The Mercedes had survived a volley of AK bullets and an exhausting hour-long chase before McClain had gotten away from the Stasi agents.

He eased up on the gas pedal as he came to Chemin Robert Stewart and turned left. A four-story complex of luxury condos appeared to his left, while a row of million-dollar houses stretched on the right side. McClain always marveled at the masonry skills involved in the magnificent look of the mansions in this highly sought-after neighborhood. Backing on the private, eighteen-hole Rivermead Golf Club, a few steps away from the nature trails along the river, and a short drive from downtown Ottawa across the river, the neighborhood was home to some pretty influential people. People like Quan Van Tran, the CIS Director General of Intelligence, South Asia Division.

Quan—whose name meant "soldier" and was pronounced like "Kwan"—was a first-generation Canadian born to Vietnamese parents. Saved from the clutches of death by execution in the last few days of the Vietnam War, Quan had grown to become a fiery patriot, putting to shame many Canadians whose families had lived in Canada for as long as the nation's history. Quan had been a smart, efficient, and brave field agent all over Asia and the Arabian Peninsula for over two decades. Then a stray bullet to his left leg had ended his clandestine operation career one fateful night off the shores of Thailand and left Quan with a slight limp. Quan did not turn to drinking, did not quit, but refocused his energies and his skills to become the youngest man in the history of the CIS to hold the powerful position of director general.

A quiet, reserved man, confident of his own abilities and of the men serving under his command, Quan rarely sought assistance from other divisions within the service—unless there was a national emergency or an operation had gone sideways. Which made tonight's meeting even more interesting, since Quan had reached out to McClain, inviting him to his house to go over a matter so important and sensitive that it could not wait until tomorrow and had to be discussed outside the CIS Ottawa headquarters.

After a couple of right turns McClain was on Rue Félix Leclerc, the street circling most of the neighborhood. The beautiful houses had red brick or natural-looking stone facades, and the street was well lit by fancy decorative street lights. A relatively new neighborhood, most of its houses were built in the last ten years. The trees were still young, but what the front yards lacked in mature vegetation they more than made up for in manicured lawns, elaborate driveways, and cobblestone pathways.

McClain parked behind Quan's black Lincoln Navigator on the street and made his way up the four steps leading to the main entrance of the house. A large bronze planter was neatly placed near the wooden door with a thick, tempered opaque glass. A clematis plant had climbed over a trellis and was crawling toward the red brick wall and the door.

Before he could knock, a woman opened the door. "Welcome, James. Nice to see you again."

It was Lien, Quan's wife. She was dressed in a floral maxi dress and had wrapped a comfortable-looking maroon cardigan around her shoulders. She held a book in her left hand, still opened at the page she had probably just been reading when McClain parked out in the front.

"A pleasure to see you, Lien."

"Come in, come in."

McClain stepped inside the spacious hall and removed his dress shoes and his coat. Lien hung the coat in the closet next to the door.

"How's Martha doing?" Lien asked as they came into the living room.

"She's doing well, thanks for asking. Are those new?" He pointed at the dark brown leather couches that matched perfectly with the maple hardwood floor and the beige walls.

"Yes, a gift from Jen and Chrissy for Christmas. Quan's kept complaining about his bad back, and they got worried about their father. The couches are supposed to be orthopedic. They're so comfortable."

"How's Jen's and Chrissy's medical practice?"

"It has its ups and downs, but mostly it's well. There's always people getting sick, right? The government is changing the health care coverage and some insured services. It's not very clear what it means, but we hope it's not too much trouble."

McClain nodded.

"Tell Martha I love the dragonfly she made for us." Lien pointed at the stained-glass sun-catcher hanging by the large bay window across from the black stone fireplace. "Does she have any new pieces? A friend of mine is interested in buying one or two."

McClain shook his head. "Her arthritis has been quite bad over the last few weeks, so she hasn't done much. But I'll let Martha know about your friend."

"All right, I won't hold you any longer. Quan's upstairs in his studio. Would you like some coffee? Tea?"

"I'll have some tea."

"Black?"

"Too late for black. Something herbal."

"Vanilla red bush?"

"That sounds great."

"All right. I'll bring it up in a couple of minutes."

Lien dropped her book on the couch next to the fireplace and walked to the kitchen through a set of French doors.

McClain headed to the staircase to the right of the kitchen and made his way to the second floor. He knew his way around the house, since he had been here a couple of times, most recently for Quan's sixty-fifth birthday back in December. Quan's studio was in the far end corner of the hall, secluded from the rest of the house and especially the kitchen and the living room. McClain cast a quick glance at Quan's family photos hanging on the wall. Quan's and Lien's wedding picture. Graduation day with Jen, then three years later with Chrissy. Pictures from Jen's wedding.

He knocked gently on the door. Quan's strong voice came from inside. "Yes, come in."

Quan was sitting behind his large antique mahogany desk reviewing a thick report. The desk was strewn with folders and papers, but there still seemed to be some sort of order among the chaos. The papers were set in a semicircle pattern around Quan's small empty glass and a half-full bottle of Macallan Scotch Whisky.

"McClain, welcome, welcome."

Quan stood up and hobbled to meet McClain near the door. They exchanged a strong handshake. Quan was smaller than McClain, with thin shoulders, and walked with a hunch. He was dressed in a dark blue shirt with sleeves rolled up to his elbows, and black pants. Quan had embraced his receding hairline, and the gray hair around his temples and at the back of his head was cut very short. He was clean-shaven and his reddish face had crow's feet around the eyes, a deep crease on his forehead, and thin wrinkles along his thin lips. But his small grayish eyes were alive and full of energy as he peered at McClain with a look of appreciation mixed with impatience.

"Thanks for coming right away. Please take a seat."

Quan gestured toward two overstuffed armchairs across from his desk. They matched the set of couches downstairs, and McClain was certain they were a part of the same Christmas gift from Quan's daughters. He sat on the armchair closer to the window and threw a glance outside at a glowing street light and the dark expanse of the golf course.

"A drink?" Quan said as he pointed to his desk. "I've got this superb twenty-one-year-old Macallan. It's rich, smooth."

McClain shook his head. "I'd love to, but I have to drive back."

Quan shrugged, then poured about two fingers from the bottle into his glass. He picked up a green folder from his desk, then stumbled into the other armchair. He laid the folder on his lap and took a quick sip of his whisky, as if to gather his courage before starting the conversation.

"What is this all about?" McClain asked.

He had never been a fan of chit-chat, especially when time was of the essence. Quan had approached McClain in the parking lot of the CIS headquarters about four hours ago, but had not given him any details. He had only said it was urgent and of great consequence.

Quan looked at McClain. His eyes carried a sense of hesitation, but he offered a small nod. "I don't really know how it happened, James. I've . . . I've lost two agents."

McClain frowned and his body went limp. He sat up straight. "Lost as in they're dead?"

"I'm not a hundred percent sure. That would be the best-case scenario under the circumstances."

"I'm not following."

Quan leaned forward and handed his folder to McClain. "Let me explain. Isaac Schultz and Park Min-joon. Two of my best field operatives in Beijing. Schultz is of Hebrew descent but was born and raised in China. Fluent in Chinese and Japanese. Park is from South Korea, speaks Chinese like a native, and has strong ties to the military and secret services of both Korea and China. Both naturalized Canadians, Schultz and Park were trained at The Plant and graduated with excellent marks. They've been working in South Asia, mainly in China, over the last seven years."

McClain nodded and flipped through the first couple of pages of the folder. Two photographs of the agents were clipped to the records of their files. Schultz was tall and broad-shouldered, with reddish-blond hair and an explosion of freckles on his cheeks and his chin. Park was of smaller stature, black-haired, with thin lips and a scar stretched along the right side of his face, by his ear.

Quan had stopped talking, so McClain raised his head. "Go on," he said.

"Last year, the agents began an operation to turn North Korean scientists or members of its armed forces into double agents. We have very little accurate intelligence about the true nuclear capacities of North Korea. While we believe that they can launch a ballistic missile with a nuclear warhead, the range and the reliability of such an attack are uncertain. There's always a sharp warmongering rhetoric from Pyongyang, so we are trying to separate fact from fiction."

McClain nodded. He was familiar with the general situation in the Korean Peninsula. Divided along the 38th Parallel after the end of the Second World War into a communist state in the north part and a pro-Western state in the south, the area still remained quite volatile and a powder keg. North Korea repeatedly threatened the South and its allies with complete annihilation.

McClain dropped his gaze to the folder, then looked up at Quan so that he could continue his explanation.

Quan took another sip of his drink. He licked his lips, then said, "North Korea carried out two underground nuclear tests last year. Its Musudan missiles have a range of about 2,500 miles. If they're moved to the Sea of Japan, all of South Korea and Japan are within their reach. Earlier this year, we received reports of such movements of missiles. The South Korea-US Combined Forces Command raised their threat level to WatchCon 2, the highest level in peacetime."

He sighed and began to scratch at his chin.

"What happened?" McClain asked.

"Schultz and Park were scheduled to meet with an army colonel in South Korea ten days ago. He approached them through a series of mutually trusted contacts in the Chinese Ministry of State Security. The recent political infighting at the top level of the Political Bureau of North Korea's Communist Party threatened to spread down the ranks and spill over throughout the army. We had high hopes the army colonel would agree to provide actionable intel and even defect to our side. But he was a no-show."

"Was he setting a trap?"

Quan shook his head. "I'm not sure. Schultz and Park reported to their HQ in Beijing and were expected to take a flight out of Seoul on the next day. They never made it."

A light rap came from the door. "It's me," Lien said. "The tea's ready."

She waltzed in with a silver tray in her hands, which she gently placed on the glass-top coffee table between the two armchairs. "Sugar and cream on the side," she said to McClain. "Honey, do you need anything?"

Quan shrugged, then raised his glass toward Lien. "Thanks, I'm good."

"Okay, enjoy." Lien said and closed the door.

McClain glanced at the tea's steam rising from the cup. The delicious aroma of vanilla was very tempting, but he decided to wait for a minute or two before picking it up. "What do you think happened to the agents?"

Quan closed his eyes for a moment and let out a sigh. "I'm still determining the severity of this situation. After Schultz and Park missed their flight, they went incommunicado. We attempted to reach them on their secured cellphones, but they were off the grid. I dispatched a team of agents to the Seoul safe house, but it was empty. Not in disarray, and there were no signs Schultz and Park had left in a hurry or were in trouble. Not as far as we could tell from the safe house."

"When was the last time you heard from the agents?"

"They called in to inform me that the colonel never made it to the meeting. They called four hours after the scheduled time, as per our established protocol."

McClain frowned. "The colonel doesn't show up, then the agents disappear. Not a coincidence."

"No, it's not. I had another team look over the files and the reports of their operation. I sought the assistance of the British Secret Intelligence Service, since we've run joint ops in China and South Korea."

"And what did the British say?"

"They had no intel until three days ago. Then they heard some chatter coming from a North Korean military installation, a camp near the demilitarized zone, about five miles from the border with South Korea. The chatter seemed to indicate the North Koreans have a trusted source of intel about Western ops in South Korea. Then the next day, the safe house in Seoul was turned upside down."

"North Korean State Security operatives?" McClain asked.

"Yes. Thankfully, my team had cleared the safe house of all sensitive materials. So there was no damage to our current or planned missions in the country. But yesterday, a bomb exploded at a safe house in Beijing, killing one of my agents. Another one is in critical condition."

"Again, no coincidence."

Quan nursed his glass. "Absolutely not. Schultz and Park had set up that safe house and used it as one of their main bases of operations."

"And you have more bad news?" McClain said in a flat voice.

"Unfortunately. I have a couple of old friends at the NSA and pulled in some favors. They repositioned one of their recon satellites to listen to conversations inside the North Korean military installation and some of their bases. You can guess what they heard."

McClain's frown grew deeper and wider and he leaned back in his seat. "Park's name came up, along with Schultz's."

Quan's nodded. "The worst-case scenario. My two agents captured by the enemy and giving up intel as a result of torture."

He finished up the rest of his whisky in a big swig. He pursed his lips, then said, "I've asked the NSA to double-check and reconfirm. And hopefully they can establish Schultz's and Park's location. Then I'll give my orders."

McClain looked at Quan's face. The man was visibly in pain, and every word he was saying seemed to hurt him more and more.

"I need another drink," Quan said and struggled to get to his feet.

"I think I'm going to have one as well," McClain said in a low voice. "I'll take a cab home."

Quan nodded. He found another glass inside a cabinet behind his desk by a large bookcase, and brought the Macallan's bottle to the coffee table. He poured about three fingers into McClain's glass and his glass.

McClain took a small sip of the amber liquid and felt the whisky's instant warmth. "What orders?"

Quan paused for a long moment, holding the glass in his hand, but not bringing it to his lips. He heaved a sigh and spoke in a slow, tense voice. "Once we've determined the location where they're being held inside North Korea, I'll have to dispatch a cleanup team."

He dragged the last two words and kept his eyes glued to his glass. His words had sealed Schultz's and Park's fate. The cleanup team's mission was going to be the elimination of the two agents.

McClain pondered Quan's words. He could see the dilemma clearly.

"It pains me, James, but I just can't have two rogue agents revealing our agency's secrets under torture. The North Koreans are breaking my men, slowly but surely, and we're already seeing our operations threatened. Good agents are dying. I may not be able to save Schultz and Park, but I can save the rest. I *will* save the rest."

McClain said nothing. Quan had already made up his mind. It was a heart-wrenching decision that a director or a team leader wished they would never have to make, but when the time came, they gave the order. It was established protocol, familiar to field agents and their handlers. And McClain knew where Quan was going with his line of reasoning.

Quan gave McClain an intense look. "You know what I'm going to ask from you, James. I wanted to discuss this with you in person, before submitting an official request to the director. My South Asia teams have been compromised and I don't know yet the full extent of the breach and of the damage. Schultz and Park had vast knowledge of many operations throughout Asia. So the cleanup team has to be from another region, remote and separate from mine. Perhaps from your section."

McClain kept his eye contact with Quan but did not give him any hint of what he was thinking at that moment. The truth was, McClain needed more information and more time to decide on a course of action. His initial reaction was that it would be suicide to send a team inside North Korea. The CIS and most Western intelligence agencies had no assets in the hostile Communist country. The cleanup team needed a clear infiltration plan and a solid exit strategy.

On the other hand, the need to stop the gush of intelligence was very real and urgent, even if it meant silencing Schultz and Park in order to save the lives of many other agents. But this situation was unique because of the fact that the agents' initial mission had not been to infiltrate North Korea. That country was off limits to all agents operating in South Korea and other areas of South Asia. McClain was wondering how Schultz and Park had ended up in the hands of the North Koreans, and he also wondered why Quan was not interested that much in finding out those reasons.

"I gave Schultz and Park specific instructions not to cross the border with North Korea. This meeting and all other previous meetings with potential assets or defectors had taken place either in South Korea or China, never in the forbidden land," Quan said slowly, as if he had read McClain's mind.

"And you have no idea why or how they ended up in a prison up there?"

"I can make an educated guess that they were either following a lead—the promise of intelligence or other sensitive material from the colonel or someone he could have sent in his place—and decided to continue with their mission, in violation of my direct orders. Or maybe they were captured, and if that's the case, the North Koreans know we'll deny any connection to them. Schultz and Park know this as well, and they can't expect us to risk more agents' lives on a rescue mission."

McClain cleared this throat. "But do they expect us to insert an assassination team, which of course will put the lives of more agents in harm's way?"

Quan's eyes turned into small, fiery slits. He placed his glass on the coffee table and spread his hands in front of him. "I didn't want this and neither did they. But we're doing what must be done and choosing the lesser of two evils."

McClain nodded. "Yes, for us. If I were in their shoes, I would strongly disagree."

"I wouldn't pick this option either, but the choice has been removed from my hands." Quan gave McClain a shrug, then added in a warmer voice, "Please take this operation under consideration. I will not make a recommendation to the director unless you give me your approval."

McClain raised his glass and finished his drink. "Okay, I'll let you know tomorrow."

"Thank you, James. I know I'm laying a heavy burden on you. I appreciate your help."

McClain said nothing. He reached for his BlackBerry in his waist holster. "I'm calling a cab. And I'll finish my tea before heading out."

CHAPTER THREE

Toronto, Canada
April 25, 4:45 p.m.

Justin gazed out the kitchen window at a gathering of clouds moving menacingly over the tall maples and pines at the end of his father's backyard. A large grove stretched beyond the property line and between the houses of the neighborhood. Justin remembered when he was seven or eight years old and he would sneak out of the house around midnight to watch the coyotes roaming the grove. When the winter got harsh and the animals grew hungry, they dared to venture right into the Halls' backyard.

His father, Carter, caught Justin one of those times and gave him a severe scolding. Justin learned his lesson: always watch your back and vary your pattern. Then his mother discovered meat disappearing from the freezer on a regular basis, as Justin would occasionally toss small chunks of meat to one of the coyotes, a scraggly little fellow that was missing a part of his tail and dragged its left hind foot. Justin learned another important lesson: save your supplies. He began to put aside small portions from his lunches and suppers for the furry friend he named White Fang.

Justin heard the floorboards creak as someone stepped inside the spacious kitchen. The slight scent of bergamot filled the air, the unmistakable signature of his fiancée, Anna.

"Hi, how's the party going?" Justin said and gestured to the right, beyond the window, toward the gazebo. He could not see it, but the sounds of hushed conversations of adults and joyful shouts of children came loud and clear.

Anna whispered, "They're wondering what happened to you." Then she leaned in for a kiss.

Justin kissed her back, then brushed one of Anna's curls out of her face. Her blue eyes carried a soft glow as she looked at Justin from behind her square, rimless glasses. She had permed her raven-black hair that afternoon, and she was beautiful in her natural look with a peach-tone blush, a light brown eyeliner, and a nude lip balm. Anna wore a snug-fitting red woolen turtleneck and black dress pants. Justin had gone with a more casual look: light blue Levi's jeans and a gray long-sleeved polo shirt.

His clothes were a small sign of rebellion and a slight hint of his passive-aggressive behavior. He did not really want to be here for his nephew's seventh birthday party. This house where he was born and raised brought back many memories. Some were sweet, but most of them were bitter.

"I was waiting for the coffee maker to finish its job." Justin glanced at the machine at the corner of the quartz countertop, then at his wristwatch. He had been gone for over ten minutes. "Would you like some?"

Anna shook her head. "No, too late for me. I don't want a sleepless night."

Justin shrugged, then fetched a cup from the cupboard.

"Let's go." Anna took hold of his hand. "It's your family. You can do this."

"I can, but I'd rather I didn't have to."

They walked out to the patio, then along the beige limestone pathway that snaked through the yard and led to the wooden gazebo. The left side of the yard was landscaped to perfection, with a couple of terraces full of different plants and shrubs. There were ornamental grasses, ferns, and barberries in the back and hydrangeas, peonies, and pulsatilas in the front. *Carter must have had the gardener come and tidy up the yard yesterday or earlier today,* Justin thought. His father disliked any landscaping or yard work involving manual labor or getting dirty, but did not think twice about hiring professionals to do the job. As the CEO of Hall & Brown Equity Investments Inc., one of the largest brokerages in Toronto, he could afford to hire gardeners and even renovate or redo the entire yard, which he did every couple of years or so.

A long stretch of carpet junipers and a heart-shaped patch of tulips and irises covered a section of the yard by the red brick wall of the house. Justin's mother, Caterina, loved gardening, and irises were her favorite flowers. Justin frowned at the memory of his mother. He was only eleven years old when she had driven off a bridge in her car. The police investigation ruled it as an unfortunate accident caused by the dark night and icy roads. But Justin knew his mother was escaping from a life that had turned into a nightmare. He had witnessed the verbal abuse and the physical threats when his father was around and the neglect and the abandonment when he was gone on his long business trips. His mother's death had not been an accident.

Justin grew up fast and strong, so he could stand up to his father and to everyone else who threatened the people he loved. He had been too young and powerless to be there for his mother, but was not going to let that happen again to anyone else in his life. As soon as he could, he joined the Service, which gave him a second family, or perhaps the only family he ever had.

Carter had been diagnosed with stage 3A non-small cell lung cancer about a year ago. He had undergone preoperative chemotherapy, a surgery in California, and adjuvant chemotherapy, and was taking a number of controversial new treatments, considering the cancer's survival rate of less than fifteen percent. The cancer had disappeared but doctors were worried about its recurrence and kept Carter under constant observation.

The illness had brought Justin closer to his dad and his estranged older brother Seth, who had always been Carter's favorite son, but the reconciliation process was slow and difficult. They could not make up for almost two decades of absence and bitterness through the occasional phone calls and rare visits. With Justin's unpredictable schedule and Carter's illness, it felt like they were not making much progress. So Seth's wife, Tiffany, had organized this impromptu birthday party for their son, Theodore, who was turning seven in a couple of weeks. She had invited a couple of Theodore's friends and had convinced Anna, who then had convinced Justin to take the hour-long flight from Ottawa.

Justin ducked as he walked underneath an arbor lush with clematis at the end of the pathway, then climbed up the three stairs leading to the large rectangular gazebo. Carter was half-sitting, half-lying in a comfortable armchair full of cream-colored pillows. He was dressed in a tweed jacket, black sweater, and brown slacks. Tiffany was sitting on another armchair next to Carter and was sipping from a large mug that Justin assumed contained hot chocolate, since Tiffany swore by her Ghirardelli Double Chocolate.

"Eh, there you are," Carter said as Justin took a patio chair across from the steel-framed bistro table with a glass top, while Anna sat to his left. "What, no coffee for me?"

Justin found Carter's voice gruff and his tone patronizing even though the old man was probably joking, since a Molson beer bottle stood half-full at the corner of the table in front of him. Justin was not sure if Carter was supposed to drink alcohol or coffee because of his condition, but then Carter was never known as a man who followed rules.

"I . . . I had no idea you wanted a drink," Justin said, then lifted his cup to his lips. The gesture expressed much better than words his actual sentiment.

"I'll go grab you some, Father." Tiffany straightened her black-and-blue sweater dress with a cowl neckline and stood up. "Anything else?"

"No, just black coffee, dear."

Tiffany smiled at Justin and left, long blonde braid swinging behind her with every step, the heels of her boots clicking on the floor panels of the gazebo.

"When's the next time you see the doctors?" Justin asked with genuine interest. His father's illness was one of the few things they could discuss freely without provoking bitter feelings or fits of anger. Carter was confident he would beat cancer and was treating the situation in the same way he had handled pretty much every crisis in his life for as long as Justin could remember: throw money at the problem.

"In two weeks," Carter replied in a low voice. "Doctors at St. Mark have these new drugs they want me to try as part of my therapy. I have to pay an arm and a leg for those, of course, but they've given excellent results during clinical trials."

Justin nodded.

"I told them money was no problem, as long as they work. I'm getting tired of being poked and probed, and nobody can give me clear answers."

That's because there are no clear answers, Justin thought, but said nothing. He nodded again and took a sip of his coffee.

"How long are you staying in Ottawa?" Carter asked.

"A few more days, maybe a week. Unless I'm ordered otherwise."

Carter opened his mouth to talk but instead he let out a loud cough, then a wheezing sigh as he made an effort to draw in a deep breath. He coughed again.

"Dad, are you okay?" Seth's voice came from the outdoor kitchen behind the gazebo along with the aroma of meat cooking on the barbeque grill.

"I'm all right, I'm all right," Carter said as he held his chest. "Just . . . having trouble . . . breathing."

Justin sat up straight in his chair. "Dad, do you need anything?"

"No, no, I'm all right." Carter reached for a Kleenex from one of his pockets and wiped his lips. "It's this stupid cancer, that's all. But I'm not dying."

Justin looked at Seth through the gazebo's trellis. Seth shook his head, then mouthed something indistinct. Justin returned his glance to his father before Carter could notice their exchange and become angry about whatever it was that his sons were plotting behind his back.

Carter sipped his Molson, then took a few shallow breaths.

A moment later, Theodore dashed through the grove and the backyard. He jumped on his grandfather's lap and rested his head on Carter's chest. A frown creased his small brow and his blue eyes looked like they were going to burst into tears.

"What's the matter, Theo?" Carter ruffled the reddish hair framing Theo's freckled face.

Justin smiled at the great resemblance between grandfather and grandson.

"I can't find them, I just can't." Theo spoke in a low, desperate voice.

"Who are they?" Carter asked.

"My friends. We're playing hide-and-seek and they always hide so well. I can never find them. Ever!" Theo let out a deep sigh. "That is, without cheating and taking a peek while I count the numbers."

"No, no cheating and no pouting either. And we Halls, we're not losers. Now go get them." Carter gave Theo a gentle nudge and a pat on his back.

Justin put his coffee cup down. "Theo, come here for a second. Let me see if I can help." He stood up and walked to the edge of the gazebo facing the grove.

Theo reluctantly left Carter's side and dragged his feet toward Justin. "How do I find them?"

Justin pointed at the grove. "You can't see them, but you can see their tracks, what they left behind when they scattered to find their hiding spots. Look and listen."

"For what?" Theo's voice rang with frustration.

Justin crouched down so his field of vision would be the same as Theo's. "There are only so many thick trees. There, at four o'clock, I mean to your right, see that cluster there. I bet you one of your friends is there. Look carefully; one of the branches is moving, but there's no gust of wind."

"Jimmy is probably there," Theo blurted out.

Justin nodded. "It could be. The trail is still muddy there, so look for footsteps, especially the ones going toward the big thick trees. And remember to also look and listen for what's not obvious. What should there be at this time all over the forest?"

Theo took a moment to do some thinking. Then he said, "Birds, crows, blue jays, woodpeckers."

"Right. If you can't hear them, it means something or someone spooked them. And that someone could be . . ."

"Emilie, it could be Emilie."

Justin nodded.

"I think I found them," Theo said, and turned on his heels and darted through the gazebo, almost knocking over Carter's bottle. As he climbed down the stairs he seemed to remember something as he stopped and turned his head. "Thank you, Uncle," he said, then resumed his sprint.

Justin returned to the table as the shouts of the three children filled the grove and the backyard.

"What got them so excited?" Tiffany asked as she handed Carter a large porcelain mug.

"Justin was teaching Theo some tricks of his trade," Carter said with a wry grin on his face.

Tiffany frowned. "You didn't give him any ideas, did you? We don't want him to grow up wanting to be a spy."

Justin burned on the inside at the way Tiffany pronounced "spy" as if it were a dirty word. *No, you want him to become a banker like his daddy, so he can please Grandpa and get his inheritance,* he thought. But he decided to keep his cool. "Just giving him a few tips about hide-and-seek." He returned to his chair and hid behind his cup.

"Oh, well, he needs to get better at that. He always complains he can't find his friends. I don't understand why they keep playing that silly game," Tiffany said with a shrug.

Justin glanced at Anna. *What are we doing here?* his eyes said.

"Tiffany, where did you get that dress? It's absolutely gorgeous," Anna said, eager to change the subject.

"Oh, there's this store that just opened by our place. They have all sorts of dresses—maxi, mini—and the selection is simply incredible," Tiffany replied with great excitement. "You should come with me one day and we'll have some girly time together."

Justin rolled his eyes discreetly as he looked at the smoke curling up from Seth's barbeque. Seth was elbows-deep in the grill, meticulously using a pair of tongs to gently flip over each T-bone steak. He took great pride in his culinary skills, aiming for a golden-brown crust covering both sides of the steak.

Seth turned his head and caught Justin's look. "Five more minutes or so and we'll be ready to have supper."

Justin nodded. *Yes, we'll eat and get out of here.*

His BlackBerry vibrated inside the right front pocket of his jeans. Justin leaned back in his seat and pulled out the smartphone. The caller ID showed his boss's last name: McClain.

Justin stood up. "I have to take this," he said to Carter and took a few quick steps. When he was out of earshot, he answered the call. "Yes, sir."

"Justin, how are you?" McClain's voice was low and edgy, with a clear hint of impatience.

"Good. What's the problem, sir?"

"I need to see you right away."

"I'm in Toronto, but I'll catch the next flight."

"Great. Meet me at the Langevin Block."

Prime Minister's Office? Must be a serious crisis if the PM wants to talk to intel officers. If it were one of the prime minister's aides, McClain would have made them come to the CIS headquarters, which was just a short drive away from the Langevin Block.

"Will do."

"Talk to you soon." McClain hung up without another word.

Justin looked at the phone in his hand, then lifted his eyes up to the gazebo. He had mixed feelings about cutting short his visit. He was relieved but he also felt a tinge of guilt, as he did not know when or if he would be able to come down to see his father again.

"Is everything okay?" Anna asked when Justin returned to the gazebo.

"Yes, but—"

"You have to leave, right?" Carter asked.

Justin recognized the cold disappointed tone, the same one that had so often expressed disapproval of Justin's choices over the years. Carter's narrowed eyes conveyed the same emotion.

"Something important came up. I have to get back to Ottawa."

"Oh, but we're almost ready," Tiffany said in a high-pitched tone full of regret. "Can't this wait until after supper?"

Justin was tempted to tell Tiffany that the Prime Minister of Canada and the national security emergency could not wait until he had enjoyed his steak. Instead, he shook his head. "I'm very sorry. We'll have to take a rain check."

Tiffany puckered her lips for a moment, then looked at Anna. "But you don't have to go, right?"

Anna looked at Justin and gave him a smile and a nod. *I'll stay,* her look told him.

"My boss didn't say anything about her," Justin said.

"Great, maybe we'll go shopping in the evening."

Justin walked over to his dad and leaned in for a hug. "Sorry," he said. "I'll see you again soon."

Carter nodded but the frown remained stamped on his face.

Seth came around to shake hands.

Justin said, "I hope Theo likes his present."

"What is it?" Seth asked.

"A surprise," Justin said with a small smile.

"It's not an airsoft AK is it?" Seth furrowed his brow.

"Well, he's not old enough for the real thing yet," Justin replied with a straight face, then smiled again. "No, it's not a rifle. But you'll see the surprise when you open the present."

Seth grinned but did not say anything.

Justin gave Anna a kiss. Tiffany stood up, gave him a big hug, and kissed him on both cheeks. *An Italian thing,* Justin thought, and once again was reminded of his mom, who used to cover him in wet kisses every morning before he left for school.

"Have fun," Justin said as he cast a final glance at his family and stepped down from the gazebo. He picked up his black felt coat from the house, then got into the Nissan rental on the driveway.

CHAPTER FOUR

Ottawa, Canada
April 25, 9:05 p.m.

Justin got out of the taxi at the corner of Elgin and Wellington Streets. He took in the Langevin Block, an impressive four-story structure built in the Second Empire style from olive sandstone and polished granite and completed in 1889. Across from Parliament Hill, the Langevin Block had been the home of Canada's Prime Minister's Office and the Privy Council Office since 1975.

Justin had called McClain five minutes ago to inform him of his exact time of arrival. McClain had told him the meeting was taking place in room 307-S, Prime Minister Joseph Williams's private office on the third floor in the Centre Block. Justin had never been there, and a large tall man from Williams's security detail waited for him by one of the side doors of the building.

They climbed the stairs at a brisk pace and walked fast through the large corridors, ignoring the curious looks of a couple of aides passing by in the other direction. The guard and Justin stopped in front of the door of the prime minister's office. The guard gestured toward the door, then turned around and left. Justin took a deep breath, then rapped quietly on the door.

A man about Justin's age but dressed in a navy blue suit opened the door slightly and gestured for him to come in. Justin immediately felt uncomfortable and out of place. *I should have listened to Anna and dressed in business casual for Theo's party. But at least there are no holes or tears in my jeans.* He stepped inside the office and stood by the door next to the man in the suit.

Prime Minister Williams was sitting behind a sizable light mahogany desk—the centerpiece of the room, flanked by two large Canadian flags. An avalanche of folders and papers had covered every possible inch of the desk's top, unlike in the photos of the meticulously clean workspace Justin had seen on the pages of newspapers. Williams was listening attentively to someone on a corded phone and nodding occasionally. He was dressed in a black suit and white shirt but no tie.

McClain was sitting across from Williams on a burgundy leather sofa along the wood-paneled wall with elaborate designs and underneath a large portrait of Sir John A. Macdonald, the Father of Confederation. Another man whom Justin recognized as Raphael Gauthier, the Minister of Public Safety, was reading a thick folder resting on his lap as he sat in an armchair to the right of McClain.

Williams gave Justin a slight nod and pointed at an empty seat on the sofa. Justin sat next to McClain while the man in the navy-blue suit sat in the other armchair. McClain handed Justin a manila folder that was labelled TOP SECRET. Justin opened it and read the first page. The classified document provided an abbreviated report of a CIS unauthorized operation in North Korea, which had resulted in the capture of two Canadian agents. Their names were not in the report but the suspected location where they were being held was at a site near Prison Camp 37 in North Hamgyong province.

Williams said, "All right, Jack, you do that." He waited for a moment while he ran his left hand through his silver hair. "Of course, of course, I understand. Inform me of your decision. Yes, you too. Take care." He sighed and the frown on his forehead grew deeper and wider. Then he placed the phone handset on the receiver.

"Mr. Hall, a pleasure to meet you." Williams came around his desk and shook Justin's hand. "You know Mr. Gauthier, and this is my National Security Advisor, Mr. Foster."

They exchanged pleasantries and handshakes.

"I've heard excellent things about you, Mr. Hall," Williams said in a pleasant voice as he reached for one of the folders on top of his desk. "Your skills brought home Mr. Duncan safe and sound after his long and terrible captivity in Nigeria."

Justin nodded. "Thank you, sir."

"Some people are unhappy with the turn of events, but as far as I am concerned you did a very fine service for our country."

Justin said nothing but kept his eyes fixed on Williams's face.

"And your operation this week in Syria resulted in the elimination of two terrorist leaders while entailing no Canadian casualties or collateral damage caused by us, unlike in the event of a drone strike. Excellent job."

"Thank you, sir," Justin said, truly pleased by the compliment.

Williams moved the folder to the side. "Now, the other reason why I've called you here is because our country needs your services again, this time to deal with a new, even more serious crisis."

Justin nodded and waited.

Williams groped around the desk for his glasses, lifting and shifting papers around, then found them and settled them at the bridge of his long, narrow nose. His black eyes now looked bigger and more serious than before as he looked at Justin from behind his thick, round glasses with a horn-rimmed frame. "McClain, do you want to fill in Hall about the details?" Williams asked.

"Yes, sir."

McClain took the next few minutes to update Justin on the situation on the ground. He talked about the most recent operations of the two agents and how they had tried to entice North Korean nuclear scientists to give up that country's atomic bomb program. He mentioned the scheduled meeting with the North Korean army colonel who never showed up, the raid on the safe house in Seoul, and the bomb explosion in the safe house in Beijing.

McClain continued his explanation, and Justin's mind began to play him flashbacks from six years ago when he had ended up in the deepest, darkest cells of Iran's most brutal prison. That long week in Evin Prison in Tehran was a nightmare he would never forget. The jailers fed him moldy bread and foul water but put him on a healthy diet of daily beatings. Justin was allowed to go home only after complicated negotiations, the intervention of Williams's predecessor, and an exchange of favors.

"I want you to lead a team of elite CIS agents in this mission," Williams said when McClain was finished.

Justin nodded. He had wanted to speak up and volunteer for a rescue mission, but he did not want to interrupt McClain.

"It's a mission like nothing you've done before," Williams said in a low but steady voice. "Not only because of the location but also because of the purpose of this mission. It's something extremely dangerous—and frankly, it's something no leader ever wants to order done to his people, brave agents who have given so much to their country." Williams sighed. "Hall, you will go to North Korea to put an end to the agents' sufferings."

Justin understood Williams's order but still a small part of his mind refused to believe he was being dispatched to eliminate two agents of his own agency. His face remained calm but his voice wavered a bit as he asked, "Pardon, sir?"

Williams's shoulders slumped, and he removed his glasses and tossed them on his desk. He massaged his temples with both hands as if to fend off a headache. He paused for a long moment then said, "I know, Hall, it's not the order you expected. But it's the only possible option at the moment and under these circumstances."

Justin unlocked his tightened jaws to object to the claim that the agents' fate was sealed and the only possible mission was an authorized kill. But before he had a chance to say a word, Foster let out a low cough. Williams noticed it and made a hand gesture for Foster to speak.

Foster said, "As we know, the Communist Party and its leaders have a stranglehold on North Korea and its people. They rule with an iron fist. The army and the secret services of that country control pretty much every aspect of the people's lives. They have no freedom of any kind; they cannot watch foreign television and their Internet access is heavily restricted. They cannot even travel to the capital without permission. The communist propaganda has brainwashed them into worshipping and bowing down before their leaders. They aren't allowed to think or do as they like. Now the men are being forced to wear the same hairstyle as their leader. They are starving, as the famine of the nineties showed, when over three million of the twenty-two million population of the country died. Now food is rationed or lacking altogether. Yet, North Korea's army is the fourth largest in the world and they spent one-third of their national income on their army."

Justin nodded and wished Foster would move along and tell him something he did not know. Anyone with a computer and Internet access and ten spare minutes could learn these facts for themselves after a simple Google search.

Foster exchanged a glance with Williams, then looked at Gauthier before he pushed up his metal-framed glasses, which had slid to the tip of his nose. "I didn't mention the extraordinary network of informal spies, but we estimate that one in three people regularly monitors and reports to the government about the activities of their relatives, neighbors, and friends. In this situation, a rescue operation is tantamount to suicide. The agents are held in a well-protected location, near a maximum-security prison camp, a short distance away from hundreds of soldiers. A prison break would require a large team—at least a dozen men—which would make a stealthy insertion and a clean exit very difficult if not impossible."

Justin frowned and swallowed hard. Foster's words made sense and gave a fair assessment of the situation.

"What makes this particular case even worse is the fact that we're not completely sure about the integrity of our agents," Gauthier said as he leaned forward in his seat. "They were not cleared for an operation inside the territory of North Korea. Their safe house in Seoul was found clean and tidy. No signs of a struggle there or anywhere else, and nothing to indicate the agents were kidnapped or forced to cross the border."

"Are you saying they're defectors? Traitors?" Justin asked in a loud, gruff voice that sounded like an open accusation.

Gauthier was not expecting Justin's reaction. At first he looked confused, then annoyed at the interruption. He rubbed his bushy gray-and-black goatee and narrowed his small gray eyes. "Eh, no, I am not saying anything like that, Mr. Hall. The facts, the evidence shows that Mr. Schultz and Park at the moment are giving sensitive information to our enemies. We have to put an end to this flow of intelligence that's crippling our mission, threatening our security, and costing the lives of our agents."

Justin fell back on the sofa. A heavy burden was laid on his shoulders. He knew Isaac Schultz personally. They had been good friends at The Plant and had graduated the same year. They had never worked together, because they were posted to different areas of the world, and had since lost touch. But there was no way, absolutely no way that Isaac Schultz would betray his country and go rogue inside North Korea.

He thought for a quick moment about the implications of having a personal connection with one of the missing agents. *I'm sure McClain knows about it, and thus the prime minister and everyone else is aware of that piece of intel. Perhaps that's why they selected me for this mission. Schultz's betrayal of his country is also a personal betrayal.*

Foster said, "Regardless of how or why our agents ended up in the hands of the North Korean army, the undeniable truth is that we have a considerable leak of intelligence. The agents could be willfully cooperating with the North Koreans—a possibility which I wish I could dismiss—or they could be tortured to reveal what they know. I believe the latter is the situation we have in our hands."

Justin nodded. He took advantage of a small pause and said, "Shouldn't we at least give them a chance to explain themselves? Tell us exactly what happened? We can at least try a rescue mission." He looked at Foster, then at Williams for a reply.

Williams shook his head. "We have spent the last two days going over many scenarios, and rescuing them was at the top of the list and the highest priority. But after the bomb explosion in Beijing, it has become very clear that a rescue mission is no longer on the table. Our agents *are* giving away secret intel." Williams stopped for a moment, seemingly to organize his thoughts. He nodded to himself and said, "We could start negotiations for their release, of course, but the North Koreans have not officially or unofficially acknowledged their capture. If we admit the two agents belong to us, it will cause a scandal and a diplomatic crisis, causing irreparable damage to many other ongoing CIS operations in that part of the world."

Justin opened his mouth but Williams stopped him with a hand raised in his direction. "I know what you are going to say and trust me, this is not about politics or about me heading a minority government that can collapse at the first hint of a scandal. It's far from it. And this is different from your capture in Iran a few years back. You were carrying out a sanctioned operation in that country, you did not break under pressure, and the Iranians made it exceptionally clear they were looking for a trade. The North Koreans are notorious for never negotiating the release of captives, especially the ones they have not admitted to having."

Justin sighed.

"This is extremely difficult, Justin," McClain said slowly, and placed an arm on Justin's shoulder. "We just want to make it absolutely clear that this operation is our last and only resort."

Justin nodded but his hands were balled into fists. He let out a deep breath, then said, "How do you want me to proceed?"

McClain reached for a folder in the briefcase on the floor next to his feet. "Schultz and Park were working on developing potential assets among Korean nuclear scientists. One of them, a certain Hong Song-Ok, was the best candidate. Hong works at the Yongbyon Nuclear Scientific Research Center, which is the largest complex in North Korea. And the government is expanding its facilities and operations. Our agents met with Hong twice in China when he was travelling for conferences. He's always chaperoned by an agent who's better at chasing tail and drinking himself stupid than keeping a watchful eye on his man. Hong was on the fence, but our agents' reports indicate a strong possibility Hong was going to defect and provide us with a trove of secrets about Korea's nuclear program." He handed the folder to Justin, then continued, "Hong is travelling tomorrow to Dubai for yet another conference.

You'll have to turn him and convince him to provide you safe travel within Korea, as we have no assets on the ground."

Justin looked at the thin, pale face of Hong in the first page of the report. He was in his early fifties but looked much older, with a wrinkled and pockmarked face. His grin showed his uneven yellow teeth, and there was an overall sadness in the man's appearance. "And the infil and exfil?"

McClain said, "The agents are held near Camp 37. It's only five miles away from the border with China and about sixty miles from the border with Russia. Infiltration from Russia across the Tumen River that serves as the border between the countries is easier. The border is porous, the area sparsely populated, and your appearance will not attract much attention, considering you speak Russian and you fit in."

Justin nodded. "A four-man team should be sufficient for a hit op. I will need Carrie and Nathan and another man, someone who's also familiar with the terrain, in case the Hong option doesn't work or something happens to him and then—"

Williams interrupted him. "The man earlier on the phone was the British Prime Minister, Jack Edwards. The British have two great MI6 agents who operated in North Korea over the last two months on reconnaissance missions and one of them speaks Korean. Edwards is still deciding on whether to support our mission, and if he says 'yes,' those two operatives would be the rest of your team, along with O'Connor."

Justin held his tongue. He did not like the idea of working with agents of another service. Their skills and abilities may appear as great in their files, but he would be the one trusting them with his life in the middle of a hostile North Korea, surrounded by countless enemies. But they came highly recommended by Williams, and their knowledge of the Korean language and the terrain could provide the team's winning card.

"As far as the details of the operation, that's up to you to decide, Hall," Williams said. "But you need to move fast. Meet with Hong the day after tomorrow in Dubai and then infiltrate North Korea as soon as possible after that."

"Understood, sir," Justin said in a strong, confident voice, although he had many doubts about the objective and the execution of the operation.

Williams said, "Gauthier and Foster will provide you any assistance you may need, but you'll report to McClain on the mission's progress."

Justin nodded and looked at McClain, who gave him a small smile.

"Will do, sir," Justin said.

Williams stood up. "Thank you, Hall, on behalf of our country." Then he shook Justin's hand.

Justin said goodbye to Foster, Gauthier, and McClain. He tried to look upbeat but he found it difficult. He was going deep inside a hostile country to kill two agents of his own agency whose only mistake was to fall into the hands of the enemy. He did not feel the mission was something he should be thanked for. But he had received his marching orders and he needed to make preparations.

CHAPTER FIVE

Military outpost fifteen miles north of Hoeryong
North Hamgyong Province, North Korea
April 26, 8:15 a.m.

Kim Jong-nam drew in a long puff on his cigarette and blew out the smoke slowly through his nose and his mouth. A thin gray cloud formed in front of his cold face, then a sharp wind gust carried it away. Kim tried to follow the vanishing spiral of smoke, but he saw nothing but the hill slopes and the valleys beyond the barbed-wire fence surrounding this remote outpost, about ten miles away from the prison camp.

His small gray eyes followed the Tumen River snaking at the bottom of the valley and separating these forests from those on the other side belonging to China. Kim wondered for a moment about the thousands of people who had tried to cross the river with hopes and dreams of a better life. Instead most of them had found death in the cold waters or the volleys of gunfire from soldiers chasing them like dogs. The ones who were caught alive were most often executed for treason, if the starvation and the daily beatings in prison camps did not kill them. And Chinese authorities routinely returned many of the escapees back to their homeland, considering them economic immigrants and not refugees, denying them asylum and protection.

The few that actually survived the ordeal had to live in constant fear about the fate looming over the family members and relatives they had left behind. Even if they were lucky enough to avoid the firing squad or the prison camps, they were branded as enemies of the state, and shame, misery, and humiliation would follow them for the rest of their lives. *Their families and relatives deserve it, since they raised such fools. But that will never happen to my family. My wife and my daughters will never live in terror.*

Kim took the last drag and flicked the cigarette butt into the bushes about four feet away. He did not worry about starting a fire. The ground and the plants were still damp from the long winter, which this year had dragged on longer than everyone had expected. He tapped the front pocket of his coat—a drab olive military trench coat that hung heavy on his small frame—and wondered whether he should smoke another cigarette. He was down to the last two Marlboros that a friend of a friend had bought in the black market fueled by shadowy Chinese and Russian characters. Then he would have to go back to smoking local brands like Gohyang, produced in the Paeksan Cigarette Company in Hoeryong. They were cheap but they tasted like crap. *Americans may be evil but their factories make really good stuff.* Smoking smuggled cigarettes was frowned upon and if caught, Kim might be subjected to some tongue-lashing from his superiors. But they were far away in Pyongyang, and he was the highest-ranking officer on this station and the man who ran the show.

Kim was smart enough to understand the politics of his country and to know when to keep his mouth shut. Which was all the time. The nail that sticks out gets hammered down, as the old saying went. Kim allowed himself the occasional American cigarette or whisky, his only vices, but otherwise was extremely careful not to stick out, especially considering his job with the Ministry of State Security, the most powerful of the four intelligence agencies of the country. The MSS was under the direct control of the country's Supreme Leader and responsible among other things for investigating domestic espionage and counterespionage activities. And today Kim was investigating the case of a nuclear scientist suspected of planning to defect to two Canadian agents, who had been caught and brought to his station.

Kim took in a deep breath and decided to save his Marlboros for the next time he felt the cigarette craving. He walked slowly on the dirt path toward the main complex station, once a large barracks that had been converted into a prison, which at the moment held twenty-one detainees. To his right, about a hundred yards from the prison, there was a small cinderblock barracks painted gray, with offices and dormitories for the station's personnel and the soldiers, a total of forty people. Four Chaju ten-ton trucks were parked near the barracks. A little further away stood Kim's beauty: a black Ppeokpuggi, an off-road vehicle, assembled in the country from Chinese parts. It handled the rough country roads very well and Kim was very proud of it.

"Good morning, Comrade Kim," a soldier greeted him as Kim climbed up the five steps leading to the prison's main entrance.

Kim nodded at the soldier, who began to march away in haste with an AK hanging over his left shoulder. "Where are you going?"

"Down to the camp."

Kim stopped, turned around, and grabbed the soldier by the arm. "Why? Who ordered you?"

"Comrade Jang. He said he needed someone to examine a few files."

Kim frowned and he felt his heart drumming in his chest. Jang was the commander of the prison camp, but he could not pull rank and order Kim's soldiers around. Not without Kim's knowledge and authorization. And the task of reviewing papers sounded quite routine to Kim, something one of the hundreds of Jang's men could do very well.

"Go back to your post, patrolling the fence," Kim ordered the soldier and pointed toward the west.

"But . . . what about—"

"I'll handle Jang . . . if he is man enough to call me."

The soldier grimaced, then gave Kim a quick nod and jogged up the hill.

Kim cursed Jang under his breath, pushed open the gray metallic door with peeling paint and rust marks around the hinges, and stepped inside the prison. The door creaked, and two soldiers huddling next to a wooden stove behind a small desk right inside the entrance got up and greeted Kim in a single voice.

He saluted the life-sized bronze statue of the Supreme Leader standing on the other side of the entrance as it waved and smiled at him. He nodded at the soldiers and continued down the long, narrow hall. Small windowless cells stretched along the length of the building. They had steel-plated doors and were simple eight-foot-by-eight-foot squares, each with a narrow iron-framed bed and a concrete floor with a hole that served as the toilet. There were no light bulbs, so prisoners would never know if it was day or night. Not that it would matter, since their fate was in Kim's hands. If they confessed their crimes against the state and the people and provided him the intelligence and the answers that he and his superiors demanded, the prisoners could save themselves a great amount of pain and suffering.

Two soldiers were sitting on wooden chairs in front of the last two cells near the end of the hall. They stood up as Kim approached them.

"Good morning, Comrade Kim," said one of them, the taller of the two.

Kim nodded. "How are they?" He nodded toward the cell to the right.

The number 19 had been scrawled on the door a long time ago. The black color had faded and the number was almost illegible against the brown, rusting door. One of the captured Canadian agents, Park Min-joon, had been held in that cell for the last three days.

The tall soldier said, "This one made no sound all night, since their transfer from the camp. Then he complained of chest pain about an hour ago. The doctor came and fed him a couple of pills. Now he's sleeping."

Kim glanced at the small viewing slit, covered by a shutter, in the cell door. "Did he say whether he's getting better?"

"He didn't say," the tall soldier replied.

"And this one?" Kim gestured with his right hand at the cell across from Park's and looked at the short soldier.

"He's been singing for the last hour or so," the short soldier said in an annoyed voice.

Kim flinched, then scratched his head. "Singing?"

"Yes. Songs about his god. Something about a shepherd and grace and other stories like that."

"Huh. Well, his god is not going to save him from my hands. Bring him out to the interrogation room."

Kim walked up ahead and turned left. The interrogation room was the only heated part of the building beside the soldiers' corner at the entrance. Kim had instructed the soldiers to start the heating stove, as he was planning to spend the first part of his work day interrogating the Canadian agents, and perhaps a couple of the other prisoners who had been jailed for having political views contrary to the Supreme Leader and for criticizing his regime.

The room was about the size of four cells put together, and the black rectangular stove had begun to warm the room. Kim found the temperature still not to his liking, so he frowned and cursed the stupid soldiers. He stomped toward the pile of firewood behind the stove, picked up a couple of large logs and fed them into the mouth of the stove. He sneered at the meager fire inside the stove and cursed the soldiers again.

He retreated to a desk near the stove and removed his coat. He placed it carefully over the wooden chair's back before sitting down. Then he began to roll up the sleeves of his gray woolen sweater. He did not want to get them dirty, and his interrogations tended to turn bloody more often than not.

The door opened and the two soldiers dragged in the other Canadian agent, who Kim knew was called Isaac Schultz. He was the one who was not wounded during the shootout at Kaesong last week. It had killed two MSS agents and the nuclear physicist working on the uranium mine complex at Sunchon in the South Pyongan province. MSS agents had given chase and had caught the agent and his partner Park and seized fifteen pounds of weapons-grade uranium in the back of their van. Now Kim wanted some answers about the whole affair and he was determined to get them. His superior in Pyongyang—a powerful and fearsome man he did not dare cross— had made it abundantly clear that Kim could not return to the country's capital unless he had precise intelligence about the Canadian agents' operations and their network of spies in North Korea.

The soldiers held the agent by his arms and shoved him onto the chair across the table. Kim looked at the face of his enemy. Schultz's lips and eyes were swollen and he had bruises and cuts along the side of his face, on his forehead, and near his ears. A couple of his front teeth were missing, revealing black gaps. The soldiers down at the camp had beaten him with bamboo sticks and had kicked him, so Schultz probably had other wounds all over his body. The front of his white shirt and black pants were caked with dried blood. But still Schultz had a small but defiant smile on his face, and he was already getting on Kim's nerves.

"My name is Kim Jong-nam and I'm an officer with the Ministry of State Security," Kim said slowly in a warm tone in English. He had learned it in elementary school and was told he spoke it rather well but had quite the accent. Kim had not practiced it very often and when he did, it was mostly with other North Koreans. English-speaking visitors were very rare in the country, and his line of work was not the ideal setting to have lengthy English-practicing conversations. "I'm in charge of your case and from now one you will communicate with me. Do you understand what I'm saying?" He looked at Schultz's blue eyes and offered him a genuine smile. Kim truly wished the Canadian would cooperate so he could return to his family in Pyongyang.

Schultz kept his gaze on Kim, then winced. "What happened to Jang?" He slurred his words and his voice was hoarse and low.

"He and his men are no longer a concern. They are in the past, the same as the torture and the beating. Very shortly you will go back home."

"Yes, but only after I've given you everything I know."

Kim smiled and leaned forward. "Very good. We are coming to an understanding, Mr. Schultz. I like that. Now would you like something to eat? Or perhaps something to drink?"

"No," Schultz said.

"Bring me two cups of citron tea," Kim ordered one of the soldiers, the short one. "You'll like it. Very good with honey. Now tell me: what were you doing in Kaesong?"

Schultz gave Kim a wry smile. "Will you believe me if I said we were there as tourists?"

"I wish I could. But unless your tourism involved purchasing some uranium made in the Democratic People's Republic of Korea, I would say you were trying to lie to me. And I don't appreciate liars. Do you understand what I'm saying?"

Schultz just stared at Kim.

"Let's start at the beginning: how did you cross the border?"

Schultz began to shake his head but Kim stopped him with a dismissive hand gesture. "Don't tell me you flew to Pyongyang, because your passports show no stamps. So how did you get into the country? Did you break through the fence? Did you get in by boat? Or did you bribe any of our border guards?"

Schultz winced as if a jolt of pain was shooting through his body. He closed his eyes for a moment, and when he opened them again he seemed calm and collected. "Since you have my passport, you've probably noticed it's of a diplomatic type. That means it affords me protection and—"

"It doesn't afford you anything." Kim cut him off in a stern voice. "You entered illegally into my country. You tried to smuggle nuclear material from my country. And you shot and killed two agents, colleagues of mine, and upstanding citizens of my homeland. You can be executed for these crimes. I'm offering you a very good trade: your life in exchange for some information. You don't value your life?"

"You should contact my ambassador in Seoul, who can negotiate my release with your politicians or your Supreme Leader—"

Kim pushed back his chair and jumped to his feet. He slammed his fist on the table as he towered over Schultz. "Don't you mention his name, you imperialist aggressor, you scum of a spy. You came here to fuel discontent among our peaceful people, to find renegades willing to betray their country and rebel against their loving leaders. But you failed, and you will rot and die in this very place if you do not tell me everything. Right now! Start talking, you scum!" Kim slammed his fist on the table again, and a fleck of spit flew out of his mouth and landed on Schultz's face.

Schultz did not say a word but the defiant look remained stamped on his face. He showed no fear. He raised his hands, handcuffed in front of him, to clean his face, but Kim grabbed one of his arms. "You talk or I will pry the words out of your mouth."

Kim seized Schultz by the throat, his fingers digging deep into the man's skin. Schultz struggled for breath and tried to resist by elbowing Kim. The soldier stepped forward and kicked Schultz to the side, throwing him off the chair.

"Talk or I will kill you, slowly and painfully, ripping you to pieces." Kim leaned over the captive and yelled in his ear.

He stomped on Schultz's back, and his boot formed a large smudge on the man's shirt. Kim put his boot to Schultz's head and leaned on him with his full weight. Schultz moaned and whimpered. But there was nowhere to go. Kim kicked Schultz, then shoved his head against the whitewashed wall, stained with other prisoners' blood.

"Get up, get up, you wicked running dog," Kim shouted and spat on Schultz.

The soldier hoisted Schultz in his arms and shoved him onto the chair. Schultz sighed and wheezed as he tried to get some air into his lungs. Blood was oozing from a cut running from the left to the right side of his face. Two wounds on his forehead had also burst open and a blood trickle was making its way along the side of his nose.

Kim said, "My actions are just a sample of what will happen and continue to happen to you until you talk and tell me everything about your informants, about all the traitors that are helping you plot the collapse of our socialist system. But the masses of the people are masters of our revolution and reconstruction, and we will not allow capitalist jerks to destroy it."

Schultz said nothing. He let out a weak sigh and his face slowly began to resume its bold, defiant look.

Kim said, "You have nothing to gain and everything to lose by being stubborn and refusing to confess to what we already know. We have the human scum you had convinced to betray his country, and we are going to find all the other traitors that worked with him. And if you do not talk to me, I will get my answers from your comrade, that swollen-headed, loud-mouthed traitor."

Schultz began to shake his head. "No, don't hurt Park or I will—"

"What? You will do what?" Kim screamed.

The interrogation room door opened and the short soldier strode in, balancing in his hands a wooden tray with a white porcelain pot decorated with a blue-and-green flowery motif and two matching cups. Kim turned to the guard and stared at him with rage pouring forth from his eyes.

"The tea you ordered, sir?" the short guard said with a sense of insecurity and fear in his voice, especially after glancing at Schultz's face.

"This jerk doesn't deserve a cup of tea." Kim spat out his words. "He deserves the whole pot."

He clutched his fingers around the teapot handle, ignoring the heat that started to burn his hand. He swung the teapot around— tea spilled all over the table as the cover flew across the room—and smashed it against Schultz's head. The spout caught him right above the left ear, carving a deep gash. The scalding liquid poured over the captive's face and neck. The force of the blow knocked him to the ground, where Schultz writhed and screamed in agony.

"That's where you'll be, where you belong, eating dirt underneath my foot." Kim jammed the heel of his boot on Schultz's neck and pressed the captive's face against the coarse cement floor and the pool of blistering hot water. "And while you take some time to rethink your position, I will have a little talk with our Comrade Park."

"No, no," Schultz shouted, and tried to grab Kim's boot, but the man had already stepped beyond his reach.

"Enjoy your tea." Kim spat in Schultz's direction and headed toward the desk. He picked up his coat and put it on calmly and slowly while his eyes were focused on Schultz's face, distorted because of his pain. Then Kim looked at the soldiers. "Bring the doctor to treat his wounds," he told the tall soldier in Korean.

The tall soldier nodded and hurried along with the short soldier to pick up Schultz and take him to his cell.

Kim sighed as he stepped outside in the hall. He had truly hoped one of the captives would have started to talk and give away their secrets by now. *I'll need to change tactics if I am to show results to my superiors. Beatings and threats do not seem to work.* Kim frowned and realized he might have to call the man he hated owing a favor, since he usually ended up paying a very steep price in return. Jaw-long was an influential man in China's Political Bureau and had strong ties to political counterparts in Korea's Workers' Party and National Defense Commission, the top government branch responsible for all military and security policies. *It's like dealing with a snake,* Kim thought, *but it is better to keep an eye on the snake and watch its sharp teeth than turn my back and suffer the venomous bite.*

CHAPTER SIX

Shangri-La Hotel, Dubai, United Arab Emirates
April 28, 10:20 a.m.

Justin glanced at the clock in the bottom right corner of his laptop screen, wondering when the morning session would end. He had been able to follow the speaker—a renowned engineer from the French National Centre for Scientific Research—for the first five minutes as he covered the latest developments in nuclear fusion research. The man was quite animated as he spoke passionately from the podium of the large Nasreen conference hall, on the third floor of the hotel, and his PowerPoint presentation beamed onto three huge screens behind him. Once the engineer began to expand on the incubation period, particle size, and absorption rates, Justin was all but lost. He tuned out the speaker and nursed his coffee cup as he kept a close eye on Hong, sitting at the other table about ten feet away and across from Justin's table.

Justin and Carrie—who was sitting on the other side of the conference hall near the exit and keeping an eye on Hong's chaperone—had yet to make the initial contact with Hong. They had planned to approach him the previous evening at the reception welcoming the participants to "The Future of Nuclear Energy: Visions and Strategies," a two-day conference hosted by the Emirates Nuclear Energy Corporation (ENEC), a public entity of Abu Dhabi, one of the UAE's emirates. But a delay in their flight had derailed them and they had not arrived at the Shangri-La Hotel until after midnight.

Their next chance to casually run into Hong without arousing the suspicions of the chaperone—who was most likely a member of the MSS—was the day after, at the breakfast event for the conference participants. Justin and Carrie attended as representatives from the Atomic Energy Institute of Canada, as Schultz and Park had done in the past, but Hong and his chaperone were a no-show. They came to the conference hall only a couple of minutes before the start of the morning session, looking tired and upset. They sat next to one another and kept to themselves but for the shaking of hands with the people at their table.

Justin had studied Hong's file during the long flight from Ottawa. Schultz and Park had scheduled this meeting with Hong about a week before their disappearance, and their goal was to make an offer to Hong in Dubai. If he agreed to defect, they had been authorized to give Hong political asylum in Canada for him, his wife, and his two teenage sons. It was now Justin's job to convince Hong to trust a complete stranger and agree to betray his country.

A defection in a sense was the final stage of an asset development for intelligence gathering. Once a person defected, there was no turning back, no change of heart, no second chance. An asset in development could decide at any time to stop providing intelligence to their handler and hope and pray their actions would go unnoticed by the authorities and the secret agencies of their countries. Sometimes they could even switch sides and become double agents, giving false reports to misinform and mislead their adversaries. While this was still possible in a defection scenario, its likelihood was very small because of the publicity that generally accompanied a defection, since defectors were branded as traitors by their home countries and kept under strict surveillance in the host country.

Convincing an asset to make the final step of defection was a long, tedious process, requiring a close personal relationship with the defector. It took time to build the trust and the ties to make possible the crossover. Justin had at the most a day and a half, so he hoped Schultz and Park were right and had laid carefully and correctly most of the groundwork.

Justin took a sip from his coffee. It was still hot, as he had just poured a fresh cup from a carafe at one of the tables at the end of the large conference hall. He liked his coffee hot, black, and bitter, as it helped keep him attentive at all times. He glanced again at Hong, then at the French engineer still rambling about vacuum vessels and concentration saturation. Another ten long minutes of boredom, then a faint round of applause and no questions or comments. All of the sixty or so participants seemed to be happy to go for a break.

The man sitting next to Justin turned to him and asked him how he had enjoyed the session. Justin shrugged, picked up his BlackBerry, and excused himself. He lifted up his shoulders and tilted his head while standing a few steps away from his table, feigning stretching his neck muscles. His eyes followed Hong, who made a beeline for the coffee tables. The chaperone stood up and caught up with Hong. They chatted for a moment while Hong was refilling his mug and helping himself to a Danish pastry. Hong frowned while getting an earful from the chaperone, who at some point even wagged his finger in front of Hong's face. Then the chaperone left the conference hall, followed quickly by Carrie.

Justin took advantage of the small window of opportunity and walked over to Hong. The nuclear scientist looked dazed and shocked, holding in his hands his mug and his plate with the half-eaten pastry.

"Is it good?" Justin asked in a low voice, pointing at the pastry.

"Huh? What?" Hong replied in an absentminded voice.

"The pastry. How is it?"

Hong shrugged and took a small bite. "It's all right. It's good," he replied in a thick accent.

Justin looked at his BlackBerry, then at the door. Carrie was going to send him a text message if and when the chaperone was to return to the hall.

"What delegation do you belong to?" Hong asked and peered at the badge hanging around Justin's neck.

The nametag had twisted slightly and Justin's name was not visible.

"I'm with AEIC. Like Schultz and Park." Justin turned the nametag over. It identified him as Timothy McNally.

Hong frowned for a split second when he heard the Canadian agents' names. "Why aren't *they* here?"

"Change of plans." Justin dropped his voice to barely a whisper. "We don't have much time before your handler comes back. We need to talk."

Hong put his plate and mug down and crossed his arms in front of him. "How do I know you are truly who you say you are?"

Justin smiled. *He's careful. I like that.*

"I have something for you," Justin said. "Come to my table."

Hong reluctantly followed two steps behind him. Justin had anticipated Hong's reaction and had prepared a thin folder with a few pictures of Hong talking to Park during their last meeting two months ago in Beijing. Justin picked up the folder, held it close to his chest, and opened it just a hair so that only Hong could see its contents.

"Convinced?" Justin asked as he closed the folder and placed it back on the table.

Hong hesitated for a moment, looked around the hall, then gave Justin a slight nod. "What do you want?" His voice was low and nervous.

"We want you to make a decision. If you come with us, you and your family can start a new life in Canada, away from your current nightmare. New identities, protection, money, and most importantly, freedom."

Hong pondered Justin's offer. He looked at the folder, then at Justin, while the frown never left his face. His wrinkles seemed to multiply by the second and his eyes grew darker and gloomier. The man appeared to age by a few years within a few seconds.

"You have twenty-four hours to think about it," Justin said in a soft voice. "Of course, the sooner you decide, the more time we have to plan your exit and that of your family."

The last word brightened Hong's eyes, which glinted with a spark of hope.

Justin read the sign and seized the moment. "My partner will take care of your 'colleague' so that he'll not bother us. We'll have complete privacy to discuss our strategy."

Justin's BlackBerry beeped with the arrival of a text message. He glanced at the screen: *You have 30 secs.*

"He's coming back." Justin looked over Hong's shoulder. "What was he furious about?"

Hong's chin dropped and he looked at the floor. "He's suspicious of me and told me he'll kill me if he notices something that does not feel right."

Justin nodded. "Then we'll be extra careful. I need you to go straight to the men's washroom after the next session is over. Got it?"

Hong nodded. "Got it."

Justin stepped away from Hong as his chaperone appeared at the doors. Justin sat at the next table and struck up a conversation with a German researcher, a blonde woman in her forties. Out of the corner of his eye, he saw the chaperone talking to Hong. Their conversation seemed friendlier than earlier and Hong kept nodding, although he mostly avoided the chaperone's icy eyes.

Carrie stepped inside the conference hall. Justin gave her a quick gesture with his head and they made eye contact. He smiled at her and Carrie smiled back. She came over and introduced herself to the German researcher as Sophie Bertillon.

"How are things going?" Carrie asked after they shook hands.

"Wonderful," Justin asked. "This is a great venue. We learned some positive news and perhaps we'll have even more in the afternoon."

The German arched her left eyebrow. "But the lecture was so long and dry," she said. "And some of the information was outdated and irrelevant."

Justin smiled at her. Of course she had no reason to believe they were discussing something else beside the conference keynote speaker's presentation.

A man dressed in a *thawb*—the traditional white robe of Saudi men—and a red-and-white-checkered headdress invited the participants to take their seats. The conference was going to continue with a presentation from one of the ENEC's directors.

Justin returned to his table and tried to pay attention to the presenter. He was also dressed in a thawb, but his was golden, with elaborate black embroidery. The man was in his fifties, with a big bushy moustache and a strong baritone voice. Justin learned that the UAE was in the process of expanding its commercial nuclear power reactors and was close to completing its second power plant fueled by uranium at Barakah, about 185 miles west of Abu Dhabi, in close cooperation with a Canada-based corporation. The board executive gave an update on the progress, the billions of dollars flowing to the project and the billions of kilowatt-hours of electricity expected in return. Fascinating as it may have been, Justin tuned him out and returned to his long list of pressing tasks.

He used his laptop to log onto the CIS encrypted state-of-the-art security online server and accessed some of the files he had requested from the office. Justin was working on several fronts at the same time. He was trying to identify the best location for infiltration into North Korea across the Russian border. Some of the areas along the ten-mile border were too close to security installments and watch towers. A couple of points were known crossings used by local gangsters involved in drug and cigarette smuggling. Justin had sought the assistance of a contact within the FSB, Russia's internal security and counterintelligence service. Yuliya Markov was an operative with whom he had shared more than one mission, a few months ago in Yemen and then in Russia. Hopefully, Markov would be able to find someone among the Russian border guards who could give Justin's team a hand during their infiltration into North Korea. Justin did not want to fight Russian border guards or run the risk of being discovered by them before even crossing into North Korea. He needed to reach a workable compromise.

The next task on his list was Quan. Justin was troubled by the determination of the CIS director to eliminate his agents without giving them an opportunity to explain themselves and their actions. Justin was not having doubts about his orders and his mission in North Korea, but he was hoping to find some evidence in the files to justify a stay of execution.

Thus he had asked McClain to provide him with a higher level of security clearance, so he could review all the files related to operations run by or tied to Schultz and Park over the last year. There was a mountain of reports and notes, as the two agents were true worker bees and liked to document their actions very thoroughly. And then there was a web of agents reporting to Quan as their director, and Justin had obtained access to their reports as well. He had cast an immense net, not wanting to miss anything, since this was a matter of certain death for the two agents.

The third item on Justin's agenda was becoming familiar with half of his team. Earlier that morning, McClain had confirmed that the SIS—better known as MI6—were going to provide their assistance with the mission. Their operatives— Reginald "Rex" Phillips and Evelyn "Eve" Davis—were going to meet up with them in Vladivostok, Russia, in two days. Rex was a skilled sniper, having joined the ranks of MI6 from the Special Air Service (SAS), one of the special forces units of the British Army. Eve spoke Korean like a native and had a great sense of orientation in pretty much any type of terrain. Justin was hoping to convince Hong to meet them near the Korean-Russian border and drive them to the camp where the agents were being held captive. The MI6 contact that Rex and Eve had used eight weeks ago during their stint in North Korea had vanished without a trace. MI6 believed he had been killed or captured by the wide network of North Korean secret agents.

Justin sighed as he looked at Eve's classified file on his laptop's screen, then reached for his mug. He frowned as he founded it empty. Justin clicked a few keys on the keyboard and locked the laptop. Then he walked to the table, where he refilled his mug. He took a long swig, enjoying the hot liquid that was perking up his senses. Then he walked back to his table.

He plowed through the reports while only occasionally glancing around him and at the speaker. His back was against the wall so no one could sneak up on him. There were no cameras in the conference hall and he was holding his laptop near his chest. The only set of eyes he had to worry about were those of the two men sitting to his left and right. But they were completely absorbed in the presentation and were oblivious to pretty much everything else taking place around them.

A round of applause signaled the end of the speech. Justin logged out of the server and feigned attention while the ENEC director took a couple of questions. Then he dismissed the participants for lunch.

As the stream of people began to slowly make their way toward the door, Justin's eyes followed Hong and his chaperone. They were the first ones to leave their table, and the chaperone seemed to insist they get out of the conference hall as soon as possible, even if it meant elbowing their way through the people already ahead of them. Justin gestured to Carrie, who nodded back as she also hurried her pace to keep up with her target.

* * *

Carrie hated this part of the job: seducing Shin, the chaperone, to have dinner with her up in his room on the fortieth floor of the Shangri-La Hotel. It was like enticing a snake to come and crawl onto your bare chest. She had never liked this whore-like tactic, and had almost failed the class on sexual seduction and honeypot techniques back on the training course at The Plant. "I will kill for my country and I will die for my country, but I *will not* become a whore for my country," were the words Carrie had shouted at her instructor at the time. And now she had agreed *only* to convince Shin to take her to his room and then slip a concoction of sedatives into his food or drink, which would cause Shin to be incapacitated for the rest of the day. The next morning he would wake up without as much as a headache, but by then Justin and Hong would have sealed their deal.

She hurried to catch up to Shin and Hong, who were marching with a fast pace down the cream-colored marble corridor, seemingly headed toward the men's washroom. Shin turned his head and gave Carrie a stern glare with his piercing black eyes, as if he was wondering why she was following them.

"Hey," Carrie said with a smile and a nod as she walked past them.

She stopped near a window and looked at her image in the reflection on the glass. She fixed a few hair strands for a moment, then looked at Shin, who was standing alone by the door to the men's washroom.

"I think you were at my conference, the one on nukes' energy," Carrie said and took a couple of steps in Shin's direction.

Shin nodded. "I saw you too, and you were looking at me."

His accent was thick and his voice was strong.

"Where are you from?" Carrie advanced another few steps. She was now about three feet away from Shin.

"I'm from Korea."

"Oh, South Korea?"

Shin frowned. "No, not South Korea. The Democratic People's Republic of Korea, the true Korea."

Carrie arched her eyebrows. "Fascinating," she said in a genuinely surprised tone of voice. "I've never met anyone from DPRK. We don't hear much about you but I can see that the men from there are so . . . so handsome." She gave her tone a playful twist.

She was not exactly telling the truth but she was not lying either. Shin was tall and broad-shouldered, with a clean-shaven face and high cheekbones. He was in his late thirties or early forties but still had all his hair, albeit some of it had turned silver, especially around his temples. His eyes were deep black and he had a high forehead and a small, narrow nose.

Shin shrugged, then cocked his head to the left. The undecided look in his eyes told Carrie he was still determining her true intentions with the compliment.

"And we Canadians are so straightforward," Carrie said, still in the same flirtatious tone. "Why don't we go for lunch and you can tell me all about yourself and your country?"

Shin looked toward the men's washroom, then back at Carrie.

"Come on, your friend is a big boy and can find his way around the hotel." Carrie stepped near Shin and gave him a slight nudge with her right elbow. "Let's go get some room service. We have a little over an hour. That gives us plenty of time to enjoy our meal, our conversation . . . and more," Carrie whispered slowly and softly in Shin's ear.

She knew she was being very direct and was moving very fast. Maybe it was because she was out of practice or maybe her disgust for this part of the operation was getting the best of her. But she was counting on Shin's reputation as a womanizer and on the prevailing belief in North Korea that everything in the Western world of capitalism is corrupt and degenerate, including the women and their sense of morality.

Shin peered at her incredulously. Carrie could tell what was going on in his mind as he measured her up with a lustful look.

"Sure, why not?" he said in a firm voice, his accent even more pronounced. "This way." He gestured down the corridor and offered her his right arm.

Carrie took it without hesitation, although her stomach almost turned at the touch. She immediately felt dirty, like she was walking barefoot and had stepped into a pile of crap, with the gooey, smelly yuck now stuck to her skin. But she smiled and nodded at Shin as they made their way through the bright corridor and reached the six elevators.

The hollow ping announced the arrival of an elevator, and Shin played the gentleman and allowed Carrie to take the first step inside. She thanked him and held her briefcase with her left hand, close to her knees. Her SIG P228 pistol was inside the briefcase, loaded and ready, along with a pair of handcuffs. She hoped there would be no need to use either one, but she was prepared in case of any contingency.

Shin pressed the correct button on the elevator panel. He smiled at Carrie, a small, hesitant smile, but she returned a big, genuine smile. They reached the fortieth floor in a matter of seconds. The elevator doors opened and Shin again gestured for Carrie to walk in front of him. She thanked him again, stepped outside into the corridor, and waited for Shin. She knew his room number, but she feigned ignorance. Shin tilted his head to the right. Carrie nodded and followed him, staying one step behind him.

"This is my room," Shin said as he stopped in front of a door.

He fished out a plastic card from his pocket and slid it into the electronic lock of the door. A moment later, the door snapped open and a dot on the lock turned from steady red to blinking green.

"It's open." Shin pushed the door a crack.

"Go ahead," Carrie said.

"Ladies first." Shin's voice turned firmer and a notch louder.

Carrie nodded. "Since you insist."

She took the first step, then realized the trap Shin had been setting for her. She made the mistake of turning her back to the North Korean agent for a split second. Before she could react, she felt Shin's strong fingers wrapped around her neck.

"Who are you?" he said as he pushed her inside the room and shut the door behind them. "American agents? CIA?"

"I . . . I don't know what you're—" Carrie said as she struggled for breath.

She raised her right hand up and tried to slip her fingers underneath Shin's powerful grip.

"Shut up." Shin tightened his chokehold. "You lured me here with offers of sex but I know what you really want. Information. Intelligence. Who do you work for? Tell me or I will kill you."

Carrie raised her shoulders and swung her body slightly to the left. She slammed her right fist into Shin's groin. He bellowed in pain and eased his grip just a little. But it was sufficient for Carrie's right hand fingers to slide underneath Shin's arm. She pushed his arm away with all her strength, while at the same time she threw her left hand back at Shin's face. She gouged at his eyes, scratching and tearing at his skin. Shin screamed and released his grip.

"You whore," he shouted. "You're dead."

Carrie stepped away and turned around. Shin was blinking and flinching and shaking his head around like a madman. He stuck his left hand inside his jacket.

Carrie knew what he was going for. She lifted her briefcase and blindly groped for her pistol. Her trained fingers found its trigger just as Shin begin to pull out his gun. Carrie fired a single shot. The bullet struck Shin in his right eye, and he collapsed against the door, dead before hitting the floor six feet away from her.

Carrie took a couple of deep breaths and fell on the couch across the room. She looked at the pool of blood forming around Shin's head, then reached for her BlackBerry. A couple of long moments passed while her call was being connected, then she said in a calm voice, "Justin, we have a situation."

CHAPTER SEVEN

Shangri-La Hotel, Dubai, United Arab Emirates
April 28, 12:05 p.m.

Justin stifled a sigh and glanced at Hong, who was sitting across from him on the earth green sofa, nervously sipping a cup of tea. His hands were shaking, causing the cup to rattle against the saucer. Hong looked at Justin, frowned, and, almost dropping the cup and saucer to the carpet, placed them on the coffee table between the two men.

"What's wrong?" Hong asked as the corners of his eyes crinkled.

"Something came up, and I need to meet my partner." Justin put his phone away as he stood up. He had just finished talking to Carrie. "Wait here. I'll be back in a few minutes."

"I thought we were going to talk."

"We will. But this matter takes priority. Don't go anywhere. And order a cup of coffee for me." Justin smiled, trying to calm down Hong.

He studied Justin's face for a moment, then nodded. "Yes, okay."

"Great."

Justin jogged through the sunlit lobby with limestone walls. He got into one of the elevators and impatiently tapped the panel. His mind was in overdrive as he considered various scenarios about how to dispose of the body.

The elevator doors opened, and Justin darted through the corridor until he found the right room. He stood very near to the door then said in a low voice just above a whisper, "Carrie, it's me."

"Watch your step," Carrie said from inside then slowly opened the door.

Justin noticed a few small stains on the beige carpet two feet away from the door. Shin's body was lying on his back two steps away. Carrie had placed towels and a housecoat around his body and his head to soak up the blood.

"How are you doing?" Justin asked as he checked on her.

"I'm fine." Carrie massaged the sides of her neck. "Unhappy about having to kill him, but he left me no other choice."

"What happened here?" Justin said.

Carrie gave him the abbreviated version. "I had to shoot him," she said as she ended her story.

Justin nodded. "I understand. Do you think anyone heard the shots?"

Carrie shook her head. "I had my suppressor on. Not many people are in their rooms at this time of day, and someone would have knocked on the door if they heard the commotion or his screams."

"All right." Justin walked to the nearest twin bed, then to the large window. It overlooked the Sheikh Zayed Road—the main artery of Dubai—and the impressive Burj Khalifa Tower, the centerpiece of downtown and the tallest skyscraper in the world, standing at over 2,716.5 feet high. The likelihood of anyone's noticing the struggle from the business towers across the street was probably nil, because of the reflective, mirror-like exterior surface of the windows. The traffic noise from the sixteen lanes of Sheikh Zayed Road did not penetrate the thick windows, and Justin wondered if the call to prayer at 5:00 a.m. would be loud enough to wake the hotel guests. He turned around and said, "Assuming there are no witnesses, our first priority is to clean up this place and get rid of the body. We'll need disinfectants to scrub the blood off the carpet and wipe away all stains. I'll buy us gloves, bags, a container and other cleaning supplies."

"And the largest heavy-duty duffel bag to move the corpse," Carrie said in a low voice.

"We'll also have to book this room for three or four more days, to make sure we're all far away from this place and have completed our mission before the cleaning crew realizes what took place in this room."

"Yes. What about Hong?"

Justin shrugged. "I don't—"

A gentle knock on the door interrupted him. Then they heard Hong's voice speaking in a language they did not understand. Justin assumed it was Korean.

He sidestepped the body as he walked to the door. He opened it a hair and looked at Hong, who returned a look of surprise mixed with shock.

"What . . . You shouldn't be here," Hong said and tried to enter the room.

"Be careful where you step," Justin replied and slowly opened the door while pointing down at the floor.

Hong took a couple of seconds to realize what had happened and the gravity of the situation as he stared speechless at Shin's dead body. He opened his mouth but no words came out as he paced around the room, waving his arms in the air. Then he sat on the edge of one of the twin beds and put his head between his hands.

"You . . . you killed him. You killed him," he said in a quavering voice.

"It was self-defense." Carrie pointed at Shin's pistol lying near his body.

Hong did not look up. "I am . . . I am a dead man, like him."

He stared at the body for a long moment, then looked at Justin. Tears had filled his eyes and the wrinkles on his face had doubled.

"No, you're not," Justin said and walked over to Hong. He sat near him on the bed. "This is okay. We're going to fix this."

"How? How is this okay? Shin is dead and nothing can bring him back to life. If I go back home tomorrow without him, the secret police will arrest me and my family and we'll end up in the prison camps. They'll torture us and we'll . . ." Hong's voice trailed off as tears began to stream down his face.

Justin stood up. He went to the minibar across the bed and filled a glass with a generous portion of whisky. He took the bottle with him and handed the glass to Hong. "Drink this."

Hong looked up and shook his head.

"It will calm your nerves." Justin held it a few inches away from Hong's face.

Hong held the glass with both his trembling hands and took a small sip. He made a face as if he was swallowing a bitter pill.

"Take a good long swig," Justin said.

Hong brought the glass to his mouth and drank another small sip.

"This is what we're going to do." Justin stood in front of Hong. "As soon as you've calmed down, you'll call home and talk to your supervisors at the Yongbyon Center. Then they'll have you talk to people from the Ministry of State Security."

Hong frowned and shook his head. "No, no, no, no, no," he said and almost spilled half of his glass.

Justin held him by his arms with a strong grip. "Hong, listen up and it will make sense. You're going to tell the MSS that Shin defected to the Americans. He asked you to join him, but you refused. You love your country and that's why you're calling home to report him."

Hong's jaw dropped. "But he *did not* defect. You killed him."

Justin sighed. "True, but you cannot tell that to the MSS. Remember that Shin suspected you were going to betray your country, and he was not going to think twice before killing you with his own hands. But now he's gone." Justin pointed at the body to emphasize his words. "And you are safe."

Hong said nothing and swallowed the rest of the whisky.

Justin reached over and refilled the glass. "The MSS is aware of Shin's suspicions of you. Maybe they expected Shin to call them and report on you tonight or tomorrow before your return flight. If you call them now, they may conclude that Shin made up the entire story to draw away attention from his own plans of defection. And especially since you're reporting it and you're planning to return home even without Shin, it will cement your cover story and remove any doubts that you were ever going to leave."

Hong gave a small nod. "Because if I had such plans I would have run away with Shin and never returned home," he said slowly, unsure if those were the right words.

"Yes," Carrie said. She leaned against the curved desk with a large flat-screen television set on top of it. "Exactly. You're proving to them you're a patriot."

Justin said, "And once you're inside North Korea, you'll prepare your family for the trip out of the country. Hong, this is good. Now we don't have to look over our shoulders, but we can plan and prepare our next steps."

Hong shook his head and more tears flowed from his eyes. "I'm . . . I'm so scared for my family. If the secret police as much as suspect I'm lying to them, I will be killed. And my family, my wife and my kids too."

"Hong, you have to help us help them," Justin said in a warm but firm voice. "You're all they have, and you're the only one who can help them escape the daily misery and the nightmares of their lives."

He wanted to add that Hong had no other options. If he chose to tell the truth, the regime would most likely believe he had orchestrated or at least not prevented Shin's death. Especially considering that Shin had already harbored suspicions about Hong's loyalty toward his country.

Hong's head swung back and forth as his body rocked involuntarily. His left foot was tapping nervously on the floor. His eyes were still dark and undecided, and his face was covered in tears. "I'm . . . I guess I don't have another way out." He studied the dead body for a moment, then looked at Justin. "Okay, tell me what I need to do."

CHAPTER EIGHT

Shangri-La Hotel, Dubai, United Arab Emirates
April 28, 1:35 p.m.

Justin and Carrie spent the next hour and a half preparing Hong for his call and his conversation with his supervisors at the Yongbyon Nuclear Scientific Research Center and the agents of the Ministry of State Security. It was crucial for Hong to follow the script and keep his story straight about what exactly Shin had told him and the order of events.

"They're going to ask you more than once," Justin said as he coached Hong. "They might yell at you and accuse you of complicity or treason. Just ignore their accusations. Stick to the story, but do not repeat it like a broken record. Use other words, emotions, expressions, but always, *always*, follow the storyline about what happened, where, and how."

Hong nodded and seemed to understand, but halfway through the preparation he broke down. He began to cry and sob uncontrollably, and nothing Justin and Carrie said brought him any consolation. He told them his life story through tears and sighs, and how his distant cousins had tried to escape into China five years ago. They were caught by border guards and sent to the prison camps. Their family never saw them again, but were told the men had been executed by firing squads. Hong and his relatives were forced to denounce and disown the cousins in order to save their own lives. Hong had been moved down the ranks at his job; at least he was still allowed to work at the nuclear facility. But there was a large stain on his family history and the authorities always kept a close eye on him.

Justin and Carrie were aware of all this information about Hong. It was in his files, and Schultz and Park had done an excellent job in double-checking all facts about Hong's past. Determining the exact motive why someone would turn their back on their country and decide to betray them to the enemy was paramount to deciding the trustworthiness of a defector and of the intelligence he was providing. Hong had made plans to defect soon after his cousins were murdered, but was worried about the government backlash against his old, bedridden mother and father. Once they had passed away, about six months ago, Hong had redoubled his efforts to escape the country.

Justin told Hong that his fears were real and valid but reassured him that there was hope for his future. Justin explained to him that if he stuck to the plan he was not going to be alone when he returned to North Korea. Justin told Hong only what he needed to know: gather as much classified intelligence as he could about the nuclear center, its current status, expansions plans, anything he could get his hands on that would have a significant value. Then he was to meet the agents near the North Korean–Russian border, drive them to an unspecified location inside the country, and then drive them and his family to freedom across the North Korean–Chinese border.

Hong took his time to ponder the plan and finally agreed to his assigned mission. They did two dry runs of how the conversation might go and then it was time for Hong to make the call.

He first reached a low-level supervisor who freaked out and almost had a heart attack during the call. Justin and Carrie could hear the loud voice and the screams of the supervisor, which needed no translation. Then Hong was patched through to a senior director of the research center, who sounded calmer and more focused. He asked a lot of questions, some of which Justin and Carrie had thought of, and others they had not. Hong handled himself quite well and overall conveyed the right message. The supervisor told Hong to call again in about half an hour, when he would have an official from the MSS present on the call.

Hong began to sweat during the wait and asked for another whisky, but Justin declined his request. Hong had to stay sober and sharp for the next discussions with the Korean secret agents, which were more important and trickier than the previous call. These operatives were trained to detect lies and deception. Hong had done well so far, but if he tripped even once or if he sowed even the slightest seed of doubt in the agents' minds, they would be on high alert. Justin's and Carrie's operation would be doomed before it even got off the ground.

The time came and Justin encouraged Hong to answer the questions in as few words as possible and to act shocked and confused by Shin's behavior. Carrie had jotted down the main points so that Hong could consult them.

The call went through and Hong began his talk in rapid Korean. He was soon interrupted by two different men—whose sharp voices and angry shouts spilled out of the phone receiver to fill the room. Justin wished he could understand what the agents were actually saying. The sweat pouring from Hong's forehead, his weak, trailing voice and trembling hands, and the constant interruptions conveyed a pretty good idea of what horrendous interrogation Hong was going through. At one point he was even flinching, as if their questions were hitting him across the face. But he was able to keep talking, struggling at times and often glancing at Carrie's notes written in large capital letters.

The angry voices seemed to calm down or at least lose their loud pitch. Hong was now more relaxed and he was constantly nodding. Finally, he lowered the phone receiver back into its cradle and heaved a deep sigh.

"So?" asked Justin.

Hong wiped the sweat off his face with his palms. "I think . . . I think they're now convinced Shin is a spy and a traitor. They've already sent people to pick up his family."

Justin nodded slowly. He wanted to say *better his family than yours*, but he was not sure that would give Hong reassurance at this moment.

"And they want me to return home immediately, to catch the first possible flight out. Oh, and they're also sending a team of agents here to fully investigate Shin's defection."

"They told you that?" Justin asked.

"Well, not in those exact terms, but one of the colonels said this matter will be analyzed thoroughly and someone will follow up on the information I gave them."

Justin exchanged a glance with Carrie.

"We don't have much time," she said.

"Yes, I'll go and prepare for the body's disposal. You stay here and brief Hong on our next steps."

Carrie nodded.

"What will happen to me now?" Hong asked. "One colonel told me they will interrogate me again when I return to my homeland."

Justin shook his head and sat on the bed next to Shin. "You will not meet them. Too dangerous at this point. We can't predict their reaction, and they might decide to torture you to see if you're telling them the truth."

"What about going back and collecting intelligence from my work at the center?" Hong asked.

"Too late for that. We'll use what you already know, what you remember," Justin said.

Hong nodded. "I have some documents at home, things I have been able to sneak out of the center while thinking about this decision. I can have my wife bring them to me, to us."

"Yes, that's a good idea," Carrie said.

Hong sighed and his face twisted into a deep frown of panic. "But . . . what do I do now?"

"You will call again in a couple of hours to inform them there's no room on any earlier flights. So they'll be waiting for you at the airport in Pyongyang in two days. But you're not going to be aboard that flight. You'll come with us and we'll leave tonight, as soon as we've taken care of Shin."

"We're not flying straight to Pyongyang, are we?" Hong asked with a certain amount of doubt.

"No. We're flying somewhere else and we're crossing the land border," Justin said, keeping his reply vague. Hong did not need to know all the exact details. "Now you'll call your family and tell them to meet you tomorrow evening in Rajin-Sonbong. Can you do that securely?"

Hong thought about it for a few seconds. Then he nodded. "Yes, one of our neighbors has a cellphone."

"And can you trust your neighbor?" Carrie asked. She was standing by the window.

"Yes . . . I mean, they have been trustworthy so far. We have watched together DVDs smuggled into the country and we've talked about our dislike for the authorities."

"Okay, your neighbor should find a vehicle, a van if possible, and drive your family to Rajin-Sonbong. I know it's difficult, but promise him you will pay him in American dollars whatever it costs him. They should wait there for further instructions."

Hong nodded.

Justin stood up. "Carrie will stay with you at all times. It may not feel like it, Hong, but you're safe now. You made the right choice. And we'll make sure your family joins you, and all of you will be safe and start a new life." He extended his hand to Hong.

Hong jumped to his feet and then gave Justin a big hug. "Thank you, thank you," he said in a low, tearful voice. "I promise to do everything it takes, everything it takes."

You might have to, and most likely you will, Justin thought.

"I'll be back soon," he said to Carrie as he walked around the body and left the hotel room.

* * *

Dubai International Airport, Dubai, United Arab Emirates
April 28, 9:25 p.m.

Justin returned in about an hour with two large duffel bags full of cleaning supplies and other items for their disposal-of-the-body operation. They scrubbed and scraped Shin's blood off the carpet, the door, and the walls. Then they wrapped Shin's body in plastic sheeting and put it into a wheelchair they had requested from the hotel's reception. They had scrapped the earlier idea of carrying the dead body in a duffel bag. It would be too bulky and heavy and cumbersome to move down the hall and into the elevator then through the lobby and the main doors without attracting curious glances. The security cameras were also unavoidable and would raise suspicions right away, or at least in a couple of days after the arrival of the North Korean agents. A woman pushing a wheelchair with a weak and elderly lady wrapped in a blanket and a black burka would look much more normal and perhaps be much less memorable.

While waiting for the sunset and the cover of darkness, Justin and Carrie wiped off all their fingerprints from the room surfaces and removed all Shin's valuables—personal belongings he would have taken with him if he had truly defected to the Americans. They left most of his clothes behind, but took one of the sets of pants and shirts hanging in the closet.

When it was around seven fifteen, Justin walked a few blocks from the hotel until he found a car rental company. He asked for a Dodge Caravan, which offered plenty of space, and used one of his many fake driver's licenses to rent the car for a day. He drove it back to the hotel. Carrie met him on the sidewalk on the left side of the hotel and together they helped their "grandmother" in the wheelchair into the back of the van.

Hong met up with them about five blocks away, south of the hotel. Justin drove south and then southeast on Highway E66 for about forty miles. They stopped on the side of the road near the village of Al Faqa and waited until there were no vehicles in sight. Then Justin and Carrie quickly lugged Shin's body to the desert. They walked among the sand dunes for a few dozen feet and then began to dig his grave. Justin had bought two shovels, and within half an hour they had dug a two-foot trench. He would have preferred a proper grave, six foot deep, so no vultures would dig up the body. But that would take hours, and he was not going to risk being discovered by curious passersby whom he would then have to eliminate and thus dig more graves.

At about 9:25 in the evening they arrived at the Dubai International Airport. The Gulfstream 450 jet that had brought them from Ottawa to Dubai through Frankfurt—owned by PrivilegeJets, a front company of the Canadian Intelligence Service operating all over the world—was ready to take them to Vladivostok. It was obvious this was the first time Hong had climbed aboard a private jet. He was mesmerized by the spacious cabin with oversized beige-colored leather seats, pull-out tables, and a four-place divan. He took in all the exquisite details of the luxurious interior as he ran his hand over his seat's armrest and looked at the sidewall panels and through the large oval windows. Valentina, the flight attendant, came to take his drink order while Hong swiveled in his seat.

Justin told Hong to enjoy the flight and to let Valentina know if he needed anything. Then Justin retreated to the back of the plane and sat across the table from Carrie. The Gulfstream interior was configured in a Universal Forward floor plan with seating for up to fourteen passengers and berthing for six. Justin and Carrie could have a quiet conversation without being heard by Hong, sitting near the galley about twenty feet away.

Carrie had already pulled out her laptop and was connecting to the CIS servers over the secure Internet connection. She looked up at Justin and gave him a big smile. "How's our guest?"

"Very excited and playing with the seat's controls."

"Let's hope he'll be that excited tomorrow night as well."

Justin nodded. "Yeah. Have you gotten in touch with Rex and Eve?"

"Not yet. I'm uploading the audio file to the server and I'll send a note to McClain to have someone translate it ASAP."

Justin glanced at Carrie's BlackBerry hooked up to her laptop. The smartphone had been customized and equipped with a long-range audio recording device. Carrie had used it to record Hong's conversation with his supervisors and the MSS agents. If Hong was not being completely honest with them, they would find out about it before they had put their plan into action in North Korea.

"I'm almost done," Carrie said.

Valentina brought them some ice-cold lemon water and they chatted for a couple of minutes. She was CIS like the two pilots and knew some of the details of the operation, as intelligence among the team members was shared on a need-to-know basis.

Ten minutes later, the captain announced they were ready for takeoff. The Gulfstream began to glide slowly over the tarmac. It was quiet inside the cabin but Justin knew the powerful engines were roaring just outside the windows. They were going to produce 13,850 lb of thrust each to fly them for the 4,400-mile-long nonstop flight. The captain mentioned that their cruising speed was going to be Mach 0.80 or almost 530 miles an hour, and they were climbing to an altitude of 41,000 feet.

After the captain levelled the plane, Justin checked on Hong. He was watching an action movie on the television screen mounted on the panel between two windows and had put the noise-cancelling earphones over his head. He had pulled out the seat's footrest, had reclined his seat, and was truly enjoying himself.

"We can speak freely now," Justin said to Carrie when he returned. "He's deeply immersed in a Hollywood flick."

Carrie removed her glasses and leaned back in her seat. "This operation didn't start on the right foot. Besides Hong, now we have another player, this Choe, his neighbor, about whom we don't know anything. We have only Hong's word that he is trustworthy."

"And we can't go on that alone. We'll give Choe a location far away from where we're actually going to cross the border. He'll hide the car—the van or whatever vehicle he's bringing—in the woods along the river, and we'll wait for nightfall before retrieving it. Then Hong will drive us and Rex and Eve to the prison camp."

Carrie nodded. "I've e-mailed McClain about the audio files." She pointed toward the laptop.

"Great. I'll write the report about today's events and send it over to McClain. Then we'll have supper, and afterwards I'll review the files about the route we're taking inside Korea. McClain was supposed to gather updated photos and maps of the area."

"Are you planning to sleep at all tonight?" Carrie asked in a tone that made it clear she was expecting "yes" as an answer.

"Oh, yeah. I'll rest for a few hours. It's going to be a busy day tomorrow and the day after that."

Carrie took a sip of her water. "That's our life, Justin. One crazy day after another crazy day with a little break in between. It's so difficult to make plans and to have a bit of a life outside work."

"I hear you. It's quite frustrating. Have you made new plans for the wedding?"

Carrie shrugged, then groaned. "Why, so I can cancel them again?"

"No, so McClain can put the date in his calendar. Then you can pray that no crisis happens on or around that time."

"I don't think my prayers get heard. The last time we booked the venue, sent out the invitations, I got my dress ready and we had to cancel three days before the wedding. An assassination planned in Cairo, and my plans ended up in smoke. And the worst thing was that the intel about the assassination was false. Go figure."

Justin nodded. He had been involved in that operation when it seemed a group of Islamic militants were planning to target the newly elected president of Egypt. Because Justin and Carrie had a wide network of contacts in North Africa, McClain had dispatched them to foil the plot, which ended up being a false alarm.

"Is Thomas getting frustrated?" Justin asked about Carrie's fiancé.

"He is, but I'm the one who's furious about it, since I'm screwing up the plan. He's in the private business and the CEO, he can take a couple of weeks off at a moment's notice and assign someone else to run the PR firm. I'm the one who can't take two days off even when I give my boss six months' notice." Carrie heaved a deep sigh.

"What are you going to do?"

"I don't know. Thomas and I have talked about just eloping, running away somewhere and tying the knot, just the two of us. But Thomas wants his family to be there and he has so many relatives. They're a tightly knit group. I want a beach wedding, but it doesn't matter if we have three or three hundred guests."

Carrie smiled and played with a few strands of hair that had come loose from her ponytail. "How are you and Anna handling the changes?"

Justin shrugged. "It has been only three months since she returned to the CIS as a surveillant, so it's hard to tell. It hasn't had any impact on our relationship, yet."

"You're still worried about her safety?"

"Well . . . yes and no. She's always a target; we're all targets, since some extremists hate us just because of who we are and how we live. But now she carries a gun and so far her assignments have been within Canada."

"But?"

Justin ran his hand through his hair. "But I don't know when she'll be deployed overseas. She's assigned to the Central Africa Section, and that area of the world is always in turmoil. Dictators, genocides, ethnic wars."

Carrie nodded. "And you guys haven't talked about a wedding date?"

"No, not really. I mean, it's in our plans for sure, but we haven't nailed down a specific time. Anna wants a Catholic church wedding, with the priest and a big cathedral."

"And what do you want?"

"I just want to make her happy."

Carrie laughed. "Good answer."

Valentina came with their food: grilled chicken salad for Carrie and crispy pork cutlets for Justin. The look and the smell of the dishes perked up Justin's appetite. The Gulfstream's fully stocked galley allowed for cooking scrumptious meals, but Valentina was not hired because of her great culinary skills as a chef. She was better at slicing someone's throat with a Ka-Bar knife than chopping carrots.

"Mmmmm, this is so good," Carrie said after tasting the first bite of chicken. "Thanks, Val."

Valentina nodded and waved from the other end of the plane, where she was serving supper to Hong.

"How's your piggy?" Carrie asked Justin.

"Couldn't be any better." Justin cut again into his first pork chop. "Crispy and crunchy on the outside, but tender and juicy on the inside. Val's cooking has gotten so much better."

They devoured their food in silence. Justin remembered they had not had any lunch because of the incident in Shin's and Hong's hotel room. In their line of work they rarely had time to sit down and slowly and thoroughly enjoy a delicious meal. Even when time was not a factor, their training and their habits got the better of them.

Carrie wiped her lips with her napkin and took a long swig of water, emptying her glass. She put her plate to the side and flipped up the lid of her laptop. "Have you found anything new on Quan?"

"No, but I'm still looking." Justin scooped the last crumbs off his plate. "I still don't have a full understanding of the circumstances that led Park and Schultz into NK. If they defected, why are they being tortured? It makes no sense. And if they were caught inside NK, what were they doing there?"

Carrie considered Justin's reply for a few moments. "What if they were caught in South Korea and then smuggled across the border?"

"In that case, it's very unfortunate." Justin paused and looked out the window. Darkness stretched as far as his eyes could see. "But we have our orders and they haven't changed. And before you ask, I haven't changed my mind."

Carrie raised up her hands. "I wasn't going to ask, but now that you brought it up, are you talking about changing your mind about Schulz and Park or about our mission's objective?"

"Both. It's not my place to determine why and how things ended up the way they did. It would be useful to know, but we may never find out the whole truth. As far as I'm concerned, there are more than sufficient reasons that these agents need to be eliminated. It's irrelevant whether they're acting upon their free will or under torture, at least for the purposes of our operation." Justin said his last words with much conviction and without the slightest hesitation.

"I see," Carrie said. "And I just wanted to make clear that I don't have second thoughts about our mission either. The only thing I wonder is if and how any of this operation would be different if instead of those two agents it was me locked up in that hole."

Justin's eyes met Carrie's blank gaze. He studied her face for a moment, then said, "If I had conclusive evidence that you had betrayed or were betraying our country . . . You know the answer to that question."

Carrie nodded. "Yeah, I guess I do," she said slowly and thoughtfully.

A tense silence followed for a few moments. Then Justin said, "I don't love what I'm doing at this moment, as I didn't sign up to kill other service agents. And I don't hate Park and Schultz for whatever led them to this trap. But it's my mission, our mission, and we've got to carry it out."

"I know you were good friends with Schultz during training," Carrie said softly, and held Justin's eyes.

"I was. Then life got very busy for both of us. But what McClain doesn't know—and you don't know it either—is that Schultz actually saved my life. And now, this is how I'm repaying him." He let out a deep sigh.

Carrie leaned forward and held Justin's hand. "What happened?"

"We had a river crossing exercise and I woke up sick with fever. Every bone in my body ached as if broken into a thousand pieces, and I was so tired I could hardly drag my feet. I should have skipped the exercise, but the trainer had ripped another recruit a new one because he tripped and sprained his arm. I didn't want to be an object of ridicule and sarcasm."

Justin stopped for a moment, looked out the plane's window, then returned his gaze to Carrie's face. She nodded at him and gave him a reassuring smile.

"So I go on, and halfway through the river the current gets to be pretty strong and starts to drag me away. Here I've got forty pounds of supplies over my dead-tired body and my feet are sliding on the slippery rocks and I can hardly get enough breath into my mucous-filled lungs as it is and now my head is underwater and I start to drown. That's when Schultz grabs me by the collar and pulls me toward him and holds on to me until we cross the river. The trainer never saw the scene, as he was focused on the other teams, and Schultz never mentioned it. He saved my life, as I would have probably drowned that day. And that would have completely wrecked my otherwise great training record at The Plant." Justin finished with a thoughtful nod.

"Yes, of course, it would have." Carrie tried to laugh at Justin's attempt at a joke.

Justin shrugged and shook his head.

Carrie went on, "As you said, you got your orders, and the intel makes it clear the agents are harming our country. I know it hurts and we don't have to love or like it. But we have to do it."

Justin nodded. "You're right. Unless we hear otherwise, we're moving forward with our plan. Now, how do you feel about our exfil?"

"I wish we had other options, but we don't. Returning to Russia after we've raised alarms in NK will take much longer and we'll be exposed during all that time. Crossing into China is not ideal, but it's the lesser of two evils."

"Yes. If faced with the choice of fighting a long battle with the NK army or explaining our trespassing into the Chinese territory, I'll take the second any time."

Carrie gave Justin a slight frown as her eyes glinted with a hint of concern. "And the Chinese, they'll accept our version of the story?"

"I hope they do. We'll do our best to avoid running into them but if it looks like that's inevitable, McClain will call his counterparts in the Chinese MSS to inform them our operation may spill across the border."

Carrie grinned. "May? More like *will*."

"Yes, but McClain will make it sound like it was a contingency plan, not a premeditated move. The Chinese will know it was the other way around, but they'll play ball. They'll be mad and demand an apology but eventually they'll allow us to return home."

"What about Hong and his family? Will they let them go or hand them over to the North Koreans to execute them?"

"Once they cross into China, they're Canadian citizens, so the authorities will have to let them go. Once they see their passports, they'll have no excuse."

Justin nodded toward his briefcase across from their table. Four Canadian passports had already been prepared with the names of Hong, his wife, and his two children. If Hong had refused to cooperate, Justin and Carrie would have gotten rid of the passports.

Carrie said, "In theory, it sounds solid. We'll see how it plays out on the ground."

The plane shook slightly and the cutlery and the dishes rattled on the table.

"Turbulence," Justin said.

Carrie nodded. "Yeah, we have to expect some of that when crossing such vast distances."

They waited for the captain to say something over the public address system but there was nothing, and the plane stopped vibrating within a minute.

Justin looked at Carrie and began to open his mouth and ask her a question, but then changed his mind and shook his head.

"Spit it out," Carrie said.

"What?"

"Your question. What is it?"

"Oh, it can wait."

"We have another ten hours. Ask me."

"No, it's okay."

Carrie frowned. "You have this heavy look on your face and I know you're not going to sleep well until you have an answer. What do you want to know?"

"All right. Have you looked at the flash drive yet?"

Carrie fell back into her chair. Her frown stayed on her face and she clenched her teeth. Her eyes turned into narrow slits. "No, I haven't . . . Well, I haven't seen everything yet."

Justin waited in silence. Back in December, Carrie had received a USB drive with classified intelligence from a former CIS agent. It contained reports and documents about Carrie's father and his covert operation in the Soviet Union, where he had disappeared in the late eighties. Carrie had recently discovered her father's remains and had given him a hero's funeral, with the flag-shrouded casket and the three-shot rifle salute, as he was laid to rest at the Beechwood Cemetery, the final home of thousands of Canadian soldiers and war veterans. But the secret documents contained the reasons why her father was dispatched on this mission, his objective, his target.

Carrie lowered her voice and leaned forward. "I read enough to know he was sent there to bring out someone willing to defect. It seemed it was a powerful leader in the Communist Party at the time. He had some explosive intelligence he was willing to exchange for his life and that of his wife."

Justin wanted to ask about the defector's name, but he knew Carrie was not going to tell him until the right moment.

"I stopped before I got to the name," Carrie said. She relaxed her shoulders and her frown was gone. One of her eyebrows was still arched a bit higher than the other, as if she could not make up her mind whether or not to let go of her anger. "I . . . I just don't know . . . Knowing the truth will further complicate my life."

Justin nodded. "You have closure. You found your dad and he's resting in peace. That's all that matters." He wanted to add "for now" but held his tongue.

"Yeah, I do. Who knows, maybe in a few months I'll check the reports again. They're in a safe place, somewhere no one will ever think to look."

Hong walked slowly toward them. His face was sweaty and he looked jittery, rubbing his hands together.

"You're not claustrophobic, are you?" Carrie asked.

"No, no, I worry about family. They alone and now with this job I expect to do I'm afraid for them, them lives and my life." His accent was more pronounced and he was making beginner's mistakes even though he usually spoke fluent English.

"Sit down." Justin moved over and tapped the seat next to him.

"I worry if Choe tells someone, the government people, then they take wife to jail and children . . . They kill them. I kill them."

"We're going to do the best we can to protect your family and you." Justin put his hand slowly over Hong's shoulder. "And you're doing a brave thing for you and for your family. Choe will not know about our plan. He's simply bringing your family to Rajin-Sonbong because you want to surprise them there. After he drops them off at a hotel, we will call Choe and ask him to drop the van somewhere near the border. After that, he will not go near your family anymore. You'll instruct your wife to leave the hotel and wait for us in another location. You understand?"

Hong still seemed nervous but he nodded as he tried to stop his hands from trembling. "You promise you not let my family die? You promise?"

Justin stole a quick glance at Carrie. She nodded at Justin.

"I promise, Hong. I will do whatever I can to bring you and your family and all of us safely out of that place."

CHAPTER NINE

Vladivostok International Airport, Russia
April 29, 4:15 p.m.

The Gulfstream jet glided through the vast umbrella of thick gray clouds hovering over Vladivostok International Airport. Justin did not need the captain informing them they were losing altitude and were going to land in a few minutes. He could feel the angle of flight change with the plane's descent, and the rising air pressure in the cabin created a slight discomfort in his ears. When the jet had cleared the last of the fluttering haze that surrounded them, he was able to see the landscape: tall cedars and spruces, birches and aspens, and the two- and three-story houses of Knevichi, the closest neighborhood to the runaway.

"We're here," Justin told Hong, whose face was stuck to the window taking in every detail. "Get ready for landing."

Hong nodded. He leaned back in his seat across from Justin and struggled to close his seatbelt buckle. Carrie was sitting next to Justin and gave him a small smile as he turned his head toward her.

"You ready?" she whispered in his ear.

"As ready as ever."

It was thirty-eight degrees when they stepped onto the newly reconstructed tarmac, and a cold drizzle extended its welcome. Justin buttoned his black windbreaker and lifted up his collar but could not do anything about the wet mist spraying his unshaven face. He dropped his two large duffel bags on the tarmac while waiting for Carrie and Hong, then they all walked with a brisk pace toward the entrance to Customs in Terminal A. Val and the pilots were going to meet them outside the airport after they filled out and submitted the necessary flight documents.

Justin and Carrie travelled under diplomatic passports, which made clearing the customs a breeze. Their luggage was also covered by the diplomatic protection and it was neither checked nor scanned by the customs X-ray machines. Otherwise, all alarms would have gone off considering the arsenal of weapons and explosives, as well as other tactical gear, they were bringing into the country. But the clearly marked label "Diplomatic Pouch" on each of their luggage pieces exempted their contents from such scrutiny.

Justin, Carrie, and Hong hurried through Terminal A of the airport, a giant structure of marble, glass, and steel with blue and beige as the dominant colors. It was recently built for an Asia-Pacific Economic Cooperation Summit and it was still in excellent shape. Passengers walked to and fro but there was not the great flow and the rush that was common to most airports. There were the usual airline counters, large flat screens hanging on the walls indicating the flights' departure and arrival times, and a few gift stores, but shopping was the last thing on Justin's mind.

They stepped outside through the glass doors and sought shelter near one of the entrances that offered some protection from the wind gusts and the sprinkling rain. Within a few seconds, a brand-new black Land Rover Defender stopped a few feet away from them. Through the thin haze Justin recognized the famous box-shape of the solid off-road vehicle. And he also recognized the face of the blond driver.

"That's Rex," Justin said. "And Eve, the passenger."

Carrie nodded. "Are we going?" She gestured toward the door. "Val and the pilots?"

"We'll call them and tell them we had to go. We'll meet up with them tonight at the hotel."

"Okay," Carrie said.

Justin picked up his duffel bags just as Rex came around the Rover. "Need a hand, mate?" He stretched his left arm to pick up one of the bags.

"Sure, thanks." Justin handed it over.

Rex took it, then extended his right arm. "Name's Rex," he said in a firm voice.

"I'm Justin."

They shook hands.

Rex's blond hair was in a buzz cut and he was sporting a small anchor beard. Justin guessed Rex's file photo must have been taken a few months back, since at that time he was clean-shaven and with longer hair. Rex was in his early thirties, and his strong jaw and protruding chin gave his face a square-shaped form. He had a high forehead, soft blue eyes, and an aquiline nose. He was dressed in a black leather bomber jacket and black designer jeans.

They were headed toward the trunk when Eve opened the Rover's door and climbed out. "I had to finish an important call," she said to Carrie. "How was the flight?"

"Long. Tiring. How're you doing?"

Eve shrugged. "Eh, it's raining. Feels like home back in London. I'm Eve, by the way."

"Carrie."

They exchanged a strong handshake.

"And this is Justin. Justin, this is Eve," Carrie said as Justin and Rex returned.

More introduction followed. Justin noticed that Eve too did not look like her file photo, and she seemed much younger in person than her age of twenty-seven. She had cut her hair short, had dyed it raven black, and had kept it sweeping across her forehead. Her eyes were brown, not blue, but the rest of her face was as gorgeous as her picture and she looked even better in person. Eve had high cheekbones, a small, narrow nose, and a tiny beauty mark just above the right corner of her upper lip. She wore a brown coat that came almost to her ankles, and light blue jeans.

They loaded all the gear in the back of the Rover and Justin introduced Hong to Rex and Eve. Then Rex sat behind the steering wheel and Eve in her old spot. Justin sat in the middle of the backseat with Carrie to his left and Hong to his right.

Carrie pulled out her BlackBerry and called Val to inform her of their change of plans.

"Our place is about fifteen minutes out," Rex said as they passed by some sort of facility at the left side of the airport that looked like it served for jet-fuel storage and refueling. They were driving on *Ulitsa na Novvy Terminal,* the New Terminal Road. "We're on the outskirts of Artyom." He pointed to his left. "I noticed you don't travel light."

"You're right. We'll need some heavy cover on our road trip."

Rex's lips formed a wry smile. "Oh, yes, our road trip."

A blue rusty cube truck cut in front of them, slightly missing the front bumper of the Rover.

Rex slammed on his horn with his fist. "Tosser," he shouted at the driver speeding away and covering their view with the black smoke from his exhaust pipe. "This country is so messed up. These drivers, they have no respect for anyone's lives, including their own. And they drive these crappy trucks that should have gone to the junkyard ages ago."

Justin nodded. Rex's English had the standard British accent one heard in movie adaptations of Jane Austen novels or if they tuned to the British Broadcasting Corporation television channel. It was called Received Pronunciation, the most famous of all British English varieties spoken in England, and it was considered posh and prestigious. During their training at The Plant, Justin and Carrie had attended a series of classes on recognizing and faking various accents of English and other languages.

"Pull over, you knobhead; can't cut in front of me, then slam on your brakes," Rex continued as the truck in front of them slowed down all of a sudden.

Justin sat up straight in his seat while Rex switched lanes and drove around the truck now stopped in the middle of the lane.

"Hey, calm down, will you?" Eve tapped Rex on his shoulder. "Save some of this anger for our road trip, will you?" She tilted her head and nodded at Justin.

Her accent sounded exactly like Rex's but rang out with a softer, more relaxed tone.

"I just can't stand wankers." Rex spat out the words. "You have no business being on the road if you don't know what you're doing. You're going to end up killing yourself and someone else. You have a problem, then pull over."

"You got yourselves a sweet ride," Justin said as he looked around the Rover and ran his hand over the leather center console box.

"I prefer cars from my country, and this Rover is a true beauty. It soldiers on even when we can't or we won't." He tapped gently on the steering wheel, then grinned. "The truth is, our HQ shipped this over, but what I said about the Rover's power is absolutely, completely true."

"I hear you," Justin said. "I love Rovers too."

"And we fit in with Russian mobsters," Eve said as she looked straight ahead. "We've seen a couple of Rovers and some fancy imports we don't even have in Britain."

Carrie said, "It's the same in Canada. I suspect car companies made some limited-edition models that only filthy-rich Russians can afford." She shook her head in disgust.

Rex turned right into the *Ulitsa na Aeroport*, Airport Road, when they arrived at the overpass. Fields stretched on both sides of the road. They drove in silence for a few moments and then slowly entered the west part of Artyom. Justin had read a bit about the area surrounding Vladivostok International Airport when he prepared for this operation. Artyom was a blue-collar city of about 120,000 people. Most of its residents worked in factories spread around the city producing construction material, in railroad transport, and in the airport. Fine porcelain and good-quality pianos were also made in the city.

Justin looked over at Hong, who had not said a word since they got in the car. *He's probably thinking about his family.* Justin put a reassuring hand on Hong's shoulder, and Hong gave him a hesitant smile.

The road grew narrower, barely enough for two cars. The blacktop was in dire need of replacement and potholes in some places looked like they were going to swallow the Rover's wheels. They passed by a series of five-story apartment buildings built with concrete panels, most likely from the times of the Soviet Union. They looked decrepit and depressing, their grayish color worsened by the rain which was now falling hard, with large drops thumping against the Rover's hood and windows.

Rex took a couple of turns and they came into a residential area with private houses. Some were built out of wood and others with cinderblocks, with shiny red roofs and painted a variety of lively colors. *What a contrast,* Justin thought. *After the gloomy years of Communist gray, they're going for anything but gray.*

They stopped in front of a low one-story house with a black metal gate. Rex jumped out and unlocked the gate, then drove the Rover inside the yard and parked it on the driveway a few feet away from the main entrance.

"This is home," he said as he turned off the car.

They unloaded their bags, ignoring the rainfall soaking their clothes. Eve opened the door and led them inside a large living room. It was sparsely but tastefully furnished with two large comfortable-looking armchairs and a matching sofa all in a calm beige color, a Persian carpet with a vivid flowery motif, and tall lampstands at two corners of the room. The walls were painted a light blue but there were no family photographs or pictures. A large window overlooked the yard with its two rows of shrubs along the driveway.

"We're safe here," Rex said. "One of our local ops in Russia found someone who was renting it out. We've checked for bugs. We can speak freely here."

Justin nodded. He removed his windbreaker and hung it in the closet near the door. Then he took off his boots, picked up his bags, and placed them in a corner of the living room. He walked through the living room and the dining room, turned to the right and found the kitchen. "Anyone want coffee?" he asked.

"I'll take a cup," Eve said. "Make it strong."

"Got it," Justin said.

Rex said, "I drink tea. And you?" he asked Carrie.

"Tea for me as well, thanks. Hong, what would you like?"

"No . . . nothing for me." Hong's voice was weak and low, as if it pained him to say the words.

"All right. I'll make us tea. Black is all right?" Rex asked Carrie.

"Black is fine."

Justin had found the coffee in one of the white kitchen cabinets when Rex walked into the kitchen. He stormed toward Justin and stopped only when he was an inch away from Justin's face. "What is *he* doing in *my* safe house?

Rex's voice was slightly louder than a whisper but it still carried his anger just as well as if he had shouted at the top of his lungs. And Rex's face, distorted in rage, his menacing frown and fiery eyes, left no doubts about his state of mind.

"Wow." Justin whispered back in a calm tone. "Chill out."

"You don't trust this man, do you?"

Justin shook his head. "No, I don't, but—"

"No buts. He should have stayed with the rest of your crew."

Justin took a deep breath and thought for a moment before replying, "You're right. Do you want him to leave?"

Rex squinted. He was not expecting Justin's reply. "Hmmm . . . no, but we can't discuss our op with him around."

Justin stifled a groan, since Rex was pointing out the obvious.

"I'll have him wait in the Rover. That's good with you?"

Rex nodded and his facial muscles relaxed.

Justin asked, "Fine. Anything else?"

"No."

"All right. Next time you have a concern with my decisions, come and talk to me. I'll listen to and consider your viewpoint. But lose the attitude."

Rex fixed Justin with a cold stare.

"Am I clear?" Justin asked. His eyes never left Rex's reddened face.

Rex said nothing for a long moment.

"Am I clear?" Justin repeated in the same firm tone but a little louder and with a hint of impatience.

"Yes, fine," Rex replied with a small nod.

"This is *our* safe house." Justin pointed around the kitchen with his left hand. "And this, you and me, we are *one* team."

"All right, all right," Rex said in a calmer voice. "I was out of line. I'm just concerned about our safety and our mission."

"It's good to have concerns, and we'll make sure we address them in our briefing. We'll go over all types of scenarios."

Rex extended his hand in a gesture of peace. Justin gave it a firm handshake and then returned to making the coffee.

He returned to the living room after five minutes with two large mugs. He offered one to Eve, who was sitting in one of the armchairs, across from Carrie on the sofa.

"Thank you," Eve said and smelled the coffee's aroma.

Justin stepped near Hong, who was standing at the window, staring thoughtfully at the rainstorm brewing outside.

"Hong, we have to discuss some sensitive matters," Justin said in a warm voice. "Do you mind waiting in the car?"

Hong's shoulders slumped and his face began to form a frown. In a moment, he nodded. "I understand. Can I call my family?"

"Sure. Eve, can you please help Hong?"

"Absolutely." Eve stood up. "This way, Hong." She led him down the hall toward the other side of the house.

Justin sat on the sofa next to Carrie. She had fired up her laptop and was evidently analyzing something on the monitor. Justin glanced over and saw it was a transcript of Hong's calls from the Shangri-La Hotel in Dubai. "So, he's clean?"

"Yes, he is. McClain sent back the translations of Hong's conversation I recorded in Dubai. There's nothing here about Hong lying or using any kinds of codes. He repeated what we told him, at times verbatim. Once or twice he even exaggerated to stress his point that his chaperone was the true defector."

Rex looked at them from the other armchair. "What happened?"

Justin gave him the abbreviated version of the developments in Dubai, but he left out the part where they buried Shin in the desert.

As he was finishing, Hong and Eve appeared in the hallway. Hong had a small smile on his face. Eve gave Justin a small nod.

"Everything's okay?" Justin asked as he stood up.

Hong nodded. "Yes, yes. They're doing well. My neighbor Choe is still willing to help. He's driving my wife and my sons to Sonbong right away."

"Excellent. Thanks, Hong. If all goes well, you'll see your family tomorrow."

"Thank you, thank you." Hong nodded and headed toward the door.

Justin's eyes followed Hong as he made his way to the Rover. "All right, why don't we start our briefing? Do we have a printer here?"

"We do," Eve replied. "I'll bring it here."

Justin pointed toward the large table in the dining room. "Let's set up there so we have everything laid out in front of us."

They sat around the black wooden table with a nice smooth veneer finish. Justin placed his laptop in front of him at the head of the table and Carrie sat to his right. Rex took the seat across from Justin, and when Eve returned with the printer she set it near Justin's laptop. She hooked up the cables, and in a matter of minutes, the mouth of the printer began to pour forth a dozen or so pages of photographs and documents. Justin collected them and piled them in a staggered order near his laptop.

"At nightfall we'll head for Khasan." Justin handed out a detailed map of the tri-state border region of Russia, China, and North Korea. "A little over a hundred and eighty miles south. We'll give ourselves four hours to get there, with plenty of time for any emergencies and so we don't draw any attention to ourselves. Hong will travel with our backup—Val and our pilots—while we're taking the Rover. All good so far?" He looked around the table.

Rex gave him a thumbs-up sign.

"All good," Eve said.

Carrie nodded.

Justin took out a couple of aerial images from the pile and pushed them toward Rex. "We stop before we enter Khasan. Hong gets into our Rover and we peel off the main route toward the point where we cross the border. Right here." He tapped at a red dot near the top right corner of the first photograph. "We leave the Rover with the backup team and at 1:00 a.m. on the dot we enter NK."

"The Russians are going to play nice?" Rex asked.

"For a hundred grand, they are. Our contact is going to turn off the main power supply of the barbed-wire electrical fence, giving us twenty or thirty seconds before the generator kicks in."

"Twenty seconds is not a lot of time," Eve said.

"We'll short out the fence if we have to. We have jumper cables and alligator clips," said Rex.

Justin nodded. "That was my initial thought and we may still use it. Killing the power will also disable any cameras and other sensors we may not even know exist. Assuming everything goes without any trouble, we'll have to cross the Tumen River." He pointed at another spot in the photograph. "The border is heavily patrolled but hopefully we'll not be made. Once we're across the river, we look for the van, our transport inside NK."

Eve tilted her head toward Justin. "We're sure the van will be there?"

"Hong's contact should drop it off about a mile south. Here." Justin's index finger pointed at a location on the photograph.

"And if there's no transport?" Rex asked.

Justin held Rex's eyes for a moment. "We decide whether we continue marching on foot or abort our mission, depending on the overall situation. The surrounding area does not have many residents and most Koreans don't own cars. We could take over one of the patrol vehicles, but that's not my preferred option."

Rex shook his head. "Even if we were quiet, the missing guards will be a clear giveaway. And we'll only get so far inside NK in an army vehicle."

"So let's hope the van is in position. Carrie, any thoughts?"

"If we have no transport, we're kind of screwed. It could be a sign that Hong's man may have given up our plan. He won't know the details, but it's pretty easy to figure out why Hong would need a van near the border with Russia, especially at a time when he's outside North Korea."

Justin nodded. "Yes, we need to double-check the van is there *before* we get near Khasan. Anything else?"

There were headshakes around the table, so Justin continued, "Hong gets behind the wheel and we'll make our way to the camp through back roads to avoid patrols. These are some recent aerial shots of the area. The NSA has been repositioning one of their satellites, and these were taken yesterday." He reached into the stack of papers for a few more photographs and began to pass them around. "They're not very useful since they were taken during the day and we're travelling at night, but they should still give us a good idea of the route and of the landscape.

"If we have safe passage, we should arrive at the camp before daybreak. I want us to concentrate mostly on this series of images that show the camp and its surrounding area." Justin picked up a new batch of pictures.

He took a sip from his mug and waited until everyone had spread the images in front of themselves. "The camp where the agents are held is a series of barracks, five or six of them, if we include this row of shacks here at the north part just inside what looks like the fence. The main building is the prison, this square here almost at the center of the complex. Across from it, there is a smaller structure, which I suspect is the kitchen and the dormitories. Maybe they have the administration tucked in there as well."

"How far apart are these two buildings?" Eve asked.

"Eighty, ninety yards, considering the dimensions and the space, but we don't have the exact measurements or any blueprint of the facility."

"What are the other structures?" Carrie asked.

"This one just south of the prison seems like a storage house or perhaps a garage. And the one north of the office block, I'm not sure. Maybe it's a gym or some place for social gatherings for the soldiers."

"Or propaganda and speeches from their supreme leader," Rex said with a groan. "Communist brainwashing."

"Very likely." Justin nodded. "And there are watchtowers at the north and the south entrances. The road leading out of the north disappears somewhere in the middle of the field, near these rice paddies and what seems to be a power station. The south road meanders through the fields and the valleys and comes to this small bridge. It's the only connection between this complex and Camp 37, which is about ten miles south."

"We blow it up," Rex said and made a gesture by opening his right-hand fist. "Cut off any reinforcements."

"Exactly. We'll lay explosives on the bridge and along the south road as soon as we arrive. Then Carrie and I will advance from the north and the east and attack the camp with heavy fire from two different positions. Some of the soldiers will engage us, others will rush the two important prisoners away from the camp. They'll leave through the south entrance coming straight to you."

Justin looked up at Rex. The man's blazing eyes told Justin he could hardly wait to get into action.

Justin continued, "Divide and conquer, that's our strategy. We can't be sure it will work right away, but eventually it will. We just need to sustain our rate of gunfire until it does. The soldiers will realize there's no fire coming from the south and will choose that direction as they make their way toward safety.

"They'll be in a convoy: three, four, or even more vehicles. They seem to have an abundance judging by the pictures. Eve, you'll set off the charges and stop their advance. Rex, you'll hit the targets, with support from Eve. Once you've confirmed they're killed, we're done and we'll start our exfil. We'll make our way through the forest, using one of these two trails." Justin tapped one of the photos. "After we get to the Wansan Line, we'll meet Val and her team. They'll take us to Yanji Airport, and we'll board the Gulfstream. Questions?"

There was a moment of hesitation around the table. Justin tried to guess their thoughts. He had made the plan sound uncomplicated and had simplified most of the steps. But Rex and Eve were seasoned MI6 agents. They knew there was no such thing as an easy mission, and even the most perfect plan would run into problems once put into execution. There were so many variables and so many things on the ground they were not even aware of, let alone able to control. And so much of this operation rested on the reaction and counteraction of the North Koreans.

Rex broke the silence. "Where's Hong during this time?"

"His wife and kids are expected to meet up with him at this point here." Justin went back to a previous photograph that showed the larger area surrounding the outpost. "Hong will take them to the border with China and wait there for our arrival. Once we're all at the rendezvous point, we'll proceed to cross into China."

Eve arched an eyebrow. "And everything will be dandy with the Chinese border guards?"

Rex nodded and waited for Justin's answer.

Justin said, "We really can't predict their reaction. McClain, that's our boss, can inform his counterparts about our op while we're in our exit phase, especially if we're sure we have the guards' attention. We'll avoid the guards as much as we can and will not engage them, unless they fire the first shots. I don't expect them to do that, but we'll need to prepare for any eventuality."

"How old are Hong's children?" Eve asked.

"Fifteen and eighteen," Carrie replied. "They know how to swim and should be able to make it across the river. The waters are quite shallow and the current is not strong in that part."

"We'll provide them cover and give them a head start," Justin said. "If we're detained by the Chinese border guards, it will be only a matter of time before we're released, after the intel about our op has trickled down the official channels of our CIS and the Chinese MSS."

Rex put up his arms and began to shake his head. "I didn't sign up to become a Chinese prisoner."

Justin stifled a frown. "We didn't either. But we have to be realistic. Once we've left the NK hole behind us, the Chinese guards will be like the welcome wagon. We're not surrendering to them, but we have to go through them and their territory. The Chinese are our safety net, because the NK army will not attempt to follow us there and risk the wrath of the dragon. Unless you're suggesting the alternative of turning around, attempting to escape through the road leading right by the prison camp, and then driving the sixty miles through NK territory and crossing the border with Russia."

It was Rex's turn to frown. He spread his hands in front of him but did not say anything. The absurdity of such a tactic was obvious. It was extremely risky and would most likely end up in their capture or death.

Justin looked at Carrie, then at Eve. He said, "We *must* go through China but let us not get caught by their border guards. We'll use a decoy or bribe them if it comes to that."

Carrie nodded. "I like the decoy idea as a contingency. A series of well-timed explosions can buy us precious time."

Rex looked unconvinced and bit his lip.

"What's on your mind, Rex?" asked Justin.

"We're crossing the Chinese border at daylight after engaging NK troops. It'll be almost impossible for us to sneak through the border undetected."

"Thousands of Koreans do it on a daily basis," Carrie said. "Albeit at night, but it's doable. And if we use decoys and bribery perhaps we can vanish as well in the Chinese forests."

"As a final resort we'll engage the border guards if we have to, but I prefer we exhaust all other options," Justin said. "This will be tough, and we all know the exfil is much harder than the insertion."

Rex and Eve nodded.

Carrie said, "That's true."

Justin said, "Now let's run a couple of scenarios about our tactics when things go to sideways, because if we've learned something during our years in the service, it's that they will."

CHAPTER TEN

Longjing, Jilin Province, China
April 29, 4:25 p.m.

Jaw-long hated everything about this city: its smell, its silence, its rain that had not stopped in almost a week. But he had to be here in Longjing to oversee the current operation himself, because as he often liked to say, "I am surrounded by incompetents."

He stared out of his second-story hotel window at the sleepy street below. Longjing had a little over a quarter of a million people and lay north of the border with North Korea. The surrounding area with plains, valleys, and forest-covered mountains was part of the Korean Autonomous Prefecture called Yanbian, which meant Chinese Korean. It was within the territory and the jurisdiction of China, but the area had a large concentration of Chinese Koreans, which made up about forty percent of the population in the province. The percentage was even higher along the Tumen River, as Korean peasants had settled there in the second half of the nineteenth century when the area had very little population.

Jaw-long had started to hate these Koreans. His problems were supposed to have been resolved when the two Canadian agents were very close to accomplishing their task. But instead of returning to South Korea with the shipment of the weapons-grade uranium, they had exchanged gunfire with North Korean MSS agents, had killed two of them, and were captured. The authorities had seized the nuclear material and the Canadian agents were jailed and kept inside a high-security interrogation camp across the border. But even now the incompetence of his lackeys continued to plague Jaw-long. Kim, the man who ran the camp and was interrogating Schultz and Park, had been unable to break them, despite his methods, which he boasted never failed.

So Jaw-long was back to his sticky situation without the goods he had promised to the Saudi Prince Ismail bin Saud, without the money he had already received and had spent almost all of, and without any clear alternatives. His first option to obtain the uranium from Chinese facilities had failed, and his men were almost caught in the act. The second attempt had been to purchase the merchandise from Pakistani smugglers, and that half-cocked plan had cost the lives of Peng and six men. And his last chance, Plan C, the Canadian connection, had also failed.

But Jaw-long was not a quitter. Quitting meant dying, and he was not ready to leave this world. He was a desperate man but it was a desperate time. Prince Bin Saud demanded his money and Jaw-long was determined to pay him back one way or the other.

Jaw-long had a wide web of informants inside China's foreign intelligence agency who provided him with constant actionable intelligence. So during the first few days after the Canadian agents' capture, Jaw-long had fed bits and pieces of intelligence to Kim and other North Korean MSS agents to give the impression it had come from the agents themselves as they spilled their guts under torture.

Jaw-long was counting on the Canadian Intelligence Service tracking the chatter among the North Korean intelligence community, the chatter stating that the two agents were cracking under pressure. If the Canadians made the mistake of believing such disinformation, the CIS and their government would scurry into action. And since North Korea was not known generally as a reasonable, level-headed negotiator, the two options left for the CIS entailed dispatching a team to either rescue or assassinate its "rogue agents."

Having nothing more than a hunch, Jaw-long had readied his men for a new operation. He dispatched two different teams of twelve people each to canvass the marshlands and the groves stretching along the Tumen River and the China-North Korea border. The camp where the Canadians were being held was not too far away, and a Canadian rescue or assassination team would have to either enter or exit North Korea from these Chinese lands. Whatever the number of this team, if captured in Jaw-long's tricky hands they would serve as much-needed leverage. He would use these hostages in his dealings with Prince Bin Saud or perhaps approach the Canadian government for a pricy ransom. As a last resort, there were many terrorist organizations all over Asia and the Middle East that would pay upwards of three million for each hostage. If Jaw-long captured five or more Canadians he would be halfway to paying his mounting debts.

Jaw-long's small smile was cut short by his BlackBerry's ringtone. He checked the ID and heaved a sigh of relief. It was Enlai, one of his best men, who was leading the first team covering the area directly across from the camp. Jaw-long had led the second team himself until early this morning, before his return to Longjing. Cellular signal coverage was spotty and unreliable in the forests, and Jaw-long was expecting a call from Prince Bin Saud. He was not looking forward to it, but it was his chance to update the prince and perhaps win back some of the lost trust.

"Enlai, good news?" Jaw-long asked in a loud voice.

"No good . . . news." Enlai's voice came across weak, with static and interruptions.

Jaw-long bit his lip. He felt the taste of blood in his mouth, and he spat on the floor as he turned his back toward the window. "So why are you on the phone and not on the ground, looking for those Canadians?"

"Boss, we have an emer . . . gency, an emergency . . ." Enlai's voice trailed off for a moment.

Jaw-long thought he had lost the call. "Enlai, you're still there?"

"Yes, yes. I was saying we have an emergency." Enlai spoke fast, as if fearing more interruptions. "The border guards are poking around. They stopped three of our men for questioning. I think we've outstayed our welcome in the area."

Jaw-long cursed the mothers of the border guards. "You stay put until I give the orders. I'll make some phone calls and straighten things out with the guards. They'll regret their actions. Anything else?"

A moment of silence and static, then Enlai said, "No, nothing."

"All right. Get back to work and call me if there's something good."

Jaw-long cursed again the border guards and his situation. Then the BlackBerry rang again. It was the dreaded call. "Prince Bin Saud. You're early. How are—"

"Do I work for you or is it the other way around, Jaw-long?" The strong baritone voice of the prince boomed into Jaw-long's ear. "I call you whenever it pleases me, and I expect you to always answer the phone promptly and politely. Why can't you get it into your thick head?"

Jaw-long almost fired back swear words that would have most likely gotten him killed. At the last moment, while the words had still not left his lips, he bit his tongue and let the string of curses echo through his mind.

"That's good, that's very good, you being silent. Never open your mouth unless you have something worth saying. Now, update me on the manhunt."

Jaw-long let out a silent sigh and took a moment to regroup his thoughts. He decided to find something positive to say even though there had been no progress. "The situation on the ground is quiet. No movements. My men are everywhere. Once the mice appear, we'll spring our traps."

"That's not good enough and you know it. You and your useless teams should work harder and faster. This is your land, and you told me you had eyes everywhere. How come, then, you don't have eyes on the Canadian operatives?"

"Well, perhaps," Jaw-long hesitated for a moment before continuing his thought, "perhaps the Canadians are not sending in a rescue team. At least they haven't sent one in yet."

"And how exactly would you know that?" The gruff voice did not just ask but rather demanded an answer.

"My contact in the Korean prison keeps me informed at all times. I know for a fact, with a hundred percent accuracy, that the two Canadian agents are still under lock and key."

A moment of silence, then the prince said in a calmer tone, "I wouldn't be so sure. Check and double-check, because Canadians are known for their lightning-fast operations. Yemen. Somalia. Russia. Dagestan. They're everywhere these days."

Jaw-long ground his teeth.

Prince Bin Saud said, "Remember, this is your final chance to make good on your promise. I paid you promptly the thirty million in exchange for the package. Then you disappoint me again and again, and even now you can't deliver on your miserable deal. You talk about hostages but you have nothing to show for it. Return to your mission, and for your own sake get me some results. Otherwise, you'll be extremely sorry you ever decided to do business with me."

Jaw-long stirred in silence.

"You understand me?" The gruffness returned to the prince's voice.

Jaw-long unclenched his teeth long enough to say, "Yes, I heard you."

"I didn't ask you if you heard me, but if you understood me. Are you clear about your fate if you fail?"

"Yes."

"Yes, what?"

"Yes, sir. I fully understand you," Jaw-long said the words with reluctance.

"You'd better have more than sad excuses the next time I call you, because I'm not going to be this patient."

The prince ended his call without another word.

Jaw-long returned his gaze to the window and saw nothing but the faint reflection of his darkened face. He closed his eyes but it was worse, for he saw the face of the prince. The man's small dark eyes always glowing like embers, his constant deep frown, and the disapproving headshake. *I will not let him kill me. I'm not going to die because of that brute or anyone else from his royal house of thugs.*

He opened his eyes and glared at the plains, valleys, and forest-covered mountains outside his window. He saw his opportunity and his moment to seize it. *This time, I'm going to find them. And I will make them curse the day they decided to cross into my path.*

CHAPTER ELEVEN

Two miles south of Khasan, Russia
April 29, 11:35 p.m.

The heavy rainstorm with blinding lightning and ear-splitting thunder had slowed down the team's advance. The soft ground had turned muddy and slippery. They were cutting their own path through the low bushes and the thin groves along the Tumen River. And it was pitch black, the darkness of the night enveloping them and covering their movements.

After confirming that Choe had dropped the van at the designated place across the border, the team had gotten off their Rover about a mile away from the place where the Kraskino-Khasan gravel road formed a fork near the edge of Lake Khasan. The right turn would take them to Khasan; straight ahead was the direction to Kraskino, another small settlement near the North Korean border. The team was going to continue on foot, sidestepping the border crossing and evading the border patrols, since even Russians needed special permission to enter the border area.

There was no traffic and no lights. As the Rover turned around with Val behind the wheel, everything sank into blackness. Justin and his team disappeared into the groves along the road, pressing forward toward their destination.

The temperature had dropped to forty degrees and the large raindrops soaked them down to their skin within the first couple of minutes. Justin had committed to memory some of the aerial photographs and was using those details to lead his team. The night-vision goggles mounted on top of their Kevlar helmets provided them with a grainy, greenish field of vision to guide their footsteps. Their forest-pattern camouflage fatigues made them almost invisible in the groves but the trees offered little protection from the storm. The constant thudding and splashing along with the frequent thunderclaps made it harder to hear anything else, any car engine sounds or distant footsteps, any warning signs of border patrols.

They covered their first mile without any incident. Hong was struggling under the weight of his bulletproof vest and his backpack, and he was not used to marching in such poor weather and in near zero lighting conditions. The rest of the team had no problems carrying their deployment gear, including bulletproof vests, chest rigs, weapons, and rucksacks containing everything they needed for this operation, from water carriers and Meals Ready-to-Eat to tourniquets and first aid supplies.

Radio communication towers loomed overhead at regular intervals, the only sign of civilization for the next few minutes. Then the bushes and the trees began to thin away. The team was nearing Kraskino.

They waited and listened for any strange noise. Hearing nothing, Justin signaled it was safe to come out in the open and cross the road. On the other side, they dropped to a crawl and continued for the next half a mile or so until the scrubland grew thicker and they could resume their marching.

Hong needed a break to catch his breath, so they stopped when they had skirted Kraskino and had come around to the other side. The aerial photos had shown a settlement of mostly abandoned or rundown buildings. About three thousand people still lived in the town and the surrounding area. Chinese funds had built a customs and immigration center here in 1995; they had also upgraded the roads and the Makhalino railway station and its infrastructure. The Chinese had been very generous with construction funds along their borderlines, since improvement of their neighbors' facilities meant faster service and greater trade volume for the burgeoning Chinese capitalism.

The team continued through the lowlands until Justin saw in the distance a complex of one- and two-story buildings. He held up his arm and his team stopped.

"That's the border guards' post," he said and pointed toward the box-shaped silhouettes. The area in front of them was dimly lit by a series of faint lights. A row of vehicles was parked to the right, by what resembled a gate. Justin was able to make out a couple of army trucks, a van, and two small sedans.

A rumble came from the road behind them.

"Down, down, down," Justin said.

They became as one with the ground as they sought cover among the sparse, low grass.

A bright flash of light sparkled from around the bend on the road. Two strong headlights of a small truck blinded Justin's goggles. He moved them upward and followed the movements of the truck with his naked eyes.

The driver rounded the curve and proceeded toward the post. The headlights gave Justin a good idea about the lay of the land, the border guards' complex, and a high barbed-wire fence surrounding it. A grayish watchtower appeared about a mile or so away across the Tumen River.

A silhouette came running out of one of the buildings and opened the gate for the truck. Its driver parked it at the closest possible place by the nearest building to shorten the distance he would have to travel in the rainstorm. Then he jumped out of the truck and ran as fast as he could while keeping his head down.

Justin and his team waited for ten minutes. There was no movement, no noise, but for the pounding rain. They resumed their crawl until they came to a dirt road. They crossed to the other side toward a thick grove, the first sign they were near the fenced borderline, as shown in the aerial images.

"Here we are," Justin said as they dropped near the seven-foot-high barbed-wire fence cutting through the middle of the grove. A concrete post stood near an old willow tree that had partly withered.

He glanced at his wristwatch and pressed a small button on the side. The screen glowed with a dim light and the digits became visible.

"It's 12:45," Justin said. "Let's find a good spot as we wait for our signal."

Rex nodded. He was lying on the ground on his stomach next to Justin and peered through his binoculars. "I see the railroad bridge," he said, then got up.

They followed along the fence line, staying at a safe distance to avoid contact in case they slipped on the slick ground or tripped on tree roots. A couple of minutes later, they came to a point where the strands of the barbed wire had been pushed to the side. It looked like someone had sneaked through the fence at this point.

Justin was not sure if an electric current was pulsating through the fence, so he took a willow leaf and touched the tip to the fence.

He did not feel any tingling sensation in his hand, so he moved the leaf further toward the fence and brought the hand closer to the wire. Still nothing. He knew some fences carried intermittent current, so he held his hand there for a minute or so. The wire was most likely dead, but he still decided it was better to wait. They already had a plan in motion. If their contact did not come through, they would go ahead as if the fence was not electric.

Justin said, "Right here looks good. Rex, monitor the bridge. When those lights go off, it's our time."

He dropped his rucksack to the ground in preparation for their crawl under the barbed wire. Then his eyes found Hong. His face was damp and blackened with specks of mud. "You're ready to do this?" Justin asked him.

Hong nodded and tried to stop his body from the involuntary shaking chills. "I can't . . . can't go back now even . . . even if I wanted to," he said in barely a whisper, his voice trembling and his teeth chattering.

"But you don't want to, right?" Justin said.

"Right. My family is there." Hong pointed toward the fence.

"You'll do well," Justin said. "We'll all do well."

He placed his C8SFW assault rifle next to himself and rubbed his gloved hands together for some warmth. But they were drenched and cold, and he just sent splashes across his chest.

Carrie had removed her gloves and was alternating between blowing on her cupped hands and rubbing them slowly. Justin gave her a small smile, unsure if she could see him in the dark, since she had flipped up her night-vision goggles.

Justin knelt near the fence, waiting for the right moment. Time seemed to slow down to a crawl as he counted the seconds in silence. He exchanged a few glances with Carrie, Eve, and Hong, and every time received reassuring nods. Hong even gave him a double thumbs-up sign.

"The bridge went dark," Rex said. "Go, go, go."

Justin hesitated for a split second as he reached for the lowest barbed wire with his gloved right hand. Then he pulled the wire up as hard as he could. He half expected the shock of an electric jolt, but nothing happened. The wire was dead. His Russian contact had come through.

"Hurry," Justin said.

Carrie was the first one to slide under the wire. She pulled her rucksack and her C8SFW assault rifle and rolled to the side. Next, it was Eve's turn. She crawled under the wire within a couple of seconds along with her L118A1 assault rifle—the British designation of the C8SFW—then Justin pushed her rucksack toward her. Eve grabbed it and moved into position next to Carrie.

"Hong, your turn," Justin said.

Hong wriggled clumsily under the wire. He raised his back abruptly while he was not yet through, and one of the barbs caught onto his jacket and dug into his skin.

"Oh," Hong cried.

"Shhhhh," Justin said.

He untangled the barb with a swift hand and shoved Hong to the other side. He handed Hong his backpack, then Rex slid his L115A3 sniper rifle and his rucksack ahead of himself and slipped under the wire without any problems. He held the barbed wire up for Justin, the last to crawl to the other side.

Rex had just let go of the wire when the lights at the bridge came back on. Justin looked at the barbed wire, and his eyes caught a small strip of Hong's camouflage jacket. He removed the piece of cloth carefully, to erase any signs of their ever being in that spot.

Justin crouched near Hong and asked him, "How are you?"

"Okay." Hong nodded. "Sorry, I got caught there."

Justin shrugged. "It's all good."

He shouldered his rucksack and looked at his team members. They were all ready.

"Let's go," he said.

They were across the border but technically still on Russia's land. The Tumen River tended to swell in spring and eat up the surrounding land, often changing its course. Theoretically, the border cut right through the middle of the river, but in practical terms a re-demarcation was often needed, especially after a number of years of heavy rainfalls and flooding.

Justin led his team through the last stretch of willows, and they came to a sandy part of the riverbank. He fell down to a low crawl, hugged his rifle, and slithered into the dark water. The bitterly cold water sent shivers down his spine, but did not slow him. He was already drenched because of the storm, and the water would probably clean off some of the mud caked to his clothes.

He kept his head and the tip of his rifle's barrel above the flowing waters as he swam with slow strokes, until he reached roughly the midpoint of the river, about a hundred feet or so from the shore. Then he stopped and looked back. Four heads bobbed in the water a few feet behind him. The right one was splashing quite loudly, and Justin hoped no guards would hear the noise over the thundering storm and the gurgling river. And he also hoped the rain curtain and the blanket of darkness would hide them.

Justin waited until Eve—the second person in the line-up—came near him.

"Problems?" she whispered.

"No, checking the advance. Keep going."

Carrie nodded at Justin as Hong and she swam toward him.

"You're doing great," Justin encouraged him. "We're halfway there. You can do this."

Hong nodded and took a few quick breaths. He pressed on, and Justin was impressed at the man's determination. They were all professionals, trained at such tests of endurance and prepared for such operations. But Hong was a scientist, a common man looking out for his family.

Rex slowed down for a moment as he brought up the rear. Justin gestured for him to carry on, then resumed his own slow strokes. In a matter of minutes, all members of the team had safely reached the other shore and rushed to hide in the nearest grove.

"Welcome to North Korea," Carrie whispered to Justin when he joined the team.

He gave her a small smile. "Everyone's okay?"

They all nodded. Hong's entire body was shaking but Justin could not do anything about it, not until they had reached the van. And hopefully, Hong's neighbor, Choe, had remembered to bring dry blankets and a change of clothes for everyone.

Justin said, "We'll proceed south according to plan. The van should be about a mile away."

He took the lead once again as they snuck through the woods alongside the river. The grove was thicker, and Justin kept his eyes open for any fences. Some areas of the border had double and even triple fences.

They came to a clearing and a narrow trail. Justin noticed a few fallen willows and a fire pit dug out of the ground. Some ashes were still at the bottom of the fire pit.

"Someone was here recently," Justin whispered slowly. His right hand hovered over the waistband holster carrying his SIG P228 pistol.

The loud gunning sound of a vehicle startled him. Before Justin could say a single word, two strong headlights fell upon the clearing. The car or the truck—he could not be sure because of the bright lights that blinded his eyes—stopped the same exact moment Justin rolled on the ground and disappeared among the thick bushes and behind a willow tree. He heard rushed footsteps approaching and loud shouts. He did not need to know what they were saying to understand their meaning: surrender or die.

He readied his pistol. He did not want to fire, for the gunshot would be heard across the grove and set off all alarms. But they also could not be captured.

The footsteps were getting closer and so was the shouting.

Justin brought his SIG in front of his face and held his breath. He popped out, but before he could pull the trigger he heard four muffled gunshots. They came from across the clearing, where Justin had last seen Carrie.

He took a couple of steps, glancing at four bodies sprawled on the ground. Carrie had fired killing shots. Two guards had wounds on their chests, the blood visible over their green uniforms. The third one was missing a big chunk from his face right near his eye, and the fourth guard was bleeding from his throat.

Justin climbed up to the road. He checked the vehicle—a battered Russian model UAZ-469 in a drab olive color—and found no one inside. A weapons cache was stored in the back: a rocket-propelled grenade launcher, a wooden box of RPG warheads and boosters, and two PK light machine guns.

He turned off the headlights and returned quickly to the clearing. Rex and Eve were carrying one of the bodies to the river, while Carrie and Hong picked up the second body. The dead guards' weapons—newer-model AK assault rifles—were stacked in a pile near the fire pit.

Justin began to scatter some of the dirt around with his boots to cover the bloodstains. "Quite the welcome," he muttered to Rex and Eve when they came back.

"Carrie's a fast shooter," Rex said. "Good to know she has our back."

"Too bad their uniforms are wrecked," Eve said as she began to pick up the feet of the third guard.

"No, I got it," Justin said. "You can load those AKs into the UAZ."

"Are we taking the UAZ?" Rex said as he lifted up the guard by the shoulders, careful not to splatter his pants with the dripping blood.

"We have to. At least until we get to the van. The UAZ has a couple of machine guns we can use during our assault on the camp and a few RPGs, which will also come in handy."

"Then we drive it into the river?"

"Yes, if we can." Justin lowered the dead guard into the water. "You think he'll stay down?"

"I hope so. For a while at least. Until we're far away from here."

On the way back, they helped Carrie and Hong with the last body. Hong's face looked pale and he seemed quite distraught at the sight of the bloodied bodies. Justin searched his mind for words of comfort but could not come up with anything encouraging. He did not want to lie to Hong, and he could not promise this operation was going to get easier. Instead, the deeper they ventured inside North Korea, the deadlier it was going to get. This was kill or be killed territory.

Justin placed a hand on Hong's shoulders, and Hong gave him a small nod.

"Thanks, Carrie," Justin said when they were finished with the bodies. "When did you screw in the suppressor onto your pistol?"

"When you were busy with the fence. I figured we would run into these guys sooner or later. Everything seemed so easy, and we know usually it's not that way."

Justin nodded. "Live and learn."

"You can't and shouldn't think of everything. You're the leader, not the team. We're here for each other."

They walked back to the clearing. Justin picked up his rucksack, took out his SIG's sound and flash suppressor and twisted it into the muzzle of his pistol. "The UAZ will be our transport to the van," he said in a quiet voice to the team gathered around him. "We'll take all the weapons, then ditch the UAZ in the river if we can. If not, we'll hide it where the grove's the thickest. Rex, take the wheel."

Rex backed the UAZ and drove slowly with no headlights. Justin felt the gravel crunch under the tires, and its noise sounded very loud. He held his SIG high and ready near the rolled down window.

A sharp crackle from the dashboard radio startled him. Then a burst of loud Korean echoed through the car. The man's strong voice was forceful and he sounded angry.

"Status check," Eve said. "He's wondering why the guards are taking so long."

"Your typical boss," Rex said with a scowl. "You can never please them."

The shouts grew louder and turned into screams. It was soon going to burst their eardrums.

"What do we do?" Eve asked.

Justin pulled the radio handset and offered it to Hong. "Answer it," he said. "Keep it short. Tell them everything's fine."

"But . . . but . . . I don't know. They'll recognize my voice and know I'm not one of the guards," Hong said with a stutter, in a terrified voice.

"Make your voice throaty and cough. And cut in and out as you talk." Justin showed him the dial in the radio handset. "If we don't answer, they'll realize something is wrong and dispatch another patrol."

Hong swallowed hard and picked up the handset with reluctance, as if it was going to burn his hand. He cleared his throat, then fiddled with the dial. He spoke in a soft, muffled tone for a few seconds, then coughed, paused, and turned the dial. The shouting erupted again, but Hong cut the voice off with a very convincing cough. Then he turned down the volume and the voice seemed to lose some of its harshness. Hong spoke again, this time a couple of short sentences, and that was it. The voice went away.

Hong gave them an easy smile. "It seemed to work. I think I convinced them."

"What did they say?" Justin asked.

"They had noticed the power failure and were wondering about it. I told them we had seen nothing and were coming back."

Eve leaned back in her seat and gave Justin a small nod. She was discreet and Hong did not notice her head gesture.

"All right, we're safe for now. Let's reach the van."

They followed the narrow road meandering through the groves as it followed the river's snakelike bends. In a matter of minutes, they came to the place where Choe was supposed to have dropped the van.

Justin was the first one to get out of the UAZ. He scanned the area up the road, then began to move carefully toward the river. Rex followed him closely, staying two steps behind him. The rest of the team stayed in the vehicle.

About ten feet away from the road, Justin spotted a black vehicle hidden in the bushes. Choe had been careful to back it up near two large willows and had broken enough tree branches to cover it. If one did not know the location or what to look for, it was fairly easy to miss the vehicle.

Justin motioned for Rex to check the other side of the windowless van, a model he had never seen before this moment. Rex went around the back while Justin approached the van with caution, behind the sight of his pistol.

No one was in the driver's or the passenger's seat. Justin took a small Maglite flashlight from his chest rig and checked underneath the van and alongside the doors for any explosives, wires, or other unusual devices. Finding nothing, he focused the small ray of light inside the van's cabin. The keys were still in the ignition, and there was nothing in the back but a heap of rolled-up clothes and blankets stuffed behind the seats.

Rex came to the front of the van. Justin flashed him the okay sign, then gestured toward the door. He grabbed the handle and began to slide the door slowly, making as little noise as possible. Once the door was fully open, he climbed inside and searched through the clothes and the blanket.

"It's all good," he said to Rex as he jumped out. "We'll drive up to the UAZ and load the weapons."

Rex nodded and swung his MP5A3 submachine gun pistol over his shoulders. They cleared the branches, then Justin got into the driver's seat and turned the key. The engine came to life with an angry roar. Justin flinched at the noise but was glad the headlights did not turn on automatically along with the engine. He pressed on the gas pedal and the van slowly began the climb up through the rain-soaked bushes and onto the road.

As soon as the van began to turn toward the UAZ parked about thirty feet away, a small thin man jumped out of the grove across the road, waving his arms in the air like a windmill.

"What in the...?" Rex said and gripped his submachine gun.

Justin hit the brakes and turned on his Maglite. He pointed the beam at the man, who had stopped right in front of the van. No weapons were visible on the man, but Justin could not be sure of what he might be hiding underneath his greenish raincoat. The man squinted and raised his left hand to his face to cover his eyes from Justin's flashlight.

"Hold your fire until we've checked him out," Justin said.

He left the engine running and they both slowly stepped out of the van. He kept his Maglite on the man at all times in case Rex needed to open fire. They flanked the man from both sides. He made no moves nor said any words, just stood there like a life-sized statue under the hard rain and the whipping wind.

"You speak English?" Justin said in a whisper when they were about six feet away from the man.

The man nodded.

"What are you doing here?" Justin asked.

Before the man could answer, Justin heard footsteps from the direction of the UAZ. He turned and looked at Hong, followed by Carrie and Eve.

"Stop, stop, don't shoot him," Hong said in a low voice when he reached them. "He's not a spy. He's my neighbor, Choe."

Justin pulled out his SIG. "Search him. Let's make sure he's not carrying."

Rex gave Choe a thorough pat-down. "He's clean," he said when he was finished. "But what is he doing here?"

Hong shrugged. He took a couple of steps forward and spoke to Choe in Korean in a loud voice. It sounded to Justin like Hong was yelling, and his tone seemed to carry a lot of anger.

"What's going on?" Justin asked Eve.

"Hong's asking Choe what he wants, and why he's still around. He was to leave after dropping the van." She listened to the exchange.

Choe spoke very animatedly, his arms pointing toward the van, toward the river, and then toward Hong.

Eve said, "He's saying that he knows about what's going on here and why Hong needed the van and the clothes. He knows we came from across the border and how we got the UAZ. And—"

"I want go America," Choe said to Justin in broken English, interrupting Eve. "You take Hong to America. You take me."

Justin shook his head. "We're not going to America. And you can't come with us."

Choe shook his head. "Hong go with you. I go with you."

"Please explain to him we *can't* take him with us," Justin said to Eve.

Eve began talking to Choe in a soft tone, but Choe interrupted her in a raised voice.

Hong jumped in and tried to calm Choe down.

Justin looked at Eve.

She said, "Choe insists we should take him. He wants freedom, he loves freedom, he wants to go to America. And he doesn't want this for himself, but for his son, his only son, the only precious thing he has left in this life. His exact words, not mine."

"Tell him. He needs to go back home, to his son," Justin said.

"No, no," Choe said.

"If he doesn't leave right now—"

A rustle came from the bushes behind Choe, as if a small animal was trying to escape a trap. Rex pointed his weapon at that location, which prompted Choe to jump forward in front of Rex's submachine gun.

"No," he said in a low but firm voice. "Son. My son." He cocked his head.

Justin looked at the bushes and a scraggly-looking, completely soaked and shivering boy came out with a slow, unsteady gait. He was no older than five and he tottered timidly toward his father. Choe crouched and wrapped him tightly into his arms. The boy started to sob quietly.

Justin sighed. "Ask him if there are others in the grove, but be gentle," he asked Eve. "And if he told anyone about the van."

Rex stepped near Justin. "What are you thinking?"

"I'm not going to kill a father in front of his son." Justin spoke slowly so Choe would not hear his words. "But this complicates our mission and our exit."

Carrie and Eve came near them. Eve said, "He says 'no.' He told no one where he's going, not even Hong's wife, even though she tormented him for an answer. His—"

Justin said, "His exact words, I know."

"If we turn him away, he might make noise and draw attention. Or he could head straight for the watchtower and alert the border guards," Rex said.

"But how will he explain what he's doing here, so close to the border?" Carrie asked. "The guards are not stupid, they'll understand Choe's involved."

Justin said, "Yes, but our cover and our operation will be blown. We can't risk him talking, even though I don't believe he will."

"So they tag along?" Carrie asked.

Justin looked at Choe still holding his little boy in his arms and gently stroking the boy's hair. The boy seemed calmer but he was still trembling. Justin sighed again.

He took another moment to think about the situation, but the choices were already made for him. He said, "We'll take them to our meeting point with Hong's family, then we split up. If Choe and his kid are not near the border with China when we get there, they're on their own."

Eve nodded, while Rex said nothing.

"Rex, what do you think?" Justin asked.

"We shouldn't take them, but we have to under the circumstances. We'll make do as we go."

"All right. Eve, explain to them our decision. Rex and Carrie, let's move all the weapons to the van," Justin said.

They stacked the wooden box and the RPG launcher, the PK machine guns, and the four AKs near the back of the van. Then Justin alone drove the UAZ between the trees where Choe had previously hidden the van, and continued further down, all the way to the riverbank. Then he pressed hard on the gas and the UAZ's tires began kicking back water. Justin kept his foot on the gas to avoid getting stuck in the shallow muddy waters. The UAZ carried on until water and vegetation debris began to come in through the doors. Justin felt the current dragging the vehicle and the water rising quite fast, sloshing around his ankles.

He squeezed his way out of the window as the UAZ began to sink. Justin swam around and could see nothing but the dark churning waves, which had swallowed up the vehicle. He made his way to the shore, trying to contain the shivers that were sending constant jolts racing throughout his body.

Rex and Hong were changing into new sets of clothes under the willow branches. They were wearing mismatched sweaters, pants, and coats that looked worn and dirty, but Justin could not protest too much. The clothes were dry and at this point—when he was shivering through his bones and feeling like even his marrow was going to freeze at any moment—he would wear anything, even a gown or a robe made of leaves, provided they were dry.

"The ladies are changing in the van, that's why we got this place." Rex ducked nearer to the willow trunk to dodge raindrops falling from the tip of the curved branches. "It's better than out in the storm, but not by much."

Justin nodded and picked up the clothes Rex handed him. He stripped off his clothes and turned around, his back facing the men.

"Holy mother of . . ." Rex's voice trailed off. "Where'd you get those scars? Iraq?" He pointed at Justin's back.

Justin turned his head and saw Rex's outstretched hand. Rex was looking at three deep scars, almost eight inches long, carved along Justin's shoulder blades. They were reminders of the time he had been captured in Libya after a hostage rescue operation that went wrong.

Justin said, "Iraq? No, never had the pleasure of visiting those deserts."

Rex's inquisitive eyes searched Justin's face for an answer.

"Long story. Maybe I'll tell you one day."

Rex nodded.

Justin sighed as he put on a blue shirt and a pair of black corduroy pants that seemed way too thin around the knees and three inches too short. Then he donned a brown button-down sweater with what might have been a crisscross motif. He ran his hand over the front and noticed a small hole near the bottom. The clothes had the distinct musty smell of most basements. *Oh, well,* he thought, *it's only for a short time until our own clothes dry out.* Lastly, he wrapped a thin black wool jacket around himself. It was snug around his shoulders, but he did not mind. He was already starting to feel warm.

They wrung the water out of their clothes the best they could, then returned to the van. Carrie was already sitting in the driver's seat and Choe was in the passenger's seat. "What took you guys so long? Primping ourselves for the party, aren't we?"

Justin smiled. "Sure we are. You look adorable in that sweater."

Carrie gave him a sideways glance. "Ha, ha, not funny. Get in. Mind if I drive?"

"Not at all. My tired bones can use a break. If we happen to catch a break."

"Let's hope and pray," Carrie said. "We're just starting our op. The hardest part is yet to come."

CHAPTER TWELVE

Three miles inside North Hamgyong Province
North Korea
April 30, 1:40 a.m.

C arrie drove slowly through the dark night and the relentless storm. The gravel road turned steep as they left behind the Tumen River, and the groves grew smaller and thinner. Carrie kept her window slightly open so she could hear any unusual noises, although between the rain thumping and the wind whipping, the van it was quite difficult to hear anything else. The thunder and the lightning had disappeared, but large raindrops kept pounding everything with a vengeance.

They came to a small narrow road and Carrie stopped to observe the landscape. A long stretch of fields ran parallel to the road, and she assumed those were rice paddies. To the left, there were a couple of low structures. One of them was taller than the others— about three stories high—and resembled a watchtower.

"Problems?" Justin asked from the back.

"No, just studying the area. Which way, Choe?"

Hong translated the question to Choe. He pointed toward the right, then a stream of rapid words came out of his mouth. Carrie understood not one of them.

Hong told her, "He's saying we have to go right. That's how he came here. There's a border-guard post about two miles north, but he avoided it by turning left through the rice paddies at about halfway there. There's a small trail for ox-drawn carts but the van will be able to go through."

Carrie nodded. "Thanks, Choe."

Choe smiled and said, "You welcome. Good?"

"Yes, that's good," Carrie said.

She made a right turn, the van gliding through the darkness. Carrie kept her eyes to the left, looking for the right spot where they were going to cut through the fields. The rain and the pitch-black night made a difficult job even harder. She threw a glance at Choe and was glad that he was also paying attention. He was squinting and leaning forward in his seat, his neck and the upper part of his body tilted toward Carrie for a better look.

Choe let out a sharp squeak that startled her. He gestured with his hand to a point about forty yards up ahead. Carrie narrowed her eyes and strained to see what had gotten Choe so excited. The road forked into a small trail about a foot or so higher than the nearby flooded field. The turn was almost invisible, and she was glad Choe had pointed it out to her.

"Thanks again, Choe. You're a big help."

Choe smiled. "You welcome."

Carrie steered the van into the small trail, feeling the wheels sinking into the wetland. She picked up speed to avoid getting bogged down. The rice paddies stretched on both sides of the trail, and Carrie felt the van was extremely exposed. If someone was observing this stretch of land with powerful night-vision goggles they would notice the vehicle creeping forward at this ungodly hour of the night. And if a strong searchlight suddenly came on, there was nowhere to seek cover.

She held her breath and kept a constant pressure on the gas pedal. The van's roars troubled her, but she could not do anything to muffle their noise. She hoped the rain would reduce the visibility of anyone on the lookout and the howling wind would carry the van's noise in the other direction.

They reached the end of the trail and Choe pointed to the right. Carrie nodded at him and turned the wheel. The next trail was a bit wider and the ground under the van's tires was packed hard. Carrie glanced up to the rearview mirror but the faces of her team were obscured by the darkness inside the van. Justin was talking to Rex in a low voice, then Rex replied in his polished British accent. She could not tell what they were discussing, but she was sure Justin would inform her if it was relevant to their operation.

The first couple of houses appeared to her left. There were no lights in the yards, so Carrie could make out only the top of their box-shaped silhouettes as they lay sheltered behind what she assumed were fences and hedges. A thin spiral of smoke was rising up from a low chimney.

Choe began to talk and Hong translated his words. "We're getting closer to the banks of Lake Sobon, the largest lake in this area, over 1,500 hectares. We'll soon come up to a dirt road, and we have to cross it in order to avoid the nearest town of Josan-Ri."

Carrie nodded. "You came that way when you got here?"

Choe waited while Hong translated, then replied, "Yes, yes. I drove around the edge of the lake, and then through the fields and the hills. The terrain changes the further away we get from the river."

Carrie look straight ahead and then to the right. They came to a long structure that looked like a warehouse. A couple of tractors and carts were parked near a colorful wall mural. She squinted but she could not make out the mural features.

She turned to the left and they headed south. The dirt road appeared in the distance. It was wide enough for three cars, and a series of small structures appeared on both sides. A couple of small houses and a few shacks.

"This is the closest we'll get to the village houses," Choe said through Hong. "Then we should not have problems."

Carrie said nothing. Her entire concentration was on the sleepy houses. She rolled the window all the way down and shifted in her seat. She ignored the raindrops falling now on her left arm and leg. She listened for any sound, something that would signal a villager was awake and perhaps following their moves. Carrie knew it was a matter of time before the border patrols dispatched a team or more to look for their missing comrades. And Carrie did not want any witness giving clues and directions.

A light turned on in one of the houses to her left and Carrie turned the wheel. She tapped the brake pedal, and the van coasted over the dirt road and onto the other side, away from the house. It then came to a stop behind one of the shacks, and Carrie turned off the engine.

"What's going on?" Justin asked from the back of the van.

"We've got company," Carrie whispered back. "Someone's awake."

She reached for her SIG pistol with the long suppressor and put it on her lap. She glanced in her side mirror but saw nothing because of the darkness and the trickles of rain. They waited for a few moments in complete silence but for the steady drum of raindrops pitter-pattering against the van and the tin roofs of the shacks.

"What do you see?" Hong whispered.

"Shhhhh," Justin hushed him.

Carrie held her breath and she could feel her heart pounding in her chest. She heard a low rattle and a scraping sound if someone was dragging a heavy load. An ox slowly pulling a cart came into her view. The silhouettes of three men were visible in the cart.

"False alarm," Carrie whispered. "Early risers."

Her eyes followed the cart as it moved further away. It headed in the other direction, and the driver of the cart turned it into the road Carrie had just left behind. Her lips quivered. Another thirty seconds or so and they would have come face to face with the locals.

"Is it clear?" Rex asked.

Carrie shook her head. "Not yet. But they're almost gone. Do people get up this early around here?"

"Sometimes," Hong replied. "Farm work takes a lot of time. Some of the villagers work across the border in Russia's forests and factories. Better jobs and better pay."

Carrie nodded. She waited another minute or so, then started the engine. The van coughed and sputtered to life, and Carrie felt as if the noise woke up the entire village. She stepped on the gas pedal as she turned toward the south. She looked around, but saw no lights. And she breathed easier.

They left the houses behind and Choe gave directions. They came near the edge of Lake Sobon, the strong wind stirring the surface of the vast space of dark water. Then the road turned north and they went through small groves and open fields, skirting around quiet villages and climbing through terraced hills.

Finally, they came to an asphalt road and Choe took the wheel. Hong sat up in the front also. They had more chances of running into other people now, and two North Koreans in a van was a more common sight than a Westerner woman as a driver.

Carrie sat next to Justin and across from Eve. The little boy had earlier snuggled up to Hong. Now he was sleeping on the other side of Justin, his little head cushioned in the crook of Justin's arm. He was sound asleep, wrapped in one of the blankets.

Carrie smiled at Justin, who returned her smile. Carrie wished she could close her eyes and relax, like the little boy, without a care in the world. She tried it for a moment but quickly opened her eyes and shook her head. She needed to stay awake and alert. There would come a time and a place for rest. For now, she needed to focus on their mission.

CHAPTER THIRTEEN

Two miles north of Hoeryong
North Hamgyong Province, North Korea
April 30, 4:35 a.m.

Choe turned the van's steering wheel gently as they rounded a curve. They were closing in on their target. In a matter of minutes they would reach the bridge, and Carrie would lay the explosive charges.

Their insertion so far had proceeded without any major problems. They had mostly kept to back roads, avoiding villages and towns, and had run into very little traffic. North Korea did not have many cars, and some estimates placed the number of vehicles in the country of nearly 25 million people at about only 60,000. But they had passed a number of donkey- and ox-drawn carts and two old battered trucks that ran on coal. Their chimney stacks produced a cloud of thick gray smoke, but the sardine-packed crowd of men, women, and children hanging precariously from the sides and the back of the truck stoically endured the choking toxic fumes.

The most dangerous moment had come when a convoy of military vehicles overtook them as they were coming near an army base. The front Jeep had continued on its way, but the driver of the second vehicle—a large military truck full of soldiers—had honked its horn numerous times, since Choe apparently had not been driving fast enough for his liking. Then the truck had brushed past the van, almost knocking off its side mirror. Choe had been forced to drive to the edge of the road, near a cliff that ended up in jagged rocks about a hundred feet below. The soldiers had given Choe and Hong hateful glances, they explained later to Justin, but at least they had not stopped.

About an hour later, Hong, Choe, and his son had met up with Hong's family, just outside of Hoeryong. Justin had given them the coordinates and the time of their rendezvous near the border with China. He warned them to be there on time and not a minute later. Then the van had continued on, passing around Hoeryong and heading toward Camp 37.

This was going to be the next most dangerous moment during the operation. The rainstorm had stopped and with the nearing twilight hours, they were bound to see more and more activity on the roads and the countryside. Without their two North Korean guides, they had to hope and pray they did not run into any roadblocks, army troops, or locals stopping them and asking questions.

The road snaked around a few hills and the van came within a direct line of sight to the camp. Four tall watchtowers were visible, their square shapes lit dimly by faint lights. They drove about forty yards away from a ten-foot-high barbed-wire fence crowned with more barbed-wire coils. A patrol truck was lazily driving near the other side of the fence. Eve, who was in the passenger seat, looked in that direction out of the corner of her eye. The truck driver paid no attention to their vehicle.

The van reached the southern entrance to the camp. Justin did not look at the watchtower twenty feet to his right, but kept his foot on the gas pedal as the van went down the gravel road at a steady speed. He kept his eyes on the side mirror until the van rounded another curve and they left the camp behind them.

He heaved a sigh of relief and looked at Eve. She gave him a nod, then looked down at the set of photographs in the binder on her lap. "You got to love the NSA. These images are crystal clear."

"They're useful to us, but I doubt many Americans *love* the NSA," Justin said.

"When the scandal erupted about the agency spying on the top diplomats accredited to the US and other heads of state, some guy started selling these t-shirts on the Internet. They had the NSA logo and the inscription: The NSA, the only part of the government that actually listens. I bought a couple before the website was shut down," Rex said with a chuckle.

Justin smiled. "Yeah, I remember that."

They drove for the next few minutes in silence. Justin's mind was reviewing their plan and working out potential solutions for any kinks.

"We should be getting near the bridge," Eve said, and tapped one of the photographs. "I would say about half a mile."

"Hiding spots?" Justin asked.

"Perhaps here." She handed the photograph over to Justin. "Left side by those trees."

Justin nodded. "Yeah, that's good. Carrie, you ready?"

Carrie nodded and reached for her rucksack. "Yeah, ready. Let me know when we roll."

They neared a truss bridge that was about a hundred yards long. It was quite narrow, and two cars would have to slow down in order to pass without crashing into each other. Some of the beams had large brownish yellow rust marks on them. Gravel covered a large portion of the bridge deck and a small hole was in the middle. The bridge rattled as the van crossed over it, and Justin wondered if the explosive charges were unnecessary and the bridge would simply collapse if a series of military trucks rumbled over it.

He turned left and parked the van at the bottom of the hill, near some scraggly bushes. "This is it," he told Carrie. "Rex, give her a hand."

"Yes, sir," Rex said.

Carrie said, "Should be back in five."

They both jumped out of the van and disappeared into darkness.

"So, how did you learn Russian?" Eve asked.

"Huh, what? Oh, the language." Justin shrugged. "I grew up with Russian friends and had a talent for languages, I guess. My parents, well, my dad enrolled me in a Russian language course."

"And you speak Arabic as well."

"And you've read my file."

"I'm sure you've checked out ours, haven't you?"

Justin nodded. "If you want to know something, just ask."

"All right." Eve shifted in her seat and turned to face Justin. "How do you feel about this operation?"

Justin frowned. "Quite good, thank you for asking."

"I don't mean to be—"

"I wish you would cut to the chase. How do I feel about killing my brothers? What do *you* think?"

Eve looked away. "Sorry. It came out the wrong way."

Justin shrugged. "No worries. I . . . we, we'll get our job done. That's the important thing. The feelings? They'll heal. With time."

He stared out of the window into the darkness. He thought he saw something crawling among the bushes, so he asked Eve, "Eleven o'clock. See anything?"

Eve peered through the windshield and shook her head. "No."

Justin stepped outside, holding his SIG pistol low at his side, and began to tiptoe toward whatever had caught his attention. His boots crackled over a patch of rocky ground, and a small furry creature scampered through the bushes and the trees. Justin was not sure what type of animal it was, but it was not a human and that was important.

He returned to the van and stood by the door, breathing in the brisk fresh air of the morning. He and the rest of his team had changed into their camouflage fatigues a while back. The clothes were still damp and they stuck to his body. But they were going to make him almost invisible as he slithered through the plains and the hills.

Rushed footsteps came from behind the van. Justin flattened himself against the driver's door and slinked in that direction. Before he could take a peek, Eve said, "It's Rex and Carrie."

"How did it go?" Justin asked when they were near him.

"Perfect," Carrie replied. "Fewer charges than I thought, but they'll do the job."

Justin nodded. Carrie was trained as an explosives expert and had studied many improvised explosive devices during her two tours of duty in Afghanistan. She had served with the Joint Task Force Two, the elite counter-terrorism unit of the Special Operations Forces, before joining the CIS.

Carrie had used Russian-made PVV-5A plastic explosives rigged to be remotely controlled. PVV-5A explosives were available throughout the former Eastern Bloc countries once under the influence and the control of the Soviet Union. Any North Korean investigation would reveal no traces of a Canadian or British team having a hand in the destruction of the bridge. Initially, Justin had thought about using only Russian-made weapons but he had decided against it. The team members were trained to use their own weapons, and this operation demanded the utmost precision. A handful of spent cartridges alone were by no means conclusive evidence to incriminate a particular country.

They all climbed back into the van and continued toward the north. The road zigzagged through two valleys, then climbed a set of rolling hills. The outpost where Schultz and Park were being held was on the right side of the road, but Justin and Carrie would have to cover the last mile on foot, circle around the outpost, and start the raid from the north.

Justin gunned the engine, rushing to make full use of the last minutes of darkness before twilight would make their jobs much harder. He and Carrie needed to be in position before sunrise, then wait for full daybreak before attacking the outpost. Rex would need plenty of light to make his kill shots.

They checked their communication gear before making their last stop about two miles south of the base. Their throat mikes and earpieces worked without any glitch. Justin checked his emergency satellite phone batteries, and they were fully charged.

Then Carrie and Rex quickly laid a series of explosive charges along the side of the road. It was an open space without trees or any other natural protection, which would give Rex a clear shot when the detonation stopped the runaway convoy. Justin parked the van behind a small hill, out of sight of anyone walking or driving on the road.

Then it was time to split up. Justin shook Rex's hand, then gave Eve a big bear hug. "See you soon and without a scratch, okay?" he told them.

"Same for the two of you," Rex said. "You don't want to see me angry." His face struck a serious expression, then he broke it up with a toothy smile.

"Take it out on the NKs," Justin said.

Carrie gave Rex, then Eve, a tight embrace. "I want to get to know you guys better. So let's all meet up for drinks once this is over."

"You've got a deal," Eve said with a nod.

"You're buying." Rex smiled.

Justin picked up the RPG launcher and three warheads along with their booster cylinders. Carrie took one of the PK light machine guns and two long bandoliers of bullets. They slithered through the darkness, cut through the terraced hills, and advanced toward the outpost. The layout of the terrain was clear in Justin's mind, as he had analyzed a set of detailed aerial images.

As they neared the base, they came to a small creek. It formed the natural separation of this part of the hillside from the base beyond the menacing barbed-wired fence. Justin and Carrie crossed the knee-deep creek and dropped to a low crawl as they secured positions in a dry irrigation ditch. Behind them and to the left side there was an open stretch of rice paddies.

Their position offered them a good view of the two north watchtowers of the outpost. They were little more than shacks built about fifteen feet off the ground. The silhouette of a soldier was somewhat visible, illuminated by a faint light coming from inside one the shacks. A large machine gun sat at one of the corners of that watchtower.

"I'll blow up the nearest tower." Justin pointed at his target about a hundred yards away. "You'll take out the other."

Carrie nodded. "Be careful," she said.

"You too."

Carrie gave him two thumbs up, then began to crawl along the ditch. The sky had begun to turn a pale blue and there were only a few minutes until sunrise. But Rex would need more light than just the first shimmering sunrays over the horizon.

Justin placed his RPG launcher in front of him and readied the weapon. He screwed the rocket propellant cylinder into the warhead and loaded it into the RPG's muzzle. Then he checked his C8SFW assault rifle and made sure he had ten magazines within easy reach.

Then he waited and listened.

It was quiet. Too quiet. He wondered why he could not hear birds or other sounds of nature. Then Carrie's voice came over his earpiece. "I'm in position."

"Roger that," Justin said via his mike. "Rex?"

"In position."

"Eve?"

"In position."

Justin looked up at the top of the mountain to his right. The pale blue had started to turn to gold. The fence, the watchtowers, and the other structures of the base were more visible, their features still blurry but not for long.

"Ten minutes," Justin said.

He took a few deep breaths and tried to relax as he counted the slow crawling moments. Daylight was exposing the valley gradually. A couple of soldiers came out from one of the gray barracks—the one Justin suspected was a dormitory—and marched toward the nearest watchtower.

Justin flattened himself to the ground. He whispered into his mike, "Movement near the northeast tower. Two targets. Looks like shift change."

"Roger that," Carrie said. "I've got two other targets approaching my tower."

"Roger," Justin said.

Rex and Eve were silent. The outpost was beyond the effective range of their rifles. This theater of operations was solely Justin's and Carrie's. Unless they were specifically addressed, Rex and Eve were to observe but not respond to communications.

Justin examined the watchtower through his binoculars. The two soldiers whose shift had just ended looked completely exhausted, their bleary eyes and yawns showing the fatigue from the sleepless night. The new soldiers looked equally worn out, perhaps dreading the prospect of spending yet another day perched upon a shack staring at fields and hills in boredom.

Well, today's going to be different, Justin thought.

"Thirty seconds," he said in his mike.

"Roger that," Carrie replied.

Justin waited until all four soldiers were standing and talking at the watchtower balcony. He climbed to his right knee and shouldered his RPG with a swift move. He aimed it at the watchtower and looked through the weapon's optical sight.

Then he pulled the trigger.

The projectile hissed and cut a trail through the quiet morning air. It slammed right into the middle of the watchtower. The powerful explosion blew everything to pieces, which rained over that area. The bodies of the soldiers were tossed into the air like rag dolls along with the wood and metal debris.

Justin dragged his RPG launcher behind as he crawled away from his position along the irrigation ditch. The gray smoke from the RPG's cone-shaped breech was a dead giveaway. He heard the distinct thunder of Carrie's PK machine gun. Bullets were tearing the northwest tower to shreds.

He stopped when he was about twenty feet from the thinning cloud of smoke. He peeked over the ditch. A small military truck was rushing toward the destroyed watchtower. Soldiers in uniforms and some in regular civilian clothes scurried around the yard. Some were looking in Carrie's direction.

Justin aimed his C8SFW assault rifle and waited for the right moment. The truck neared what remained of the watchtower—the metal staircase and a couple of twisted posts—and five soldiers climbed out.

Justin fired a quick burst before the soldiers spread out. He struck two of the soldiers in the chest and a few bullets hit the truck. Justin fell back in the ditch and crawled to his left, again to confuse the enemy about his location.

Return fire echoed from the yard. He heard no thumps of bullets around him, so he assumed his location was still safe. He crawled another few feet, then he stopped and listened. More gunshots, but the grass and the shrubs around him remained untouched.

He took a quick glance. Soldiers were searching along the fence line. One was standing near one of the fence posts. He held the barbed wire with his hand, then stuck his head between the wires to search the other side. *The fence is not electric—or did they shut down the power to let the soldiers through?*

The soldier moved his head left and right, studying the terrain. He stopped when he was looking at the place from where Justin had fired the RPG. Then the soldier began to shout to the others as he pointed beyond the fence.

Justin fired a single shot. The bullet pierced the soldier's chest. He slumped to his right and got tangled in the barbed wire. The other soldiers looked at the fallen man, then turned their heads and looked beyond the fence.

Justin dropped back in the ditch. He hoped his rifle flash suppressor had done its job, and the rest of the soldiers still did not know his exact position. But it was only a matter of seconds before they would figure it out by the trajectory of the shots.

He crawled further to his left. A bullet zipped past him and stopped him in his tracks. Justin was not sure if it was a stray bullet or if the soldiers had discovered his position. Gunshots rang very close and more bullets whizzed by a couple of feet away. *They found me.*

He flattened himself to the soft ground of the ditch as bullets began hammering everything around him. They lifted clumps of clay and chunks of dirt and grass. Broken bush branches began to fly around him and fall on his shoulders.

Justin crawled forward at a fast pace as the volley seemed to slow down for a moment. He advanced four or five feet. The bullets were still striking his previous position. He breathed a bit easier, then popped his head a couple of inches over the grass.

Two soldiers kept firing through the fence. Justin fired quick, calculated three-round bursts and cut down both soldiers. They fell on their backs. One tried to go for his rifle and Justin fired another shot, hitting the soldier in the head.

He turned his attention toward the military truck, and saw a larger truck approaching from one of the barracks further to the south. Justin estimated it was carrying about twenty soldiers or so if it was full, but he could only see the heads of six or eight of them.

"Carrie, the fence is not live. I'm advancing to the truck."

"Roger that." Carrie's voice came amid loud machine gun fire.

Justin edged toward the fence and fired a rapid burst toward the incoming truck. A couple of bullets struck the truck's hood and windshield, but the driver kept going. Justin pushed down the last barbed wire of the fence with the stock of his rifle, then snaked inside the yard.

He planted his knee on the moist ground and mounted another warhead into his RPG launcher. He shouldered it and cocked the weapon. The truck was coming toward him. Justin aimed the launcher at the truck and pulled the trigger.

The projectile speared up from the mouth of the launcher and screamed through the yard as it whooshed toward the target. It pierced the front of the truck on the driver's side. A thick cloud of gray smoke blanketed the truck, which came to an abrupt halt.

Justin lay on his stomach and waited for the smoke to clear. A group of soldiers appeared on both sides of the truck. Justin opened fire. He hit two of the soldiers who were stumbling around, confused by the explosion.

Someone fired back at him but the shots were off target, kicking up dirt and pebbles a few feet to his left. Justin fired again and emptied his magazine. He replaced it with a fresh one from his chest rig and squeezed the trigger. The barrage of bullets sprayed the area around the truck, hitting another soldier who was peeking from behind the back wheel.

Bullets began to strike closer to his head, a few times within a couple of feet. Justin fired a long barrage and replaced the empty clip. Then he rushed to his right, toward the small truck, the only cover within a fifty-yard area. Bullets followed his spring, stitching up a crisscross pattern around his feet. Justin fired back blindly and rolled onto the ground, about ten yards behind the small truck.

He was still within enemies' reach. He was now closer to them, and their firepower had redoubled. A couple of rounds lifted specks of dirt that hit the right side of his face.

Justin fired two- and three-round bursts. Then he crawled forward as fast as he could, trying to reach the safety of the truck. A bullet bounced against the RPG launcher's metal breech and ricocheted off to the side. The launcher saved his leg, as the bullet would have blown off his kneecap or shattered his femur.

Two bullets struck up ahead, smashing the side windows of the truck. Another one whirred passed his head. More bullets spread around in front of him.

Then Justin felt a hard blow to his back, as if he had been struck with a sledgehammer. The impact sent him flying forward. He fell to the ground, just a couple of feet away from the truck.

He stayed there flat on his stomach for a long moment under enemy fire. The world was upside down and he was breathing with difficulty. His back burned with an agonizing pain.

A round thumped against the truck's cabin. The metal clang prompted Justin to pick himself up and inch forward. A sharp pain erupted from his lower back but Justin kept wriggling his body toward the back wheel of the truck.

Another bullet banged against the door, then ricocheted off his helmet. Justin shook his head, pushed hard on the soft ground with his hand and his elbows, and gave his body a last good push. A moment later, as round after round rained upon him, he rolled behind the truck.

He took a few small breaths and felt as if his lungs were on fire. He was not sure of the damage the bullet had caused but he knew the rucksack and the bulletproof vest had taken the brunt of the blow. Perhaps he had a bruised or fractured rib or a bruised lung.

He dropped the rucksack near his feet as more bullets pounded the truck. Justin found his rifle, hooked onto his left hand by the strap. He fed the rifle a fresh magazine and crept to the other side of the truck.

About six or seven soldiers were advancing toward him. They were alternating their firepower so that two or three of them were shooting at all times.

Justin aimed at the nearest soldier—about a hundred yards away—and planted two bullets into his chest. Then he shot the two soldiers to the left side, the ones who were firing at him. They took a bullet each to their heads and toppled to their backs.

"Friendly advancing to your right, at four o'clock." Carrie's voice came loud and clear in his earpiece.

"Roger that," Justin said. "Can sure use a hand."

"Roger," Carrie replied.

Justin dropped back behind the truck as a long barrage hammered it. Glass shattered and the tires exploded. The truck sank as other bullets peppered its metal frame.

He glanced around the other side. A bullet smacked the truck and skipped inches away from his face. Justin retreated, reloaded, and winced as a stab of pain cut through his back.

He cursed as his eyes searched to his right. Carrie rushed through the open yard and secured a position next to one of the shacks near the fences. She studied the terrain in front of her, then rushed toward the gray one-story barracks that hosted the camp's offices or its gym. Carrie was going to be relatively safe, since there were no windows in the wall facing her. And that area was out of the soldiers' line of sight.

He looked at the rest of the barracks and noticed a head popping out of a window. Justin fired a shot that missed the head, but shattered the window glass. The man disappeared.

A group of soldiers burst out of the barracks' side door and filed along the wall. Justin squeezed the trigger. His volley hacked down the two front soldiers. The third one turned his rifle toward Justin and fired a few rounds off the mark. Justin shot back and double-tapped the soldier, who fell against the wall.

The last three soldiers were still out in the open, but they had taken up positions around the uneven yard. Two were hidden behind a small mound and a cluster of straggly bushes. The third one was nowhere to be seen, and Justin suspected he had crawled into a small hole about ten feet away from the barracks.

Muzzle flashes erupted from the bushes, and Justin fired the rest of his magazine. He went for a new one from his chest rig as a hail of bullets rained from the other side.

Justin slithered underneath the truck and turned his attention to the old front. Muzzle flashes came from two different positions: the first one was near the front wheels of the large truck; the second was about twenty feet away where the land formed a natural mound.

Justin aimed his rifle and fired single shots. He clipped the arm of one of the soldiers who had slipped too far away from his hideout. Then he struck another soldier who peeked over the mound. His third burst missed his targets but was enough to send all the soldiers to seek cover.

He took advantage of the momentary pause in the skirmish to reach for his RPG launcher. It had fallen on the other side of the truck when he was shot in the back. Justin dragged the launcher and did a quick check. The weapon seemed fine, but for the dent in the breech caused by the bullet.

"Providing cover fire." Justin heard Carrie's voice in his earpiece. "Rush to my position."

His eyes found Carrie near the corner of the barracks. She was lying on the ground, the PK machine gun set up on its tripod in front of her.

"Roger that," Justin replied.

Carrie's PK machine gun began to roar as she fired a long barrage. Her bullets sawed through the large truck.

Justin fired a short burst toward the soldiers holed up in the second front by the wall, then picked up his rucksack, rifle, and RPG launcher and darted toward Carrie.

Someone fired a couple of rounds and their bullets lifted up dirt in front of him.

Justin ignored them and kept running in a zigzag path.

Carrie swung her machine gun to cover both fronts and blasted round after round.

Justin kept up his quick pace, regardless of the searing pain exploding in his back. He closed the distance as Carrie's gunshots began to dwindle. He sighed and took short breaths that did not overexert his flaming lungs. A couple of moments later he slid next to Carrie behind the thick concrete walls.

Carrie emptied the last of her rounds, then tossed the PK machine gun to the side. "You okay?" she asked as she sat by Justin.

"Yeah. A bullet got me in the back. The vest stopped it."

"Fractured ribs?"

"Maybe. I feel fine. Well, mostly." He let out a small cough.

"Could have bruised your lungs."

Justin nodded.

Bullets splintered the wall near them as Justin placed a new clip in his rifle. "Ready?" he asked Carrie.

She nodded.

Justin said, "We'll circle around to the other side, and use those two shacks as cover. Then, we'll advance to the fence line."

"Good plan."

They got to their feet and advanced along the wall. Justin was at the front and occasionally checked upwards, in case someone appeared at the rooftop. Carrie covered his back, following two steps behind.

They reached the other corner of the barracks and Justin took a quick peek. It was fairly quiet on this side. No shooters, but two large army trucks with canvas tops were heading out toward the south. Soldiers were sitting on two rows of benches in the back of the trucks. Justin could not tell if any prisoners were among them because the trucks were too far away in the distance.

Justin spoke softly into his mike. "Rex, Eve, two trucks coming your way."

"Roger that." Rex's voice came loud and strong in Justin's earpiece. "Targets onboard?"

"Unconfirmed," Justin said. "Go ahead with the plan."

"Roger," Rex said.

"Roger that, sir," Eve said.

Carrie glanced at Justin. "It's working."

Justin nodded. "I hope so. Let's reach the shacks and hold our ground until Rex confirms the targets have been eliminated."

"I'll cover," Carrie said.

Justin ran toward the shacks. The yard on this side of the camp was broken and uneven, with many dips and mounds. He was almost halfway to the shacks when a long barrage came from behind him. It did not sound like Carrie's C8SFW assault rifle. Bullets struck around him. Justin rolled on the ground, ignored the pain shooting from his back and his shoulders, and slid behind a mound. Dirt clods hit against his helmet and bullets flew overhead and twanged around him, tearing the ground on both sides of the mound.

Justin readied his rifle, then said, "Carrie, I'm safe."

"Roger," Carrie said.

"Now, I'll cover you."

"Roger," Carrie said.

Justin waited for a pause in the volley. When it came, he glanced over the mound. Three targets were positioned on the other side of the barracks and near another smaller, two-story building.

Justin fired at the man reloading his weapon near the barracks and struck the man in the chest and in his left leg. Then Justin fired another two-round burst at the other man, hitting him in his right arm and the lower right part of his body. The third man slipped behind the corner of the small building, but not before Justin fired four more shots that pierced the wall inches away from the man's head.

Carrie had already crossed most of the distance to Justin's position.

The third man came up again and fired a quick volley. Justin replied with two single rounds, but he missed both times. "Lucky...," he cursed.

He waited for the man to show his face again, swearing to himself he was going to nail the soldier this time around.

Carrie was about six feet away from Justin when two soldiers appeared at the other side of the yard, near Justin's and Carrie's previous position. One of them was carrying an RPG launcher over his shoulder. The other one had an AK in his hands.

"Down, down, down," Justin shouted at Carrie as he pointed his rifle toward them.

Carrie hit the ground.

Justin squeezed a quick volley but the man still fired his grenade launcher. The warhead cut across the yard as Justin dropped down and behind the mound. A moment later, the warhead smashed into one of the cinderblock shacks ten yards behind them, scattering concrete chunks and other debris over the area.

Justin peeked over the mound. The soldier with the RPG had fallen to the ground. The other one was out of sight.

"Carrie?" Justin said. "You're hurt?"

Carrie shook her head and crawled behind the mound. "Thanks."

Justin shrugged. "Good thing we didn't hide behind the shacks." He cocked his head in that direction.

"Yeah, but we still need to get out of here."

Justin nodded as he picked up his rifle. "And let's hope Rex gets his men."

CHAPTER FOURTEEN

Fifteen miles north of Hoeryong
North Hamgyong Province, North Korea
April 30, 7:05 a.m.

R ex studied the nearing army truck from the scope of his L115A3 sniper rifle. The distance was 310 yards, there was barely any wind, and the lighting conditions were close to perfection. The Schmidt & Bender 5-25×56 PM II day scope with 25x magnification brought everything up close, making these shots almost personal. The rifle chambered powerful and heavy 8.59 mm bullets.

Initially, Rex had experienced mixed feelings when assigned to this operation. His objective was to eliminate two Canadian operatives, firing the killing shots. They were suspected of betraying their country, but their guilt had not been proven. Chatter picked up by NSA surveillance had sealed their fate. No hard evidence. Not as far as he knew. But if it was sufficient for the

Canadians, it would have to do for him as well, no matter his doubts. So he stifled the sense of uneasiness building in the pit of his stomach and tightened his grip around his rifle.

Eve was positioned about a hundred feet to his left, much closer to the road than his hide further up on the hillside. Rex had checked on her two minutes ago. She was hiding behind a thick willow, her PK machine gun ready to fire.

"Eve, set off the charges in twenty," Rex said.

"Roger that," Eve replied.

Rex began to count down the seconds. His hands became one with the rifle and his finger rested on the trigger guard. His breathing slowed down almost to a stop. His body was frozen in position as he waited for his target to come into his crosshairs.

The first truck turned a bend on the road. Its driver—a skinny man maybe in his late forties or early fifties—slowed down for a moment and seemed to point at something up ahead to the front passenger. The passenger shrugged him off and the truck began to pick up speed.

Then came the explosion.

Both sides of the road erupted with a powerful and loud bang. The detonation rocked the area, and Rex felt Carrie had gone overboard with the charges. The blast spewed rubble and debris over the truck as a thick cloud of gray smoke swallowed up the convoy.

Before Rex or Eve had a chance to fire their weapons, another explosion came from the smoke cloud. This one was fiery, a blinding yellow flash; then huge flames licked at the sky. More black smoke billowed from the wreckage.

"Seriously?" Rex said, more to himself than to anyone else.

"What's the matter?" Justin's voice came over Rex's earpiece.

"Huh . . . the aftermath of the explosions."

"Any sign of the targets?" Justin asked.

"Negative," Rex replied.

"Roger that," Justin said amid gunshot rattles.

Rex examined the trucks as Eve began her PK machine gun barrage. Her rounds began to chew up the second truck as soldiers jumped off the sides to secure positions. Two men fired back toward Eve's position, but she mowed them down easily with her endless torrent of bullets.

Rex focused his attention on the first truck. Two silhouettes stumbled out of the burning inferno. They were both Asians and severely burned, flames engulfing most of their bodies. They flailed their arms as they writhed in agony.

Rex was tempted to squeeze the trigger and put them out of their misery. But he held his fire. His bullets had the names of Park and Schultz on them, but he had yet to spot his targets.

Eve continued her barrage, but more soldiers were firing in her direction. Their bullets chopped down tree branches near her position. Eve fell behind the tree trunk as she fed another belt into her machine gun.

A soldier crossed the road as he fired his rifle. He advanced toward Eve and Rex decided to engage him. He acquired his target—the soldier's head—and pulled the trigger. The soldier's head disappeared into a red mist.

A couple of soldiers came out from behind the first truck. They were cautious but confused as to the location of the shooters. Their eyes scanned the hillside. Rex waited for a moment, then spoke to Eve. "Two soldiers observing the area. Sit tight."

"Roger," Eve replied.

The soldiers turned their attention to the smoldering truck. Rex was too far away to hear their words but he read their hand gestures. They wanted to save their teammates in the truck but were unsure of how to battle the rising flames.

Four soldiers jumped out of the second truck. They shook their heads and shrugged as they stepped away from the burning hulk. None of them was Park.

They readied their rifles and headed toward the field in the direction of Eve.

"Six targets coming your way at eleven and two o'clock. Ready?" Rex said.

"Yes," came the reply.

"Engage," Rex said, and pulled the trigger.

His bullet slammed into the chest of the team's front man. He dropped onto his back while the rest of his team blasted their rifles. They were firing blindly, and their bullets struck yards away from Rex's hide. His sniper rifle was fitted with a suppressor that reduced muzzle flash and made Rex's shots almost invisible among the scrubland.

Rex fired another time. His bullet exploded on the left side of the soldier to the right. He fell sideways, but kept shooting his rifle in the air. The other soldiers took notice of Rex's position and aimed their weapons at him.

Eve slid out from behind her tree. Her machine gun erupted with a long burst. The barrage swept across the group. Two soldiers were dead before they collapsed on their backs. A third one was down on his knees, returning fire. The fourth soldier survived, unscathed by the volley. He rolled on the ground and vanished behind a cluster of bushes.

The machine gun's hail of bullets sprayed the hillside a second time. The third soldier was hit in his arms and chest. He tumbled backwards and tried to reach his rifle.

Rex fired again and pinned down the soldier with a bullet to his shoulder. Then he focused his sight on the remaining soldier.

Eve ceased fire, then said, "Status?"

"One target alive. Shrubs at my three o'clock."

"Roger that."

Eve concentrated her machine gun firepower at that location. Bullets thrashed through the bushes that concealed the soldier. But he was being smart, staying put and making no moves.

"I'm out," Eve said in Rex's earpiece.

"I've got him," Rex replied.

He fiddled with his sniper rifle scope, waiting for the soldier's head to come into his crosshairs. He took a deep breath as he counted the moments. *Come on, you little puke. Pop your head up so I can blow out your brains.*

A white handkerchief came up from behind the bushes, about four feet to the left of his perceived target location. Then a hesitant arm waved the handkerchief back and forth, the clear sign of surrender.

"Wise little puke is capitulating," Rex said.

"Let's go mop up the wreck site," Eve replied.

"Keep your eyes open. There could be others still breathing."

"Roger."

Rex got to his feet and moved forward while keeping his rifle pointed at the soldier's arm. The man slowly lifted up his other arm in the air, his confidence apparently boosted by the absence of bullets striking around him. Gunshots still echoed from the outpost, but they were distant and not an imminent threat.

Eve was closer to the surrendering soldier, so she was the first one to approach him. She said something to him while keeping her assault rifle trained on his chest. The soldier nodded and slowly removed a small pistol from his belt holster. He tossed it on the ground, then shook his head as Eve asked him another question.

Rex drew near them. The soldier was young, perhaps not even in his mid-twenties. He was clean-shaven but disheveled and his uniform was covered in dirt and grass stains. Defeat and fear were clear in his widened eyes. His anxious glance switched from Eve's face to Rex's as he tried to read their intentions and his fate.

"What did he say?" Rex asked Eve as he searched the soldier for weapons.

"The two Canadian agents were not in the trucks. They're still at the outpost."

Rex blinked his surprise. "How come?"

Eve asked the soldier.

He replied in a low, shaky voice. His hands were also trembling slightly, although he made a good effort to hide it.

Eve said, "Li, that's his name, said the outpost commander, Kim, was anticipating an ambush. They called in reinforcements from the prison camp as soon as Justin fired the first RPG."

Rex cursed. "How many soldiers in the outpost?"

"A total of forty or so," Eve said after Li gave her the answer.

Rex thought about their situation for a moment. He folded the stock of his sniper rifle, then said, "Let's check the trucks and see if Li's telling the truth. Justin, you reading this?"

A moment of pause, then Justin's voice came on the air. "Loud and clear. Mop up the place. Then Eve, take care of the bridge. Rex, report after clearing the site."

"Roger that," Rex said.

"Roger," Eve said.

"Move it." Rex shoved Li forward with the barrel of his rifle. "Tell him if he lied, I'll make him regret he waved the white flag."

Li shook his head, then spoke rapidly. His face produced a small crease of a dry smile as he waved his arms to support his claims.

"He's telling the truth," Eve said.

Rex sighed and wished Li was lying. He hoped they would find their targets burned or killed amid the rubble. Otherwise, the alternative was something he would rather not consider, especially with the North Korean Army bearing down upon them at any moment.

CHAPTER FIFTEEN

Military outpost fifteen miles north of Hoeryong
North Hamgyong Province, North Korea
April 30, 7:15 a.m.

Justin listened to Rex's report while pondering their options. But truly, there was only one. The one he had wished they were given orders for in the first place in this operation.

"You're positive, a hundred percent certain Park and Schultz are not among the dead?" he asked Rex.

"Affirmative," Rex replied. His voice carried a slight hint of frustration. "I'm staring at the bodies. There are no blonds here. And unless they dressed the agents in army uniforms and gave them side weapons, I'm absolutely certain Park did not burn to death in the explosion."

Justin glanced at Carrie, who fired a quick burst. They were crouched behind the rubble of the shacks and so far had been able to hold back the soldiers. But they were running low on ammo and soldiers seemed to come out in waves. Justin was worried one of the enemy RPG rounds would eventually hit the mark, or the soldiers would flank them from the sides and cut off their escape route.

He thought for another moment, nodded, then said, "Change of plans. We're going to attack the outpost and free Park and Schultz."

"That's craz . . . that's suicide, sir," Rex shouted in a firm, bold tone.

Justin ignored Rex's comment. "I repeat my order to attack. Blow up the bridge, then drive back with the truck. You and Eve will engage the enemy from the south. Carrie and I will advance from the northwest. Is it clear?"

A long moment of silence shattered by soldiers' gunfire and bullets slamming against the shacks' cinderblocks.

"Rex, do you read me?" Justin said.

"Yes, sir, but that's not our mission. We came here to—"

"I know why we're here, Rex. You're disobeying a direct order, and if you—"

Before he could finish his sentence, a sharp beep came from his rucksack. His emergency phone. *That must be McClain with something extremely urgent.*

"Stand by," he said to Rex and turned off his mike.

He rummaged inside his rucksack and found the satellite phone. The screen showed five missed calls and his boss's ID. "It's McClain," he told Carrie.

She nodded. "I'll take care of them."

He slid back another foot or so away from Carrie, removed his earpiece, and plugged his left ear. Then he pressed his sat phone to his other ear. "This is Justin, sir," he shouted over Carrie's gun blasts.

"Justin, I was afraid I wouldn't reach you in time." McClain spoke fast with a tone of urgency.

"What's going on?"

"We've received new, reliable intel. Our agents, Schultz and Park, haven't betrayed our country. They're not traitors."

Justin smiled. "Exactly what I needed to hear, sir."

Two bullets thumped against one of the cinderblocks and lifted concrete slivers that clanged against Justin's helmet.

"We were misled earlier, but I hope there's still time to make things right." McClain's voice turned firm. "Bring home our boys, Justin."

"Absolutely, sir."

"Godspeed."

Justin nodded, then said, "Yes, sir."

He ended the call and looked at Carrie. She loaded a fresh magazine in her assault rifle, then said, "Good news?"

"The best. Park and Schultz are clean. New orders to rescue them."

"Let's do it."

Justin tossed his sat phone back in the rucksack and put his earpiece back in place. He turned on the mike and said, "Rex, Eve, just got new orders from McClain. Park and Schultz are *not* traitors, I repeat, they're *not* traitors. We're to engage the enemy and rescue the agents."

A short pause, then Rex's voice came into Justin's earpiece. "Read you loud and clear. Heading to the camp in the mil truck as soon as Eve returns."

"It will be about two minutes, Rex. Getting ready for the blast. Fire in the hole," Eve said.

Bullets smashed against the top of the rubble. Carrie fired two rounds at a soldier who emerged from behind a mound to their left. She buried one bullet in the soldier's chest and one in his head. Then she turned her attention to another soldier holding an RPG launcher who materialized from a barracks' corner.

Justin fired toward the man as he launched his warhead. Justin dove for cover behind the rubble as the RPG arrowed toward them. It screamed a few feet to their right, and it punched the door of the last shack in the row. The explosion threw a wave of debris around them. A thick cloud of smoke covered their position.

"I can't see anything," Carrie said, firing blindly toward the place where she last saw the man with the RPG.

"We've got to move back. And fast," Justin said.

He fired a couple of rounds and waited until Carrie crawled backwards using the smoke as cover. Bullets dinged around him but he ignored them. He looked right, then left, and noticed the heavy machine gun at the top of the watchtower Carrie had attacked earlier that morning.

"Carrie, cover me. I'll get us the watchtower gun."

"Got it," Carrie replied.

Justin crawled through the scrubland and left the smoke plume behind.

Carrie fired her rifle in a long barrage.

He advanced rapidly but kept his head near the ground. Two or three bullets missed his head by mere inches. He pressed forward even faster. The staircase to the watchtower was now just twenty yards away.

Carrie kept up her suppressive fire.

Justin covered another few feet, then a hail of bullets stopped him in his tracks. Someone was firing at him with a large caliber gun. One of the rounds lifted a huge chunk of clay as it hit four feet away. Another one zinged by his head.

Justin made himself one with the ground but there was nowhere to hide. The shooter had a bad aim, or perhaps Carrie's volley was having an effect on him. The rounds kept striking off their mark and further and further away.

Justin moved forward an inch, then another, and resumed his crawl. He sprang forward as he came to the bottom of the staircase. A bullet struck the metal handrail but missed his hand. Justin climbed upward as fast as he could as more slugs clanged against the stringer and the handrails. He jumped over the last step and rolled on the watchtower's platform.

Carrie's barrage had splintered most of the wood and had drilled numerous holes in the metal baluster around the watchtower's perimeter. But a few sections were intact and they offered sufficient protection from enemy fire.

Justin pushed one of the dead soldiers to the side and sat behind the Russian-made DshKM heavy machine gun. Bullets pinged against the watchtower's frame. Justin rotated the weapon on its standard mount, looked through the sight, and fired it.

The armor-smashing 12.7 x 108 mm bullets began to pour from the mouth of the belt-fed *Dushka,* Russian for "sweetie" or "baby," as they affectionately called the brutal beast of a weapon. Justin focused the firepower to his left, where a group of soldiers were scattered around the yard. They were hidden behind small mounds but the watchtower gave Justin an excellent vantage point.

The powerful bullets tore throughout the enemy's positions. They responded with weak AK gunfire that soon turned silent. Two soldiers began to run for better cover, but the fierce barrage caught up to them. Bullets ripped through their bodies.

Justin turned the Dushka's heavy barrel toward the first barracks. The machine gun rounds found their targets and struck down four soldiers near one of the corners. Other bullets blew holes the size of basketballs through the walls.

Soldiers fell back and Justin swung his machine gun toward the other barracks. A soldier with an RPG launcher was aiming it toward the watchtower. Justin fired a long barrage. The bullets drilled through the soldier's body before he could fire his launcher.

Justin released the dual trigger and looked at the battleground in front of him. Dust rose up from three different locations. No return fire, at least not right away. He glanced at the ammunition belt connected to the machine gun from the left. *Another fifty rounds or so.*

"Looks clear," he said after tapping his mike.

"Advancing to the smaller barracks," Carrie said.

Justin fired a short burst of suppressive fire as Carrie ran through the yard.

She reached the barracks without encountering any resistance and checked the bodies of soldiers scattered around it. Then she turned around a corner. "Checking the perimeter, then entering the building." Her whisper came into Justin's earpiece.

"Roger that," Justin said.

He kept his machine gun trained on the barracks. The silence after a long skirmish was unnerving and he was expecting gun bursts from all sides.

A couple of isolated shots came from the distance. Justin glanced up toward the south. A military truck had just driven through the main gate. Then a long barrage exploded from somewhere across the other side of the yard.

"Rex, you're at the gate in a large mil truck?" Justin said.

"Yes. Got some incoming fire—"

The loud cracks of shattering glass erupted from Justin's earpiece. Then came quick two-round bursts.

"We got it, sir," Eve replied between gunshots. "And the bridge is blown to smithereens."

"All right, we'll move southward. Meet you at the prison building."

"Roger that," Rex said.

"Roger," Eve said.

Justin took another sweeping glance at the yard from behind the sight of his machine gun. Everything was quiet.

"Barracks is clear," Carrie said.

"Wait for me. We'll advance toward the prison."

"Roger," Carrie said.

Justin looked at the dreadful Dushka with admiration. He wished he could carry it with him but the gun weighted almost seventy-five pounds. Plus, it would not be very useful while they were on the move.

He took the AK assault rifle from one of the dead soldiers and stripped both bodies of their ammunition. He made out with four magazines and ran down the staircase.

Justin sprinted toward Carrie. Gunshots echoed from far away. He ducked instinctively, then realized no bullets rang or thumped near him. A few moments later, he joined Carrie behind the barracks.

"You okay?" he asked.

Carrie nodded. "Yes. And you?"

"I'm good. Let's go. Cover me."

Justin dashed toward the prison, hoping Park and Schultz were still alive.

CHAPTER SIXTEEN

Military outpost fifteen miles north of Hoeryong
North Hamgyong Province, North Korea
April 30, 7:30 a.m.

Kim examined the yard through the small windows just inside the entrance to the prison building. The attackers from the south had breached his defenses and had killed or wounded most of his soldiers. The onslaught from the north had decimated his troops. He was now trapped along with a handful of soldiers inside the outpost's last barracks still under his control.

"Where are those bloody reinforcements?" Kim shouted at the soldier fumbling with the radio near a corner to his right.

"They're coming, Comrade Kim, but the enemy has destroyed the bridge, so they—"

"Tell them to hurry up, hurry up, or all the prisoners will escape and we'll all . . . we'll all be killed."

The soldier nodded. "Immediately. Their last estimate was about ten minutes. They'll have to climb the hill and march on foot."

Kim shook his head. "Tell them to march faster. We may not have ten minutes."

A bullet shattered the glass window. A hail of shards hit his face. One sliced deep into the side of his right cheek.

Kim cursed as blood trickled down to the corner of his mouth. He wiped it with the back of his hand and cursed again.

A sharp growl came from the other corner behind the heavy wooden desk. Kim walked around and stared at the caged dog, a white *poongsan*. A soldier had stolen the dog from one of the farmers living around the outpost, and the soldiers had planned to cook and eat it for supper. Kim pointed his Makarov pistol at the animal. He neared the cage, then shouted at the dog, "You can't wait to become *boshingtang*, can you?"

The dog growled even louder, baring his teeth. He scratched the cage near the sliding bolt of the door with his right front paw.

Bullets clobbered the room's metallic door and thumped against the walls. A round pierced the other window, sending a spray of splinters all over the room.

"Get to that window," Kim ordered one of the soldiers standing near the radio. "You," he ordered another one. "Kill all the prisoners."

Kim moved to the first window. An enemy was running and shooting across the yard. Kim aimed his pistol.

Before he could pull the trigger, a gunfire burst sprayed the window. Kim was hit in his right arm and the lower right side of his body. He lurched back in agony as his feet failed to carry his weight. Kim plunged down near the base of the statue of the Supreme Leader.

* * *

Justin fired the rest of his clip at the prison window. He loaded his rifle, then quickened his pace and reached the prison wall. He looked at the door, ten feet away from him, then glanced up at the window. No return fire. Not yet.

Carrie peeked around the other corner and gave him a nod. "Good to go?"

Justin shook his head.

A rifle barrel jutted out of the window. The shooter fired a long barrage, followed by two short bursts across the yard. Rex and Eve were clearing out a pocket of resistance near the other barracks.

Justin let off a few rounds. A bullet hit the shooter's barrel and a couple ricocheted off the wall. But the narrow angle made it impossible for Justin to hit his target.

The shooter withdrew inside and fired again.

Another torrent of bullets exploded from the other window. The rifle barrel was aimed downward and to the side. The slugs smacked the ground near Justin's feet.

"Grenade," he whispered into his mike.

He pulled a fragmentation grenade from his chest rig. After he pulled the pin, he held the grenade's striker lever in place by wrapping his fingers tight around it. He counted to five in his mind, then took two quick steps and threw the grenade at the window. It bounced against the side of the window and fell inside the room.

Terrified shouts and screams tore through the room. The door was flung open. A soldier jumped out the exact moment the grenade exploded.

Justin knew the shower of fragments had shredded all shooters inside the room. They were dead or seriously wounded. Some of the shrapnel cascaded out of the door and over the soldier crawling through the yard. Other shrapnel sprayed out of the windows along with thin swirls of dust.

"Going in," Justin said.

"Got you covered," Carrie said.

Justin pointed his weapon at the wounded soldier. He was not moving and was bleeding from his back and the right side of his face.

"Down, stay down," Justin shouted at him.

The soldier turned his head and looked at Justin with his bloodshot eyes. He stretched his hands up and nodded.

Justin pushed open the bullet-ridden door and stole a peek inside the room. The walls were punctured by the grenade fragments. A large statue to the left was missing its right arm. A man was groaning in pain near the statue.

Justin stood over the man. A pool of blood was forming around his waist. A bullet had pierced his side.

The man tried to lift his left arm toward a Makarov pistol a couple of feet away.

"Don't," Justin shouted. "Don't do it."

The man opened his mouth to speak, but he coughed and spurted out blood. His dim eyes still carried a lot of hate and anger.

"I will . . . will . . . kill you," the man said between gasps.

Justin shook his head. He was tempted to just shoot the wounded soldier, but he could provide valid intelligence. Justin kicked the Makarov away.

"Carrie, backup," he said in his mike.

"Roger," Carrie said.

Justin glanced to his right. Two soldiers were lying on their backs on the floor, their bodies twisted unnaturally. They did not seem to breathe, but Justin had to double-check and make sure they were no longer a threat.

"Right behind you," Carrie said as she entered the room.

Justin pointed at the wounded man. "Watch him."

"Got it," Carrie said.

Justin checked on the two soldiers and found they were dead. Then he looked behind the desk to his right. Another soldier was slumped against the wall near a broken radio. He was bleeding from a large chest wound. Justin checked the left side of the soldier's neck. No pulse.

Justin moved to the other desk. A quiet whimper and a low rattle came from the corner. He pointed his rifle in that direction.

He dropped his glance to the floor and stared at the sad eyes of a very frightened dog.

"It's okay, little buddy," Justin said in a soft voice. "You're safe now."

The dog replied with a small whine and lowered his head.

Justin's quick check told him the dog had not been wounded by the grenade explosion. The desk had sheltered him, and God's providence had surely played a crucial part. Two shrapnel fragments had carved the wall three inches above the cage.

Justin smiled at the dog, who had placed his head between his front paws, and looked toward the hall. He took a couple of steps as he came to the corner and stopped.

He had no idea what was waiting for him in the hall. He thought about tossing a grenade to clear it up, but prisoners might be wounded from the shrapnel cutting through the doors of the barred cells.

So he dropped to his knee and glanced around the corner. It was empty. A couple of steel-plate doors were open about fifteen feet away. Justin pointed his rifle in that direction and took slow, careful steps forward.

He came to the first door and glanced inside the cell. A prisoner dressed in dirty rags was slouched in a corner. A bullet wound in his forehead told Justin the prisoner was beyond his help.

Justin returned his glance to the hall and wished he had never checked the cell. A soldier appeared twenty feet away. His pistol was aimed at Justin.

The soldier pulled the trigger.

The bullet slammed against Justin's chest right underneath his heart. The powerful punch almost threw him to the ground. He struggled for breath while his feet failed him. He leaned against the wall, groping for support, but found none.

The second round thumped against his left side. Justin winced as the sharp pain cut through his chest and almost blinded him. His knees buckled underneath him and he began to slide down.

As he fell, he raised his rifle and sprayed the hall with a long volley. Through his blurred vision, the soldier seemed to collapse to the side. But he kept firing his pistol, and Justin held his finger on his rifle's trigger.

The concrete floor came up hard and fast on his shoulder. He felt the rifle bounce on the floor, and it almost slipped from his weakened hand. But he kept squeezing the trigger and kept his cloudy eyes on his target.

More gunshots echoed behind him. Then he heard Carrie's voice. "Justin, Justin."

"I'm . . . eh, I'm fine. I think," he said slowly and tried to climb to his elbows.

"Gentle, gentle." Carrie knelt to his left and began to examine him. "Let me see before you move." She placed her hands on his chest, feeling around for wounds.

Justin dropped his glance to his chest rig and the bulletproof vest. They seemed to have stopped the rounds but he noticed the two tears. "How bad is it?"

Carrie unfastened his chest rig and his vest. "Didn't pierce through, thankfully. I don't know about your ribs and internal organs though. How do you feel?"

"Ran over by a tank," Justin said and drew in a slow breath.

"Take a moment. Rex and I will clear the rest of the prison."

Justin looked up over Carrie's shoulder and saw Rex standing guard. He nodded at Justin. Eve was further away, her rifle pointed at the wounded soldier.

"I'm fine." Justin clenched his teeth and ignored the pain shooting up from pretty much his entire body.

"And stubborn," Carrie whispered.

She offered him her hand. Justin took it and she helped pull him up. He fixed his vest and chest rig, then picked up his rifle. He loaded a new magazine in it, then said, "Let's find our men. Rex, watch our back."

"Yes, sir."

Justin moved to the next cell. He slid the rusty deadbolt and the door opened with a bone-chilling creak.

A prisoner was sitting at the foot of a small iron bed. He looked up at them. His face was bruised, his clothes were torn and dirty, and he looked thin and sick.

"Don't be afraid," Justin said, unsure if the man could understand him. "You're free now."

The man's small eyes sparked with hope and his wrinkled face produced a tiny smile. He stood up with difficulty and leaned against the wall, then took a couple of unsteady steps toward them. "You Americans?" he asked.

Justin shook his head. "No, but still your friends."

The man nodded. "Soldiers all dead?"

"Yes, well, most of them."

The man's smile grew bigger and filled his entire face. "Thank you, thank you," he said in a wavering voice.

Justin shrugged. "No need to thank us. Now, we've got to hurry and free the rest."

"I help. I come help."

"Okay."

Justin moved to the next cell and the one after that. The prisoners were all men, most in their mid-forties, but some seemed older. One or two looked like they were in their teen years. They were all weak and thin, beaten and bruised.

He was almost at the end of the hall, but he had not found Park or Schultz yet. *Maybe they've killed them? Or maybe they moved them to another prison?*

"Park, Schultz, where are you?" he shouted.

"Justin, is that . . . is that you, man?" A voice came from the last cell to his left.

Justin looked at the number 20 a hasty hand had scribbled on the brown, rusting door. It was in Korean, of course, but Justin had learned to recognize the sign that resembled two parallel lines and a cross.

"Park, you're there?" Justin asked as he pulled the deadbolt.

"No, it's Schultz," the man replied.

"I'm in here, the other cell," Park shouted.

Carrie went to free Park, while Justin stepped inside Schultz's cell. A large bloodstained bandage covered his left ear and most of his face. His right eye was slightly swollen and he had bruises on his bottom lip. His neck was blistered and his left elbow was wrapped with dirty gauzes.

"So glad to see you, man," Schultz said with a tired smile.

"Can you walk?" Justin asked.

"Yes, but I'd crawl if I had to, just to get out here."

"Let's go."

He offered Schultz his shoulder and they slowly made their way into the hall.

Carrie was helping Park, who looked in even worse shape than Schultz. Someone had carved a long cut along his left cheekbone, which matched an old scar on the other side of his face, and he was missing a couple of his front teeth. His nose was broken and bloodstains covered his mouth and his chin. Ligature marks around his neck were clear signs someone had tried to strangle him.

"Thanks," Park said in a quiet voice.

"Don't mention it," Justin said. "Let's get everyone out of here."

Loud shouts and noises came from the front. Angry voices speaking Korean and Eve replying in a similar if not louder tone.

A dozen or so prisoners had formed a small circle around the wounded soldier. They were pointing at him and shouting. One of the young prisoners spat at the soldier's face. Another one kicked him on the leg.

"Hey, cut it out. Both of you," Rex shouted at the young men.

"What's going on?" Justin asked Eve.

"They want to lynch the wounded soldier," Eve said.

"This is no soldier." The old man Justin had freed first took a step toward Justin. "This is Kim, the prison commander. He's responsible for our torture, our pain."

"He killed my son, my son," one of the prisoners shouted in a tearful voice.

"He ordered soldiers to rape my wife," cried another one.

Justin stared at Kim. The man's face registered pain and anger, but no remorse.

"What do you have to say for yourself?" Justin asked him.

Kim shrugged. "I followed orders. They . . . they would do the same. None of these people are innocent. They defied the government, the state. They deserved their punishment."

Justin shook his head. "Not your best defense."

Kim spat out his words. "I don't need to defend myself in front of human scum."

"As you wish. Have at him."

Justin stepped away as many hands reached to grab Kim by his throat, his face, his head, and everywhere else they could take hold of him. He screamed for a few moments, his voice growing weaker and weaker while the prisoners' shouts grew louder and louder. Then a bittersweet silence filled the room.

One of the young men gave the statue a strong push. It wavered but it did not topple. Another young man came to help him and they both shoved the statue. It finally leaned slowly to the left and came crushing to the ground with a loud bang. The head of the Supreme Leader broke off from the body, rolled on the ground, and lay on its side. One of the young man stomped on it, as the others cheered him on.

Justin said, "Rex, prepare our transport. Eve, help Carrie with Schultz and Park."

"What are you going to do?" Carrie asked.

"I have to free the last prisoner."

She gave him a sideways glance. "Who?"

"The dog," Justin said.

He found the cage behind the desk. The dog let out a low yelp and grunt when he saw Justin.

"Did you miss me, little buddy?"

The dog responded with a low bark.

Justin opened the cage and the dog burst out. He woofed and then licked Justin's face, wagging his tail and nuzzling Justin with his head.

"You want to come with us, eh?" Justin asked him.

The dog responded with a sharp, loud bark.

"Well, then what are we waiting for?"

The dog ran in front of Justin and headed toward the door. He stopped and turned his head for a moment, then woofed at Justin and jumped outside in the yard.

"We need to work on you following orders and heeling," Justin muttered to himself.

One of the older prisoners shuffled his feet toward Justin and began to speak to him rapidly in Korean. Justin was lost amid the stream of words but the gestures were clear. The frail old man kept pointing at one of the young men, then took him by the arm and nudged him toward Justin. The resemblance between the two was striking.

"He wants you to take his son with you," someone translated from the back of the crowd. "Other soldiers will come and they will execute us."

"Take us all. Save us all," shouted another one.

More voices called out in Korean.

"We cannot all go," said the old man, the first released prisoner, in a strong, firm voice that quieted the crowd. "Our friends need help as they sneak into China. We'll give them cover and hold back the army."

The same voice from the back that had spoken earlier said something in Korean, and Justin assumed he was translating the old man's words. Heads nodded and low shouts came from the crowd.

"But we humbly ask you to take our sons, our young men, with you. They will help you in your retreat, guide you through the forests, and fight with you. And they'll have a chance to be truly free and live in . . . freedom."

The old man's voice trailed off and his eyes turned watery. There was authority, planning, and wisdom in his words. Justin wondered if the old man had been serving in the Korean Army or had held a commanding position with other armed forces of the country.

"Great idea," Justin said in a warm, reassuring voice. "They'll be a big help. Pick the support team for our mission and have them meet me outside."

The old man didn't hold back his tears. He reached forward and hugged Justin tight against his chest. "Thank you, thank you, thank you," he whispered.

Justin smiled as he embraced the old man. "It'll be an honor to fight together, and may God bless us all."

The old man nodded. He stepped back and stood at attention. He raised his right arm and saluted Justin.

The rest of the crowd followed suit. They roared in unison in a loud battle cry.

Justin saluted them back. Then he nodded at them and marched outside.

Rex had brought around a large military truck and was sitting behind the steering wheel. Eve was in the passenger seat. The truck's windshield was missing and its cabin was bullet-ridden. But the engine was still running, albeit with the occasional cough and spurt.

"Ready?" Carrie asked from the back.

"In a moment. We're taking some of the young men. Extra support."

Carrie frowned, but did not say anything.

"I know," Justin said. "Our exfil was difficult to begin with. Now it got much harder."

"We'll do it," Carrie said.

She sat back near Park and Schultz and behind a PK machine gun.

The dog was lying by her feet. He stood up when he heard Justin's voice and let out a quick bark.

"He's telling you it's time to go," Carrie said.

"Right away," Justin replied.

Two wounded soldiers were sitting handcuffed near the door. Justin thought about freeing them, but he knew they stood no chance against the violent horde of the released prisoners. The soldiers had probably committed brutal crimes and those actions had sealed their fate.

Four young men burst out of the door. They were carrying AKs and pistols.

"Hop in." Justin pointed at the truck.

They nodded and got in.

Justin was the last one to jump inside the truck. He lifted the wooden tailgate and struggled to close it with the rusted, rattling bolts. Once he had secured it in place, he shouted at Rex, "Good to go, Rex. Let's get out of this place."

"Yes, sir," Rex yelled back.

He gunned the engine and the truck rumbled forward.

Justin sat on the dusty truck bed near the cabin, next to Schultz. Across from him, Park held an AK in his hands.

The truck had not reached the gate when a huge explosion obliterated a huge section of one of the barracks. It was the one across from the prison building. A large dust cloud began to rise up from the rubble.

"Mortars," Justin shouted.

Another round blasted about a hundred yards away, outside the fence line but in front of the gate. The enemy was trying to cover a large area, and their tactic told Justin they did not have eyes on them. Otherwise, they would concentrate their firepower on the target. The broken terrain and the forested hills provided sufficient cover. At least, he hoped, for a little while, until they crossed the border.

The freed prisoners spread out in the yard. Some began to run toward the back of the prison. They would be able to hold off the advancing North Korean army for only so long, even with the right weapons and under the right command.

Justin pulled out his satellite phone from his rucksack and tossed it at Carrie. "Update McClain. Tell him we're en route to China and may need him to make a couple of calls. It will depend on how fast the enemy advances and what the situation looks like at the border."

Carrie nodded and began dialing the number.

Rex turned the wheel and the truck swerved around a curve. Justin was thrown against the cabin and was glad he was holding on to one of the legs of the bench. The PK machine gun slid forward and one of the young men caught it.

The dog also slipped a foot or so away. He whimpered, then barked his protest.

Justin called him over. The dog hesitated for a moment, then ran toward Justin, dropped by his legs, and put his head on Justin's lap.

Justin petted the dog's head for a couple of seconds, then moved his hand to his rifle. The truck zoomed through the gate as another mortar round exploded behind them, perhaps seventy yards away. *We've won the battle at the outpost, but this war is far from over.*

He tightened his grip around his rifle, determined more than ever to save the people who trusted in him.

CHAPTER SEVENTEEN

Outside the military outpost fifteen miles north of Hoeryong
North Hamgyong Province, North Korea
April 30, 7:45 a.m.

The road rounded a couple of sharp bends as it took them south, closer to where the enemy was pounding them with mortar rounds. Justin frowned but he could not do anything to change the route or the terrain. They could try to cut through the fields and make their way to the treed hills, but he was uncertain how much more of a beating their old, battered truck could endure.

The mortar fire had intensified, but thankfully the rounds were still a long way off their mark. Mortars were notoriously inaccurate against moving targets, and were generally used as an area weapon, to suppress enemy forces. But the enemy had them and were using them in hopes a lucky one would hit the runaway truck or destroy the road in front of them.

Heavy gunshots sounded from the outpost. The freed prisoners had armed themselves with heavy machine guns, and it seemed they were mounting a good resistance. Unsure about their training and marksmanship, Justin could only hope they would put up a fierce fight. For their own sake and for the sake of his team.

The truck turned sharply around another curve. Two more turns and the road cut to the right and rounded a small hill, heading northwest. According to the maps and the aerial images, the Chinese border was about five miles away.

A shell blew up near the side of the road. It raised a geyser of soil and tree branches. Then another shell exploded a few feet away from the first one.

Rex stepped on the gas and the truck leaped forward. It rounded another turn at a very unsafe speed. The tires lost traction and slid over the dirt road, but Rex was able to straighten the wheel.

Carrie said, "McClain will give the Chinese border guards the wrong coordinates of our crossing. He'll send them south. That distraction should buy us enough time to cross the border undetected and then—"

A bullet pierced a large hole in the wooden side of the truck. Splinters struck one of the young men.

"Sniper," Justin shouted. "Get down, get down."

Carrie lifted her PK machine gun over the side. She peered for a moment, then fired a long volley.

The truck came to the last turn, and Rex eased up on the gas pedal. The truck stuck to the road as it entered the curve.

A round pinged against the truck's cabin right over their heads. The North Koreans' parting shot. The truck turned around the corner and behind the hill.

Two mortar shells erupted on the other side of the hill, but the truck was out of the enemy's direct line of sight. While still not out of danger, they now had a much better chance of survival.

Carrie fell back into her seat, while Justin checked on the young man. The splinters had caused only surface wounds to his face. His vision was intact.

"I was saying McClain's maneuvering should help us sneak across the border," Carrie said.

Justin nodded. "Once in the forests, we make our way to the rendezvous point and wait for our transport."

"Everything okay back there?" Rex asked.

"Yeah, we're fine," Justin said. He looked at the young man, raised a thumb up and asked him, "Okay?"

"Yes, okay, okay," the young man replied with a nod and a big smile.

Park heaved a deep sigh, then let out a wheezing cough.

"What's the matter?" Justin asked him.

"Nothing, I'm good. Listen, I'm sorry . . . very sorry about this mess. This is my fault. My screw-up."

Schultz shook his bandaged head. "No, man, it's not your fault. I came with you, knowing full well what you *and I* were doing. We both botched our operation."

Justin looked at Park, then at Schultz. "What op?"

Park gestured with his head toward the cabin.

"We trust Rex and Eve with our lives," Justin said.

"And them?" Park asked about the young men sitting at the back of the truck about four feet away.

Justin looked at them. They were all looking behind the truck, holding their AKs ready to open fire. "Not sure if they speak English," Justin whispered. "Let's assume they do, so keep your answers general, keep your voice down, and give me just the essentials."

Park nodded. "You know we weren't authorized to be north of the border," he said in a low, weary voice.

"Yes. You were supposed to meet a contact in South Korea," Justin said.

"Even that part is not true. We needed a reason to come to Seoul." Park dropped his eyes to the truck bed in shame. "We lied to Qu . . . our chief, claiming we had arranged for a meeting with our man. In fact, we were planning to infiltrate North Korea."

"Before you even left Beijing?" Justin asked.

"Yes."

Justin cringed. The story was not good and he did not see how it would get better.

He looked at the rice paddies in the distance. A group of people were bent over, hard at work. One or two looked up at the army truck. Justin hoped they were used to gunshots, since they lived and worked so close to the outpost, or that they would think it was a military exercise.

Justin returned his gaze to Park, whose face looked ashen. "What were you planning to do in the north?" Justin asked in a hushed voice.

Park sighed and rubbed the corner of his mouth. "Over the last year or so we've tried to develop a few assets in North Korea. We targeted mostly the nuclear scientific community and the army but considered anyone who came across as promising. Initial results were discouraging, since North Korea is a hard country to penetrate and the regime is extremely strong. But we kept going.

"Two months ago, we had an interesting offer from a contact, a nuclear physicist. He expressed some interest in providing us with some intel in exchange for payment." Park stopped and exchanged a quick glance with Schultz, who nodded and gave him a reassuring yet gloomy smile.

"What happened?" Carrie asked, cradling her PK over her lap.

"Our chief ruled against pursuing that contact. He said it didn't sound like a genuine offer. That's because when we made the initial contact, this man outright refused our proposal. He even threatened to expose us to the NK authorities. Then, a month later, he came back willing to strike a deal. To Qu . . . our chief, it sounded like a trap. So he ordered us to stop all contact with that man."

Justin thought he knew where this was going. "But you didn't?"

"We ignored the first couple of calls. Then we received a package that contained traces of uranium. Weapons-grade, highly enriched uranium. A clear sign the man had the means to procure trustworthy intel based on hard facts."

"That's when you decided to move against your orders?" Justin said.

"Well, no. We reported to our chief, who again dismissed it as a play to trick us into action. Then, that's when it happened."

Park paused and sighed. He opened his mouth but no words came out.

"What happened?" Justin said.

"This is . . . this is so embarrassing. I . . ." Park's voice trailed off.

"I got it, man." Schultz jumped in. "Park and I were blackmailed."

Park shook his head. "No, I was the one blackmailed. You, you agreed to help a friend."

"Explain." Justin looked at Park and then his eyes rested on Schultz.

Schultz exchanged a quick glanced with Park, then said, "Park has a wide network of contacts in the Chinese MSS. Lots of hard work and sweat and blood has gone into creating the relationship and building the trust. Payments, exchange of favors, whatever it took. A great investment of time and effort.

"And you know the great toll our work has on our personal lives. Park hardly sees his wife and two children anymore. What is it, once, maybe twice a month?"

Park shrugged but did not answer. He stared at Schultz and licked his parched lips.

Schultz continued, "Anyway, one of our contacts is, *was*, a woman by the name of . . ." He reached over and whispered in Justin's ear, "Li Hua. She was the girlfriend of a high-level politburo member and a source of very accurate and reliable intel. Park's relationship with her goes back more than two years and has always been very professional. But then something happened and—"

"Cut to the chase," Justin said. "Park slept with her."

His raised voice caught the attention of two of the young men. They turned their heads, but Justin gave them a stern frown. They looked away, returning their gaze to the dirt path and the plume of dirt that was zigzagging behind the truck.

Park nodded, his eyes glued to the truck bed. "I did."

"And she blackmailed you," Justin said.

"Yes," Schultz said. "But not just with the sex tapes. Li Hua had stolen our intel over the last three months, and she threatened to sell it to our enemies if Park didn't satisfy her demands."

Justin frowned. "I'm sure he found many ways to satisfy Li Hua," he said with sarcasm dripping from his voice. "What did she want?"

"Someone she described as 'a very close friend' was looking for a shipment of uranium. Li Hua demanded we provide it for her ASAP."

"And she knew about your contacts in North Korea," Carrie said with a headshake.

Schultz readjusted a corner of his bandage, then said, "Yes, she knew everything. Li Hua is extremely good."

Park said, "If I didn't go along, she was going to destroy my work and my life. All our secrets, intelligence. And my family. The shame . . ." His voice trailed off.

"We already had our contact, the nuclear physicist. He worked at . . . well, somewhere he could procure the shipment of uranium. At least, that's what we hoped at the time. We contacted him and made arrangements. Then we flew to Seoul under the pretext of meeting a contact in South Korea."

The truck's horn caught Justin by surprise. He threw a quick glance up ahead through the cabin's window. No one in front of the truck. He looked over the side and his eyes caught a glimpse of the tops of a man's and a woman's heads. The truck rumbled forward and climbed a small hill, and the pair on bicycles became visible behind the truck. They waved at the people in the truck, and one of the young men waved back.

Justin returned his gaze to Schultz. "How did you get across the border?"

"Li Hua's contacts. They bribed a couple of the border guards and drove us to the meeting place with our scientist. He was late, but eventually showed up, along with the package. Fifteen pounds of highly enriched uranium. He was ready to defect but we didn't have his paperwork."

"Yes, unauthorized op, plenty of obstacles," Carrie said.

"Right, so we had an argument. Park and I wanted the shipment but he wasn't willing to leave it in our hands unless we smuggled him across the border, with or without papers." Schultz stopped to catch his breath, as he was now speaking faster and louder than earlier.

Justin signaled for him to keep his voice down.

Schultz continued, "Eventually he calmed down and we agreed for him to come with us. But we fell into an ambush just outside our apartment."

"Li Hua's men betrayed you?" Justin asked.

Park nodded. His face had regained some color but he still looked pale and sick. "We were going to pull this off, authorized or not," he said in a low, yet convincing voice. "We had the defector, the uranium, and a cache of other evidence about North Korea's nuclear program. At a time when our service, the CIA, MI6, and other intel agencies have no clues about what the Koreans are up to, this was going to be a major breakthrough, a true success."

"But?" Carrie said.

Park sighed. "But someone betrayed us, most likely one of Li Hua's contacts. I remember the driver, always checking his cellphone and messaging. I never liked the guy."

Schultz scratched the top of his head, where his hair was caked with blood. He winced and checked the tips of his fingers. He rubbed off some of the dirt, shifted his body weight, and turned more toward Justin. "We tried to shoot our way through the ambush. But there were so many MSS agents and policemen. Our contact died in the firefight and they caught us. They took away the package and threw us in jail, first in Pyongyang, then at the camp down south." Schultz pointed with his hand to his left, toward the east. "They interrogated us, tortured us, but we never said a word, never gave up a single piece of intel. Then, they brought us up to the outpost, about five, six days ago. I've lost track of time."

Justin nodded.

"Kim, the man who ran the camp, promised to have us skewered with bayonets if we didn't spill our guts. He said he was going to make sure we did, one way or the other. Then, thankfully, you came to rescue us." Schultz smiled.

Justin nodded and avoided looking Schultz in the eye. His glance fell on Carrie, who gave him a wry smile.

They were all silent for a few moments, then Rex said, "We're coming up to our meeting point. Another minute or so and we'll see the river."

Justin looked over the side of the truck. A few houses appeared among the trees on the hillside across from wide-open fields. No border guard posts for at least another three miles.

He said, "Let's get ready."

CHAPTER EIGHTEEN

Twenty miles north of Hoeryong
North Hamgyong Province, North Korea
April 30, 8:00 a.m.

They crossed the railroad tracks that followed the meandering of the river, and Rex steered the truck deep into the grove near the river. The thick, dense trees covered most of it, leaving only the back end. Someone driving on the dirt road could still see it if they were looking in the right place at the right time. Justin hoped his team would be across the river and long gone when the North Korean army came looking for them.

Justin helped Park and Schultz down from the truck. Carrie left her PK machine gun on the truck bed, and Justin thought he saw some regret in her eyes. You never knew when you would need the fierce firepower and the long reach of a machine gun.

Eve and Rex came around and Eve explained the plan to the four young men. They nodded and told her they understood the instructions. Then the team began their march through the grove. Justin led the way, with the dog following closely behind and generally obeying Justin's gestures to "heel" and "be quiet."

About half a mile away, they came to a small clearing some sixty feet wide. Justin stopped their advance, and they surveyed the area on both sides of the border. On the Korean side, a train station rose up in the distance, about three miles away. A few warehouses were lined up near the whitewashed one-story station and a grayish watchtower looming over the area. A barbed-wire fence was visible along the river on the Chinese side near a dirt road. A small red-roofed building appeared in Justin's binocular view about fifty yards away from the fence. A guard post was almost in a straight line from the train station. Then a thick forest covering the hillside stretched on both sides behind the guard post.

Justin peered through his binoculars at the grove across the clearing. It took him a few moments, but he detected two silhouettes hiding behind the tall grass and the shrubs. Hong and Choe.

The dog had also discovered the two men in the grove. He lifted up his muzzle and let out a sharp bark.

"Good boy," Justin said and petted the dog's neck. "I saw them. Good boy. But you have to be quiet now. Understand? Quiet. Shhhhhh!"

The dog looked at Justin with his bright, fiery eyes. He whimpered, cocked his head to the side, then lay down near Justin's feet.

"Good boy, good quiet boy," Justin said.

He turned to his team, huddled near the trees at the edge of the clearing. "Hong and Choe are waiting for us. So now we'll split up. Rex and Carrie, you'll be in charge of the first group." Justin gestured with his head toward Hong's and Choe's location. "I'll take care of us here. Let me know when you're ready."

Rex nodded. "Will do." He turned toward Carrie and asked, "Shall we?"

"Lead the way," Carrie replied. "Be safe," she said to Justin and the rest of the team.

"Yes, you too," Eve replied.

Justin raised his binoculars back to his eyes. He searched the train station and the watchtower. No movement.

"Good to go," he told Rex and Carrie.

They rushed through the clearing and made it to the other side in a matter of seconds.

Justin continued to observe the train station and the buildings around it. Everything was quiet. Then a small truck appeared on the road. It was painted black and brown in a camouflage pattern.

"We might have company," Justin said into his mike. "A camo truck from the train station. Looks military."

"Roger that," Rex said. "Got eyes on it."

"Everybody down, down," Justin said. "Stay hidden and do not fire. I repeat, *do not* fire. It will give away our location."

Eve translated his words in hushed tones. The young men replied they understood the orders. They all spread out, hiding behind trees and shrubs as they kept their eyes on the road up ahead.

Justin convinced the dog to lie next to him by placing his hand over him. He petted the dog's neck and held him down. The dog playfully agreed, wagged his tail, and replied to the received attention with low grunts.

The truck reached the clearing and slowed down as it came to the edge of the road. Justin lowered his head as much as he could amid the grass. His eyes stayed with the truck.

The front passenger jumped out. It was a soldier in an olive green military uniform similar to the ones worn by the soldiers in the outpost. His jacket looked worn, the color faded and the elbows patched up. He scanned the clearing, his head slowly moving from left to right. Then he seemed to look straight at Justin's and his team's hiding spot.

Justin clutched his rifle. He wanted to be ready if the soldier stepped down to the clearing.

The soldier continued to check the grove. He took a couple of steps to his right, then stooped down to a crouching position.

"Has he made you?" Rex's voice came in Justin's ear.

"Negative," Justin replied. "But he's determined."

A strong voice came from behind the soldier. The driver was calling to him. The soldier replied with a dismissive hand wave and a headshake. He stood up and began to reverse his steps, still searching among the woodland.

Justin eased his grip on his rifle. "He's leaving. Stay down and keep calm."

The soldier gave a final sweeping gaze to the area, then jumped back in the truck. The driver started the engine and the truck's rumble died down in a few moments.

"Let's make sure they're truly gone and this is not a trick to draw us out," Justin said.

Eve repeated his words in Korean.

They all remained in their spots as Justin counted the tense moments of waiting. Silence slowly returned to the grove apart from the gurgling of the river, a bird croaking a sharp, strange sound, and the dog's soft panting.

"I think we're clear," Justin whispered.

"All quiet here as well," Rex replied.

"We must cross the river right away." Justin climbed to his knees, still halfway hidden behind the bushes. "They're looking for us, and soon enough they'll discover the abandoned truck. Once they're—"

A loud, heavy thunder shattered the silence. Justin looked to his right, toward the train station. The noise sounded like it came from that direction but there were no running trucks or locomotives. Then the roar echoed from the other side and above their heads.

"Helo," Justin said, looking through the thick canopy of treetops.

Eve nodded. She did not need to translate it. The young men had also figured out a helicopter was circling the area. One of them looked at Justin, nodded, and made a rotating hand gesture.

"Rex, get everyone ready," Justin said. "We're sitting ducks here. The helo or the ground troops will soon spot us. And they'll draw Chinese attention to this area."

"Roger that," Rex said. "But they might see us in the water, as we'll have no cover."

Justin sighed. "I know that, Rex. But they'll find us for sure if we stay here. If we make it across the river, they'll not dare to follow us inside China." He said the last words without much conviction, although he hoped the North Koreans would not give chase beyond their territory. Considering the attack against the outpost and its outcome, a deranged commander would not care about international laws and borderlines, but would seek revenge at all costs.

"Roger. Will report when ready to advance," Rex replied.

Justin turned to Eve. "We'll crawl to the edge of the river. Watch out for the fence line, and don't forget they have eyes in the sky."

Eve relayed the order to the young men, who nodded their understanding.

"It'll be tough, but you guys will make it," Justin said to Park and Schultz.

"You got it," Park replied.

"You came so far for us. We're not going to slow you down," Schultz said.

"All right. Follow me," Justin said.

The dog grunted and walked next to Justin. They all began to crawl toward the river. About ten yards away, they came to a barbed-wire fence about six feet high. Justin signaled for the team to stop, and gently held the dog down by its neck. He tore a leaf from one of the bushes to check the fence for electricity.

One of the young men said something in a quick voice.

"The fence is not live," Eve said. "That's what he's saying."

The young man crawled forward and grabbed the lowest strand of barbed wire with his left hand. He turned his head toward Justin and smiled. Then he spoke again.

"The government wants us to believe fences have electricity but we know better. Fences can't stop us. Nothing will stop us from wanting freedom," Eve said.

Justin smiled at the young man. "Good job," he said.

He crawled to the side and pushed up the wire. "Go, go, go," he said.

Eve slid underneath the fence, dragged over her rucksack, and helped Park and Schultz. Next it was the turn of the young men, and they slipped under the fence. Then the dog dropped to his belly and crawled to the other side. His wagging tail was almost caught on the sharp barbed wire.

Justin checked behind, then glanced above. The helicopter's roar had died down, but it was still flying around the area. He handed his rucksack to Eve and slid under the fence, while Eve held up the wire.

They resumed their crawl and were soon near the riverbank, which sloped gently into the water. This was the most dangerous part. The tree branches offered little protection, and once they were in shallow water, they would be completely exposed to the helicopter.

"Rex, you're in position?" Justin asked.

"Yes, we are," came the reply.

"Move forward," Justin said.

He dashed over the sandbar and glanced upwards. No sign of the helicopter. He entered the cold, muddy waters. The Tumen River was shallower here than on the Russian side, but as soon as the water rose to above his knees, Justin dropped down and only the top of his head was above the water.

He half-crawled and half-swam for a few yards, then looked to his right. Rex's group was making more splashes than Justin would have preferred but they were advancing. He looked behind to his own group. Schultz was about two yards behind, followed by Park and the young men.

Justin continued his swim with slow yet powerful strokes. He propelled himself forward fast and without splatters. His boots touched the slippery bottom of the river, and he used it to gain extra momentum.

The helicopter rumble returned from his left side. Justin turned his head but did not see it. The noise continued, and Justin assumed the helicopter was hovering over the groves or making a sweep over the road alongside the river.

The splashes from Rex's group had gotten bigger, and they were spraying a lot of water around. Someone began to wade through the water. It was Choe, holding his son in his arms.

"Rex, keep them down. The helo will make you and us," Justin said.

"They're panicking, sir," Rex replied.

Justin heard Carrie's voice calling at Choe and the others to stay calm and down in the water.

Choe pushed his way through the water for another few yards, ignoring Carrie's shouts.

The helicopter appeared at Justin's right. The rumble grew louder.

"Get down, down," Rex shouted at Choe.

He sank in the water, but the damage was done.

The helicopter dove over the river. It banked to the left and began to approach Rex's group.

Justin harbored a faint hope the helicopter had not made them yet. He kept his head down, praying the helicopter would pass over them and away without spotting the two groups. But he knew those chances were pretty slim, so he readied his rifle for a firefight.

A barrage of gunfire rippled the water between the two groups. The helicopter swooped down for the kill. More bullets cut among Rex's group and peppered the water around them.

Justin stood up and fired a short burst at the moving target. He was not sure if his bullets had hit the large black helicopter. He emptied his clip and found another one in his chest rig. He reloaded and waited for the enemy's certain return.

The young men had taken positions around him. Justin waved at them to keep going and reach the other shore. "Eve, take everyone across. I'll cover."

Schultz said, "I'll stay with you."

Justin turned around to face Schultz, who was holding up his AK. "No. Reach the trees and then provide cover for my advance. Go. Now."

Schultz nodded with reluctance and began to swim next to Park and Eve.

Justin looked at Rex's group. People were shouting and swimming in chaos.

"Rex, status," Justin asked.

"Hong's injured, but he'll make it. Carrie's making sure they reach the other side. I've got your back."

Justin nodded. The helicopter was nowhere to be seen. He took a few slippery steps to the side, then swam forward with powerful strokes, keeping an eye on the sky.

Then the helicopter rattle returned. Justin stopped and raised his rifle over the surface of the water. He paddled with his legs and aimed in the direction of the sound.

The helicopter appeared over the groves to his left. Justin looked through the rifle's sight and fired three-round bursts.

Rex had also noticed the bird and was firing his AK.

The helicopter dropped over the river. Heavy machine gun fire erupted from its starboard side. Justin dove as slugs struck the water. He kept his eyes open as more bullets torpedoed around him.

Then he heard a distant yet powerful explosion. Shrapnel peppered the water. Grenade. Justin dove, glad that he was at a deeper section of the river. He guessed it had to be near the middle, as he turned around and swam away from the area under attack.

Another explosion echoed from above the water. It sounded more distant than the first one, but shrapnel still whirled around him. And a string of bullets plunged near his arms, missing his hands by mere inches.

Justin felt a bursting sensation deep in his lungs. He needed to come up to the surface for air, but the helicopter was still hovering over the river, pouring an endless torrent of bullets. He was trained to hold his breath longer than the average person, so he kept swimming.

Everything seemed to go silent for a moment. Justin listened for the engine roar. It came to his ears faded and distant, but it was still there, still a deadly threat.

A strong spasm erupted from his ribcage. He was reaching the critical line. He pushed himself upward and raised his head slowly above the water's surface.

The helicopter was veering to the right. There was no gunner on the port side, but the retractable door was left open wide enough for someone to fire through it.

Justin took a deep breath, refilling his lungs with much-needed oxygen. He pondered for a split second whether to dive and continue swimming or fire at the helicopter. The Chinese shore was still at least fifty yards away, and he would have to rise to the surface again. The next time, he might not be this lucky.

He raised his rifle, aimed at the helicopter's tail rotor, and fired a long barrage. The bullets struck the rotor and the tail boom. A few hit the door and the fuselage as Justin held his finger on the trigger.

He emptied the magazine and took another one from his chest rig. He reloaded but the helicopter had completed its turn. Now it was fast approaching for another fierce pounce.

Justin took another deep breath and dove as fast as he could. He sank quickly, the weight of his rucksack helping his efforts. And he swam forward and away from his last seen location.

A huge explosion erupted behind him, followed by more bullets zipping past him. One of them struck him in his back, plunging him forward. The water absorbed most of the bullet's energy, and his rucksack and vest stopped the bullet itself. Still the round packed a heavy punch, and a wave of pain rippled through Justin's body.

Another bullet grazed his left arm. It tore through his jacket sleeve and his skin. Blood began to ooze but Justin kept swimming.

He soon felt his feet resting against the slippery bottom of the river. Justin was getting closer to the shore. He pressed forward, ignoring the tightening of his lungs.

A few more strokes and his knees touched slimy plants growing along the shore. He looked over his shoulder while keeping his head near the water surface. The helicopter was gone.

Justin climbed to his feet and rushed toward the grove. Eve and Schultz had set up positions near a row of thick trees. They waved at him.

Justin slowed down his pace and took a few deep breaths. He headed in their direction and glanced around the area. Park and two of the young men were crouched further away among the trees.

The dog was sitting next to them. He noticed Justin's arrival and got up to his feet, but Park held him down by his neck.

"Where are the other two Koreans? They didn't make it?" Justin asked when he got close to Eve.

She shook her head. "The helo barrage cut them down. But they died fighting."

"And how are you doing?" His eyes went from Eve to Schultz and then to Park.

"I got a flesh wound," Eve replied. "One of the boys is wounded in his arm, but it's not serious."

"Park and I are okay," Schultz said. "And the helo is gone."

Justin nodded. He hoped they would not see the helicopter anymore, but he could not be certain at this point. He reached for his mike. "Rex, status."

No answer.

"Rex, do you read me?"

A burst of static, then he heard Rex's strong voice. "Yes. We've . . . we've lost Hong. His wife's also wounded on her leg. His children are devastated."

Justin swore under his breath. "We need to get moving. The gunfight has alerted the Chinese border guards. They'll be here any second."

Eve was already on her feet. She offered to help Schultz up but he leaned on his AK and stood up on his own.

Justin took a moment to get his bearings. The helicopter's attack had pushed them toward the south. In a sense, that was good since they were now further away from the guard post across from the train station. But there was the possibility of other guard posts or watchtowers in the area.

He tried to remember the layout of the land from the aerial images. A couple of trails cut through the hills. If they could cross the fence and make it to the forest, their odds of survival would greatly improve.

"Rex, we're heading northeast and taking the southern trail as originally planned. Meet us at the trail head."

"Roger," said Rex.

They marched up the hill. Justin could still hear the helicopter's rumble, a distant yet constant ringing in his ears. He wondered if it was his imagination or if the bird was still flying over the North Korean territory. *Maybe we damaged it enough to force it to land.*

They reached the fence and slid underneath it just as they had done on the Korean side. Again Justin was the last one to slither to the other side. Just as he threw his rucksack over his shoulder, a loud truck engine roared down the dirt road.

"Hide, quick," Justin said. "Someone's coming."

CHAPTER NINETEEN

One hundred yards inside Jilin Province, China
April 30, 8:20 a.m.

They scrambled to secure positions. Justin made it across the road and dropped behind a cluster of thick pines and cedars. Park lay next to him near a thick hedge of bushes. Eve and the rest of Justin's group took cover among the thinning grove by the fence.

"Maybe they haven't seen us," Park whispered.

"I hope so," Justin replied. Then he spoke softly into his mike. "Rex, you have eyes on the truck?"

A woman's loud and sharp wailing came from up ahead. Justin peered through the bushes. Nothing. No people and no truck.

Justin said, "Rex, what's going on?"

More shouting ensued, and this time there were two different men's voices. The language they were speaking was unfamiliar to Justin. He wondered if it was Chinese or Korean.

"Rex, do you read me?" Justin's hushed voice took on a hint of concern. "What's your status?"

"We've been . . . compromised." Rex's words came through his earpiece.

Then a short burst of gunfire went off in the distance. Automatic rifle. Most likely an AK.

"Rex? Carrie?" Justin shouted. "Are you taking fire? What's your position?"

No answer.

"What's going on, Rex? Talk to me," Eve said in a worried tone.

Still no answer.

Another gunfire explosion rang out from the forest up ahead. Justin could not place the exact location, but it was probably a hundred or so yards away.

"What do we do?" Park asked.

"We stay put," Justin replied. "Perhaps the guards are trying to draw us out, hoping we'll panic and give away our position."

Eve said, "But Rex is under fire."

Justin replied, "We need to know exactly what's going on, Eve."

"And we'll not do that by staying hidden, sir," she said.

Justin thought about it for a moment. It was not clear if Rex and Carrie were holding back the guards or whether they needed any help. But they were now incommunicado, and Justin had to find out about their situation.

"All right, Eve," he whispered. "Move forward along the fence. I'll advance on the other side. Park and Schultz will provide cover."

"Roger that," Eve replied. "And the Koreans?"

"They'll stay back and cover the south side, in case more guards appear from that direction."

"Roger," Eve said.

Justin nodded at Park, who gave him a small smile and a thumbs-up.

"Stay safe," Park said.

"You too," Justin replied.

In a high crawl he got behind the trees and advanced about twenty yards. A couple of single gunshots. Pistol fire. He moved fast to his left, climbing along the hillside for a better vantage point. His arms and feet slipped over the moss growing along fallen trees' trunks and protruding roots. He tried to make as little noise as possible while slithering over dry foliage and fallen branches that carpeted the ground.

The dirt road curved about twenty feet below. Justin gained another thirty yards, then looked around the corner. A small military truck and a green SUV. It looked like a Hummer, but smaller and skinnier.

"Eve, what's your position? Do you see the vehicles?" Justin called over his throat mike.

"Negative. Oh, wait. I see a man in uniform, another man . . . a total of three men coming out of the grove."

Justin squinted but did not see anyone. The vehicles sheltered the men from his view. He advanced another couple of feet and aimed his rifle at the SUV. The driver—a young man in his twenties—was still inside, drumming his fingers on the steering wheel. He was wearing an olive green uniform and was looking to his left, toward the grove.

Justin scanned the area in front of the SUV through his C8SFW rifle's scope. The sight troubled him and his heart almost stopped beating. Two uniformed soldiers had grabbed Carrie's arms and were bringing her to the road. She was stripped of her weapons and her chest rig. A third man had an assault rifle pointed at her back.

Rex and the rest of his group appeared behind them. Four other soldiers had flanked them, their rifles and pistols trained on them. Rex was limping from his left leg, while one of the soldiers next to him was bleeding from a large shoulder wound.

The SUV driver jumped out of his seat and pointed a pistol at Carrie's head. She responded with a defiant glare.

Eve's voice came into his earpiece. "Justin—"

"I see them," he said.

Justin positioned his rifle's rubber buttplate against his shoulder. His fingers went to the trigger guard. He wanted to open fire and rescue Carrie and the other captives. The scope's crosshairs fell on the soldier to Carrie's right. He could blow off his head with a single round. But the others would open fire and kill or wound most of the captives.

He cursed, then heaved a deep sigh. He quickly considered his other option: negotiate their release. The guards would first arrest them, but once they learned they were special operatives of a foreign agency, they would have to take them to their command center. Someone at a higher position than border patrol guards would have to determine their fate. A fate that in all likelihood was already sealed in their favor because of McClain's intervention.

Before Justin could say any words, his earpiece crackled with static. Then he heard a deep man's voice speaking in heavily accented, broken English, but still full of authority and power. "We captured you comrades. If you not come out, we kill them."

The man was speaking in Carrie's mike while holding it in his left hand. His right hand clasped a small pistol. Justin moved his hand up, and his rifle's scope gave him a clear picture of the man's facial features. He was in his fifties, with sunken black eyes, a colorless face, and a square jaw. A small, thin beard covered his drooping chin.

"Justin?" Eve said. "You reading this?"

"Yes," Justin said. "Follow my lead."

The Chinese were listening to their communications, so he did not say anything else. He took a deep breath, hoping everything would work out well with their plan. "We're coming out,

Commander," Justin said via his mike, but loud enough so the man would hear his words even if he was not using Carrie's earpiece. "Do not fire, *nobody* fire a round."

He walked with a swift pace through the woods and appeared at the left side of the dirt road. His rifle's stock was in the crook of his elbow, and his finger rested on the trigger. The weapon was aimed at no one specifically, and the barrel was pointed slightly upwards and to the left. In a split second, Justin could correct his aim and fire at the target.

Eve stepped out of the grove a moment later. Her eyes met Justin's and she gave him a reassuring nod. She was cradling her weapon in a way similar to Justin.

He did not turn his head, but expected Park, Schultz and the other two men to follow behind him, their weapons locked and loaded and ready for action.

The commander raised his left hand toward Justin, while pointing his pistol at them. He was about thirty yards away. "Stop, stop. No move. And put down you weapons."

His words were followed by his men's realigning their weapons. Some trained them at Justin and Eve; others at Choe and Hong's wife and children.

Justin stopped, but did not drop his rifle. Instead, he pointed it at the commander. While Justin wanted to avoid a shootout or a standoff with the border guards, he also wanted to make sure they were not going to be shot before the commander spoke to his superiors. He needed some leverage to ensure that was going to happen, and their weapons were all their leverage at this moment.

He said, "Commander, we obeyed your order and came out. We're not your enemy, and we're not at war with you. We need your help to contact—"

The commander cut him off. "Put down you weapons, you rifles. Do now!"

Justin shook his head but made no other moves. "Commander, listen, we—"

"No, you listen. I kill you, I kill them if no weapons down."

Justin sighed but his eyes never left the commander's face. The man clenched his square jaw and was clearly running out of patience. His men were also shifting and clenching their weapons. If someone slipped and fired off a round, the resulting gunfire would not end well for anyone.

Justin said, "I'll lay down my rifle, we'll all give up our weapons, if you call your chief, the one who gives you orders—"

"No one order me here," the commander burst out. "I order you, but you no listen."

He looked to his right, toward the group of captives. He stormed toward them and grabbed Choe's little boy by the neck. Choe lurched forward, trying to stop him, but the commander raised his arm and pistol-whipped Choe across the face. His slap sent Choe toppling to the ground.

Carrie threw a punch at the soldier to her left, but the one behind her jammed his rifle muzzle into her back. She fell to one knee for a moment, but got up at once. She pulled her arm back and prepared to deliver another blow, but the other soldier hit her with his rifle buttstock to her left side. Carrie fell down a foot away from Choe.

The commander dragged the screaming and kicking little boy forward. They took a few steps toward Justin, then the commander pressed his pistol to the back of the boy's head and shouted at Justin, "I kill him. Put down weapons. Now. Now!"

Justin gazed at the boy's terrified face. He saw Ayoub, the little Syrian boy he had saved from the executioner's talons. And he saw Theodore, his seven-year-old nephew, who only knew of battles and wars in videogames. *You're not going to kill him on my watch.*

"All right, all right." Justin began to lower his rifle. "Don't hurt him. Let the boy go. We're laying down our guns."

The commander shouted, "Do it. Now. All you." He gestured with his head to the left, then to the right.

Justin did not look back, but gave the order. "Everyone, hold your fire and put down your weapons."

He stooped down but kept his gaze on the commander. The rifle was still in his hands. He was about to place it in front of his feet, when a gunshot shattered the tense air. The commander's head exploded as a bullet hit him from the back.

Then chaos erupted all around them.

Synchronized bursts of gunfire came from the forest. Justin lay flat on the ground while aiming his rifle toward the soldiers. But they had turned their attention toward the invisible shooters and were blasting their weapons.

The boy screamed in panic and ran toward his father.

The soldier who had hit Carrie was struck by a bullet in his chest and fell on his back. Carrie grabbed his rifle, then dashed toward the SUV. She shouted at the other two soldiers to take positions beside her as she knelt by the front wheels. They raced in that direction, but the first one was cut down by two bullets before he could take cover. Another round thumped against the chest of the second soldier, knocking him to the ground.

Justin zipped to the edge of the forest as bullets kicked up dirt around him. He fired blindly into the forest, spraying a long barrage. Then he dropped behind the thick bushes just as more bullets whizzed over his head.

Across the dirt road, Eve was rushing to join Rex and his group. Rex was already firing an automatic rifle he had seized from one of the Chinese soldiers.

Carrie fired a few bursts as Justin reloaded his rifle. He tapped his chest rig and realized he only had two magazines left in their pouches. "Rex, Eve, let's get to those vehicles and make our exit."

"Roger," Rex replied.

"I'll get to Carrie," Eve said.

"Roger that," Justin said.

He peered through the bushes. Two muzzle flashes betrayed the attackers' positions. Justin fired twice, single shots, aimed center mass. Both muzzle flashes stopped.

Eve hurried toward the SUV while Rex covered her advance with a long barrage.

Justin switched his rifle fire selector to single shots, then scouted the forest for targets. Two men in camouflage clothes appeared among the trees. Justin fired two rounds, but missed both times.

The men returned fire, stripping the bark off the cedar trees in front of Justin. He ducked down, then crawled forward to his right. He fired two more rounds. He missed again, but his shots were sufficient to send the two men diving for cover.

Eve had reached the SUV, and Carrie was climbing inside it. She pulled out the body of the dead driver, then steered the car slowly toward Justin. The SUV offered cover for Eve, who sprayed the forest with continued bursts of her rifle.

A large military truck appeared on the road, and it came to a halt about two hundred yards away. A group of men in camouflage uniforms similar to the gunmen firing from the forest jumped from the back and took positions along the truck and the edge of the forest. Two of them began pounding everything with their machine guns; others blasted away with their assault rifles.

Carrie stopped the SUV and Justin hurried toward it. He fell near the front of the SUV as bullets hailed from all sides, pinging off the vehicle.

"You okay?" he asked Carrie, who stayed in the SUV.

She nodded. "Yeah, I'm fine."

"More of them in the large truck," Justin said. "And that's our only way out."

Eve pointed at the forest. "Can't we cut through there?"

"No. They'll catch up to us or call ahead for troops to lie in wait. We have to overtake them."

"How?" Rex's voice came in his earpiece.

"Any RPGs in the SUV?" Justin asked.

Carrie shook her head. "And we don't have PKs either." Her voice expressed regret for leaving her PK machine gun across the river.

"I've got a couple of grenades," Rex said. "And there's a machine gun in the small truck."

Justin glanced over the side of the SUV. The truck was about fifty yards away, stopped in the middle of the road and providing somewhat of a barricade. The bodies of a few dead soldiers were scattered around the truck.

"Here's the plan," Justin said as bullets thumped against the SUV. "Carrie and I will use the SUV to reach the truck. Once we have the machine gun, we'll attack their position and force them to withdraw to the forest."

Carrie and Eve nodded.

"Eve and Rex, save your ammo," Justin said into his mike. "Shoot only what you can hit."

"Roger," Rex said.

Eve nodded.

"Climb in," Carrie said.

As soon as he got in the seat behind her, Carrie put the SUV in reverse and hit the gas. Justin fired through the shattered back window at the gunmen around the large truck. Then he tossed a grenade to his left, near the place he had seen a couple of muzzle flashes.

Bullets struck the side of the SUV but they missed him. One zipped near his head as it ricocheted off the back door. Two more bounced inside the vehicle, but without hitting him or Carrie.

She slammed on the brakes as they got to the truck. Justin shoved open the back door, which was immediately hammered by bullets. He fired toward the forest, then crawled underneath the small truck. He peered up ahead and to the sides, using the wheels for cover.

Carrie knelt near him. "Ready?" she asked.

"Go," Justin said.

She nodded and fired what appeared to be a QC, a Chinese-made assault rifle.

Justin crawled out and climbed over the side of the truck. He rolled onto the truck bed as a bullet almost blew his head off. It missed by a few inches and broke one of the windows.

A Type 80 machine gun was stashed on one side of the truck. Justin unfolded its bipod, hooked the ammunition belt to the gun, then slid the bolt into firing position. He unlatched the truck's tailgate and pulled the trigger.

The loud rattle covered all other noises around Justin. He focused his immense firepower on the left side of the large military truck. Then he pivoted the gun on its bipod and made a tight stitch along the edge of the forest. His barrage chopped down tree branches and lifted huge chunks of dirt, the bullets chewing through the tree trunks.

Rounds from incoming fire slammed against the side of the truck just as two grenade explosions came from the right and the left. Justin assumed it was Rex, but did not look back. He swung the gun back to the left side of the truck and continued his barrage.

One of the gunmen popped up near the truck's door. Justin fired at him but his machine gun jammed. It was overheated, and he could not do anything about it at that moment. He picked up the gun and dropped over the side of the truck behind Carrie, who was firing her shots in two- and three-round bursts.

"Gun jammed," Justin said and picked up his rifle.

"Did your job," Carrie replied. "They're retreating."

Justin glanced over the rear wheel mud flap. A gunman climbed through the front passenger door, then the driver reversed the truck and began a three-point turn.

"We can't let them go," Justin said. "They'll inform others."

"Let's give chase in the truck," Carrie said.

Justin left the machine gun on the ground and walked along the side of the truck. Park was advancing toward the SUV, and Schultz was laying a suppressive fire for him. Then Justin's eyes went to the grove along the fence as something white and furry darted across the road. The dog barked as it jumped into the bushes.

Justin turned his rifle in that direction. A gunman stepped into the open, flushed out by the dog. He raised his pistol, but Justin was faster on the trigger. He fired once and buried a bullet in the gunman's chest.

The dog kept barking and howling at the woods. Someone fired at him, but it missed. The dog backed away a few steps, but as he circled around the area he snapped his teeth and woofed at the gunman.

Justin could not see the gunman, but fired into the forest in a wide spray pattern, hoping his bullets would hit the target.

Park was now almost at the SUV and stopped for a moment to catch his breath.

Justin cast a glance at him, then over his shoulders. No visible shooters in the forest, so he turned his attention toward the grove. His eyes fell on a gunman who had just materialized through the woods, his rifle pointed at Justin.

"Get down, down," Park shouted as he ran in front of Justin.

Justin rolled on the ground while Park fired his AK rifle. The bullets pierced the gunman's body but he was also able to squeeze his trigger. Thankfully, his rounds were off target, thumping against the SUV's door.

"Thanks—" Justin's words were cut short by a single shot.

The round slammed into the left side of Park's chest. Park's AK rifle fell out of his hands as he collapsed to the ground. Blood spurted out of the gaping wound.

"No, no, no," Justin shouted.

He bolted toward Park and took his head in his hands. Park's eyes were closed and blood was trickling out of the left corner of his lips. He was gone.

Another bullet struck near them, stabbing into Park's left thigh. Justin glanced back and his fiery eyes locked onto a gunman shooting from the back of the military truck. A third bullet hit Park's rifle two feet away from his head. Then the truck rounded the curve and disappeared from Justin's sight. *You're not getting away that easy.*

He looked at Carrie, who offered him a sorrowful glance.

Justin shook his head and jumped to his feet. "Park's dead, but this is not over."

Carrie said, "Let's go get them."

Justin picked up his rifle and Park's AK. "Rex, Eve, Schultz, mop up the area and secure the civilians. We're going after the truck, and we'll meet you down the trail."

"Roger," Rex replied.

Justin got into the front passenger seat and dropped his rucksack by his feet. Carrie sat behind the wheel. She stepped on the gas, made a tight turn, and sped off behind the large truck.

Justin put a new clip into his rifle and held it up with the muzzle jutting out of the window. He refastened his helmet, pulling at the left strap. He thought about Park lying dead and bleeding on the road. After surviving North Korea's torture camps, when they thought it was all over, death still reached with its grim claws and took him.

He swore out loud and punched the dashboard. "Faster, faster," he shouted at Carrie.

She nodded and stomped on the gas pedal.

The truck swerved around the curve and they were swallowed up by a thick gray dust cloud. Carrie switched on the headlights. The two powerful beams cut through the cloud and gave them the outline of the road snaking alongside the river. The truck in front of them was stirring up a long trail of dust.

"We'll get them," Carrie said as she cast a fleeting glance at him.

Justin nodded. "Yeah."

He looked straight ahead, squinted, and thought he made out the box shape of the truck for a split second as it rounded a turn. He calculated the distance at about three hundred yards. Too far away for a clean shot, considering the terrain and their high speed.

Carrie was holding her foot on the gas and they were gaining on their target. Justin thought about asking her to push the truck even harder, but was worried about oversteering and ending up in the grove or in the river.

The truck bounced over a bump in the road, and they were airborne for a few moments. Gravity did its job, and the truck dropped back onto the road. Its front wheels slid a couple of feet and Carrie fought to regain control. The truck veered dangerously close to the side of the road. The right side tires drove over the overgrown grass and shrubs, and a couple of low-hanging branches scraped the top and the side of the truck.

Justin brought his rifle closer to himself to avoid its catching on a branch.

Carrie pulled hard on the steering wheel and the truck returned to the road. She sighed and stepped slowly on the gas pedal. They began to pick up speed again as they zipped through a straight patch on the road.

Justin said, "When we get to the—"

He was interrupted by a shudder filling the sky to their right. The vibrations grew louder and heavier, until the rumble almost burst their eardrums. A black helicopter filled Justin's field of vision.

"The helo's back," Justin shouted.

The helicopter zoomed ahead of them, gliding over the river. Then it banked sharply to the left and into the Chinese airspace. It hovered about two hundred yards over the road.

Carrie turned off her headlights and zigzagged just as the helicopter launched an aerial assault. Its bullets tore through the road. The dust cloud offered the truck some protection but not much. A round pinged against the back of the truck.

Justin fired a long barrage. He waited until Carrie straightened the wheel, then squeezed off a few more rounds.

"We need to get away from the road," she said. "They'll hit us sooner or later."

Justin did not answer her. Carrie was right, but he was not ready to end the chase. He fired another burst.

The road made a couple of soft turns. As they rounded the first one, Justin noticed the runaway truck was slowing down. Through the dispersing dust cloud he saw a man in the back of the truck shouldering a weapon.

"Possible RPG, watch out," he called at Carrie.

She spun the steering wheel and hit the brake. The truck drifted into the grove as a rocket-propelled warhead cut a trail of smoke through the road. It missed the truck by about ten feet and exploded somewhere behind them.

Before Carrie could bring the truck back onto the road, the helicopter overtook them. Another barrage erupted and bullets, broken branches, and leaves rained upon them. Justin emptied the rest of his clip, firing at the helicopter veering to the right over the river, then inserted the last clip into his rifle.

Carrie gunned the engine and they were back on the road. The truck up ahead was moving away fast. The gunman in the back was gone, but a muzzle flash from the left side revealed his position.

"We can't do this for long, Justin," Carrie said.

"I know, but keep going."

The helicopter completed a turn and descended over the river. Justin aimed his rifle and glanced through the scope. The target was on the move, they themselves were bouncing and sliding over the slippery dirt road, so it was impossible to align his crosshairs with the helicopter's gunner.

Justin fired a couple of rounds, then a three-round burst. He readjusted his aim and fired again. He waited a few more seconds, ignoring two bullets that spattered against the truck's sides. When the body of the gunner came into the crosshairs for a split second, Justin pulled the trigger.

He could not tell if he hit the mark, as Carrie swung the truck to avoid another RPG warhead that struck a tree and exploded to their left side. He refocused his attention on the truck and blasted it with a few well-aimed and well-calculated bursts. A couple of his rounds hit the sides of the truck, and one smashed a window.

The helicopter rattle returned behind them. Justin turned in his seat and fired the last bullets of his last magazine through the dust cloud. He replaced his rifle with the AK he had taken from Park, realizing he had no idea how many bullets were in the clip, and he had no extra clips.

"You got ammo?" he asked Carrie.

She shook her head. "Just the mag in my AK." She nodded toward her rifle lying between their seats.

Justin thought of the SIG P228 pistol in his waistband holster, but it would not do much damage against the heavily armored helicopter. If the gunner was still alive and able to shoot or if there was a second gunner, Justin would be not only outnumbered but also outgunned.

The helicopter's nose appeared through the veil of dust. Justin fired a few rounds, then the AK's hollow click informed him the clip was empty. The helicopter was now hovering a dozen or so feet away from the truck.

It was a Russian-made helicopter of the Mil series, probably a Mil Mi-8, but Justin could not be a hundred percent certain. The fuselage had undergone a serious facelift, with numerous modifications, like nothing he had seen before.

He braced himself for the powerful wash from the main rotor blades. Dust began to swirl around the truck, and branches were hurled against them. The pilot kept the helicopter sliding just a few feet over the treetops as it followed them, but no one was shooting at the truck.

"Use my AK," Carrie said.

Justin shook his head. "That's the last mag," he said. "We'll need it for them." He gestured toward the truck and pulled out his pistol.

Carrie bit her lips. "I wish we had an RPG," she blurted.

Justin thought about her words for a moment, then gave her a smile. "Grenades," he said, and tapped his chest rig. "These should bring down the helo."

Carrie nodded. "You need to get closer."

"I will. Slow down."

She stepped on the brakes, and Justin opened the door on his side. He planted his foot firmly on the truck's bolt-on step on the side of the chassis. Then he swung his body outside while holding on tight to the handle on the truck's interior roof with his right hand. The tires kicked dust into his face and the wind blurred his vision. He still reached with his left hand to the side of the truck and hooked his fingers on the stake pocket. After securing his hand he slid as far as he could on the step, then jumped into the truck box.

Justin rolled and held on to the left side as the truck picked up speed. The open tailgate rattled against the back of the truck.

The helicopter was hidden from his view, and Justin hurried to prepare his trap. He opened one of his chest rig pouches and pulled out a fragmentation grenade. He held it tight in his hand and waited for the right moment.

A barrage of bullets sprayed the truck's cabin. Justin looked to his right and noticed the military truck had slowed down. Muzzle flashes lit up from its back.

Carrie slowed down, then stopped in the middle of the road. She could not drive and fire at the same time. A moment later, she pushed her AK through the window and fired a couple of rounds.

The helicopter's whir returned as it appeared behind the truck. Justin's fingers tightened around his grenade, and he held it hidden under his right leg. He knew he had only one shot, as the pilot would realize Justin's plan and pull away or stay beyond his reach.

The pilot steered the helicopter near the truck. He was closing the distance fast. Fifty feet. Then forty. The rotor's wash grew strong. Justin held on firmly to a tie-down strap clipped to the side of the truck.

Carrie fired another burst.

The helicopter advanced another dozen or so feet. It was flying maybe twenty feet above the truck. The pilot's face became somewhat visible behind the thick, dirty glass of the fuselage. He seemed determined to maneuver his flying monster right above the truck and crush it with the helicopter's weight. Or at least run the truck off the road. And that worked well with Justin's plan.

He turned his head to the side to avoid being hit by the debris flying from the truck's bed and the dust coming from the road. Then he used his thumb to remove the grenade's pin and held the handle. A couple of seconds later, he lifted his arm and tossed the grenade as hard as he could toward the helicopter.

The pilot understood what Justin had done and swung hard to the right.

For a moment, Justin thought the grenade would miss its target and explode over his head. But he had executed an almost perfect throw. The grenade bounced on the side of the helicopter and fell inside through the port side's sliding door.

"Go, go, go," he shouted at Carrie and banged against the truck's side.

Carrie floored the engine, and the truck jerked forward with a roar.

The helicopter soared upward and veered to the left, then to the right. The pilot was trying to shake off the grenade, hoping it would roll out of the open door. He continued his movements for a few more seconds.

Then the grenade exploded inside the helicopter.

The shrapnel spewed out of the door and burst open a part of the side window. The helicopter twirled and began its downward spiral. It completed a 360-degree turn, and it dropped fast over the road.

Carrie hit the brakes as the helicopter came into her view through the windshield. It was still falling under gravity's hold. The pilot attempted to climb over the forest, and he succeeded for a few moments. The helicopter rose a few dozen feet. But then it plunged into a swift nosedive.

It swerved in a large circle, and it tilted to the left. The main rotor blades chewed through the treetops. The pilot seemed to level the helicopter for a moment, but then the rear rotor stopped spinning. The helicopter began a slow turn, tilted on its side, then crashed down on the road on its nose about twenty yards away from the large military truck.

The fierce collision tipped over the helicopter. The tail broke off and the rear rotor was hurled into the forest. One of the rotor blades folded over the mangled fuselage, while the other one cut like a sharp electric scythe through the riverside grove. Metal fragments, glass pieces, and other debris flew around the area, but there was no fiery explosion. A grayish dust and smoke cloud began to cover the area.

The driver of the large truck was not able to brake in time. He tried to swerve around the wreckage that had blocked off most of the road. But one of the front tires hit a piece of debris—a part of the tail or the blades, Justin could not be sure because of the distance and the curtain of smoke—and the truck tipped to the side. It drove unsteadily on two wheels for two or three feet, then it tore through the grove before landing in the shallow water with a loud splash.

Carrie started the engine and drove to the truck's crash site. She got out and examined the crash site through the sight of her AK.

Justin raised his pistol to eye level and walked to the other side of their truck. No one swam or walked away from the slowly sinking truck. The body of a man floated near the shore. He was on his back and motionless.

Justin stepped cautiously into the water to double-check the body. The man was dead, his neck broken as he was tossed away from the truck. Justin waded into the waist-deep water to check on the other people. Both the driver and the front passenger were still in their seats, but they had not survived the crash. The driver was a man in his mid-twenties, while the front passenger was much older, perhaps in his early sixties.

"They're all gone," Justin said when he was back on dry land.

"The helo." Carrie pointed behind them.

Justin held no hopes they were going to find the pilot or anyone else aboard the helicopter alive after the impact. As they neared the wreckage, it became obvious their search was a waste of time. The fuselage was torn into two large pieces and the pilot was hunched over his seat. He was not breathing, and neither were two other men lying over the debris. Justin was not certain which one of them was the gunner he had put in his crosshairs, but he was glad the chase was over.

"We should find the trail," he said to Carrie. "Before other border guards find us."

Carrie looked around. "It might already be too late. The helicopter crash and the gun battle must have alerted pretty much everyone. But perhaps we'll catch a break once we're deep into the forest."

"I hope so," Justin said. "And I hope Val and her team are in position, ready for our exfil."

He cast a final sweeping glance at the helicopter. Then his eyes went to the truck halfway submerged in the water.

"Let's roll," he said to Carrie.

He picked up his rucksack from the truck, and they both headed toward the forest.

CHAPTER TWENTY

Three miles inside Jilin Province, China
April 30, 9:05 a.m.

They cut through the thick forest, zigzagging and following the hilly terrain, but always advancing toward the southwest.
They made as little noise as possible and had a couple of close calls when they heard shouting in Chinese and the booming of heavy trucks. But they did not run into anyone, and reached the trail that was going to take them near the village of Dashantun, on the other side of the forest.

Justin called Rex through his mike and they met up about half a mile away. The gun battle had decimated their group and most of the survivors had suffered minor wounds. Rex and Eve were carrying Park's body on a makeshift stretcher, while one of the young Korean men was leading the way. Choe was carrying his son over his shoulders in order to keep up with the group's fast marching pace. He gave Justin a heartbreaking gaze, which acknowledged the man's mistake in giving away their position during the river crossing, a mistake that had cost Hong's life. His wife and two children were sobbing quietly. They looked at Justin with bloodshot, tearful eyes and Hong's wife reached for a hug. Justin held her in his arms for a long moment and said nothing. Nothing he could say would bring her comfort. Schultz and the other young Korean man were bringing up the rear. The Korean's left arm was pretty much useless, but he was holding an AK in his right hand.

The dog seemed to be the happiest to see Justin, covering his face in slobber. His tail was wagging furiously, but he was not barking. Even the dog had realized the need to be quiet.

Justin cuddled the dog and rubbed his neck. "You saved my life back at the river, you know that?" he whispered in the dog's ear. "I could have been dead had you not discovered that shooter."

The dog responded with more wet licks to Justin's face and hands.

"Justin," Rex said. "I spoke to Val about ten minutes ago. The Gulfstream is in place in Yanji. We just need to make our way there."

Justin stood up and walked alongside Rex, giving him a brief account of what had taken place during their chase of the runaway military truck. "As soon as we come to Dashantun, we'll secure our transport. A mid-sized truck would be enough for us all."

Carrie had replaced Rex at the head of the group and was helping Eve. The Korean gave them some directions, and they turned right through a narrow one-man trail.

"I had a chat with one of the wounded gunmen, Enlai," Rex said in a low voice, brushing away a few cedar branches from his face. "They weren't border guards, but MSS."

"What were they doing there?" Justin asked with a deep frown.

"Waiting for us. Their chief, Jaw-long—one of the men who died in the truck crash—was a member of the Chinese Politburo. This man was deep in debt to a Saudi prince named Ismail bin Saud and to pay him off, he had promised the prince a shipment of uranium."

Justin's frown was replaced by a look of concern. "The fifteen pounds of highly enriched uranium, Li Hua, her 'very close friend.' Everything is coming together. Since Enlai's not with us, I'm assuming he died."

Rex nodded. "I wanted to save him even though the wanker took shots at me. But his chest wound was so severe. Eve, or perhaps it was you, had truly nailed him well."

"That's too bad. He would have been a source of valuable intel. Oh, well, what's done is done."

"Yeah."

The group marched almost in silence for the next few minutes. Their feet crunched over dead leaves and broken branches, and their conversations were short and hushed. The two Korean men had traveled through the area about two years ago, in a failed escape attempt. A Chinese border patrol had discovered the group they were travelling with as they came to a clearing, a mistake they were determined to avoid this time around. They guided Justin and the rest of their group past grove after grove, and they crawled on those clearings and fields where the low vegetation provided little cover.

Justin updated Val on their progress and also put a call through to McClain, giving him a brief report about the exchange with Rex. McClain agreed with Justin on the urgency of finding Li Hua and getting to the bottom of the Saudi nuclear affair. A team of agents at the CIS headquarters in Ottawa was going to dig up intelligence on Li Hua's whereabouts and any Saudi Arabian involvement. Justin volunteered to first pay a visit to Ms. Hua and then meet with Prince Fouad bin al-Farhan from the House of Saud, with whom he had a history of favor exchanges. The intelligence about a member of the royal court's attempting to obtain a nuclear weapon was extremely valuable. Justin was hoping to find out if the deal was sanctioned by the king or the crown prince, or if there was just a rogue prince trying to make a name for himself.

Their trek took over four hours as they took breaks and skirted around hills to avoid any border patrols hunting them on foot, or running into villagers going about their business in and around the forested hills. Justin and Carrie shared their water and food portions with Choe and his son, while Rex and Eve split their food supplies with Hong's wife and her children. The stoic Koreans refused any food, but took a few sips of the warm canteen water.

They finally saw the first whitewashed houses, barns, and warehouses of Dashantun as they came to the edge of the forest. A small creek separated the village from the hillside. Justin and one of the Koreans—the one who was the most confident about the village's layout—crossed the creek in search of a vehicle.

Justin let the young man walk around freely, as he was unremarkable in his black pants and brown shirt, which he had borrowed from Choe. In his camouflage fatigues, Justin would stick out from a mile away, so he lurked in the shadows. He was there to provide backup for the young man in case things got out of hand.

The young man soon found a farm vehicle, a rusty tractor with a wooden trailer that had seen better days forty or fifty years ago when it had rolled off the factory's floor. The trailer did not seem very solid and Justin wondered whether it would be able to carry the weight of nine people. But with no other vehicles in sight, they could not be picky.

The young man turned on the tractor, whose owner had left the keys in the ignition, and drove it to Justin, who handed him a wad of cash. It was a thousand American dollars, which Justin assessed to be the value of the tractor and the trailer. He had probably overpriced their means of transportation, but he wanted to compensate the owner for the inconvenience of having an important part of their livelihood stolen in broad daylight. And perhaps the hefty sum would restrain the need to call the police and report the theft.

The young man did not understand Justin's line of reasoning, but nonetheless followed his order. He placed the cash near the backyard fence where the tractor had been parked until a minute ago. Then he got into the tractor's cabin, while Justin hid underneath a dirty tarp in the trailer that smelled like manure.

The trailer bed surface was coarse and dirty. Justin found a half-rotten potato in one corner, and hay strands poked at his neck along with sharp wood slivers. The sides of the trailer were about two feet high, which provided good protection from passersby or other vehicles. And the gross tarp should hide them from anyone's view until they met with Val and her convoy.

The tractor came to a stop and Justin peered through a hole in the tarp. They were near the hillside, the hideout of Carrie and the rest of their group. The tractor's driver came around the back of the trailer and Justin jumped out. Everyone hurried to climb aboard, and the trailer ended up almost full. It was going to be a rough, uncomfortable ride, but it was going to save everyone's life. And once they were beyond the cluster of small villages dotting the hills and the plains—which Justin hoped would take a little over an hour—they could breathe easier as they reached the rendezvous with Val and her crew on Wansan Line south of Longjing.

The tractor driver and Choe sat in the tractor's cabin. Justin had given Choe a communication headset and asked him to keep them constantly informed, especially when they came near other vehicles or people and if they noticed anything suspicious. Justin kept his pistol ready at all times, and once in a while peeked out to study the area.

The tractor moved slowly and pulled the trailer with difficulty. The constant clatter of the wood and metal panels followed them as they made their way through potholed dirt roads and around farmed fields. They did catch a break, and no one of the villagers they encountered gave them more than a second curious glance. Choe informed Justin when they came to a truck that bore a close resemblance to the military vehicles of the border guards. It turned out it was someone's personal vehicle parked near their front gate, but no one from that house paid any attention to the tractor as they crossed in front of the truck.

They finally reached the Wansan Line, the main artery that ran through the area. Justin called Val to confirm their location. She informed him the convoy was awaiting their arrival about two miles away, as the road forked to the right.

Ten minutes later, they left behind the rough filthy trailer and sat in the comfortable clean seats of a rental Ford SUV and a Honda van. Val drove a small Mazda sedan, and Justin gladly accepted being chauffeured by one of the pilots. He closed his eyes for a moment as he leaned back in his seat. He enjoyed a long moment of silence, knowing their mission was not finished, but the worst was over. The further away from the border, the fewer their chances of getting caught.

And once the Gulfstream 450 jet took off from the Yanji Chaoyangchuan Airport later on that evening for their direct flight to Inchon, South Korea, Justin heaved a breath of relief. Their mission in North Korea had been accomplished. He still had a few final tasks, but they ranked pretty low compared to what he and the others had faced during the last twenty-four hours.

CHAPTER TWENTY-ONE

Bali, Indonesia
May 5, 02:40 a.m.

Justin and Carrie slithered in near-complete silence through the tropic jungle-like vegetation surrounding Le Petit Jardin Villas.

CIS agents had tracked Li Hua's movements to this small luxurious oceanfront resort in Saminyak, one of Bali's exclusive playgrounds. She had arrived two days ago, but Justin and Carrie had sat tight waiting for the right moment. After her guest arrived four hours ago, it was time.

They came to the edge of the complex surrounded by an eight-foot-high wall painted a faint yellow color. The wall was mostly covered by meticulously kept palms, banyan trees, rattan, bamboo, and all types of dense low shrubs and plants. Justin scaled the wall with the help of the curved trunk of a nearby palm, then leaned to give a hand to Carrie. In a matter of seconds, they were on the other side.

The complex had four armed guards, who patrolled the grounds on thirty-minute intervals. Their shack was about three hundred yards away, and they had just covered this area. Justin and Carrie had timed their insertion to avoid being seen or heard by the foot patrol. Li Hua's guest had his own security detail, but Justin and Carrie had come well-prepared.

The two agents advanced with careful yet hasty steps toward their target. They walked on the narrow slate pathways cut through the forest. The night air was hot and humid, since May was the hottest month in Bali. Justin's black polo shirt was stuck to his back and sweat drops had covered his forehead and his neck. Carrie was wearing an army green tank top, and she seemed to be faring better under the elements.

They came to a koi fish pond and turned right. Li Hua's villa was in that direction, with a magnificent ocean view. The front desk clerk had been more than willing to give Carrie that information when she had inquired about renting that specific secluded villa.

The sharp squeal of a macaque monkey filled the night. It resembled the gut-wrenching sound of a fingernail scratching on a chalkboard. Justin and Carrie stopped and hid in the thick shrubbery.

A tall man appeared around the corner, his shoes clacking on the pathway. One of the guest's bodyguards. He was about a foot taller than Justin and had almost forty pounds on him. But Justin had the advantage of surprise.

He waited until the man had passed by them and pounced on him, striking him with a fierce blow to the back of his head. Then he reached and caught the man before his body hit the ground. Justin and Carrie carried the man quietly deep into the grove and set him against a palm tree. He would wake up wondering how he had ended up there, but not before Justin and Carrie had completed their mission.

They returned to the pathway and neared the corner of the villa. It was nestled amid the lush vegetation, with a heart-shaped swimming pool to the left and a small fountain, lounge chairs, and two white mesh hammocks underneath a cluster of tall palms. A patio area with a wood dining table and four matching chairs was to the right, inside a round cabana wrapped in a sheer cream-colored veil.

The second bodyguard was standing at a discreet distance— seven or eight feet—from the door of the villa. He was smaller than the man Justin had knocked out and seemed relaxed, his sleepy eyes almost closed. But a shiny silver pistol was visible in his waistband holster.

Justin glanced at Carrie and nodded toward the guard. "You want to use your charms?"

"Why don't we just shoot him?" Carrie raised her left hand, holding her pistol with a long sound suppressor.

"In case neighbors are listening." Justin gestured toward the other villa, whose green roof was visible through palm trees and feebly reflecting the dim moonlight glow.

Carrie nodded. She hid her armed hand behind her back, then stepped around the corner.

"Hey, sexy man, you want to dance?" Justin heard her soft whisper.

She was out of his sight, and he moved as close as he could to the villa's wall.

"Who . . . what are you doing here?" the man said in a low, angry growl.

Carrie did not answer, but a muffled shuffle came from that side. Then a muted groan, followed by a faint thump.

Justin jumped around the corner, his SIG P228 pistol ready to fire. He found Carrie removing the gun from the bodyguard's holster. He was stretched on the ground, his head resting near the bottom of a palm tree.

"Smooth and clean," Justin whispered.

Carrie nodded. "Got my hands dirty, but it was okay." She wiped her palms on the bodyguard's white shirt.

Justin stepped near the glass-paneled door. "Ready?"

"Ready."

He pulled a lock-picking set out of his pocket and fiddled with the simple deadbolt for a few moments. Then he leaned on the door handle and opened the door a hair. He looked up at Carrie.

She nodded at him and raised her pistol.

Justin pushed open the door, which swung inward without as much as a creak. The large room was half-dark, but three floor-to-ceiling windows with slightly open curtains drew in sufficient slivers of light from outside. A small table with a couple of glasses and two empty whisky and vodka bottles stood near the window, along with two foldable chairs. He made out two people lying in the king-sized bed. Li Hua and her guest, Colonel Atmaja Adianto of the Indonesian National Armed Forces. The blue sheets were near the end of the bed, covering only the lower part of their bodies. Li Hua was wearing a pink see-through camisole and was lying on her side, facing away from Justin. Colonel Adianto was on his back, showcasing his hairy chest and extended belly.

Justin exchanged a glance with Carrie and motioned for her to move to Li Hua's side. He tiptoed close to the colonel and slowly placed his pistol near the man's left temple. Then he rapped gently against the man's head.

The colonel groaned and opened his eyes slowly and lazily. It took him half a second to realize the severity of his situation, as Justin shoved the muzzle into his cheek. "What—"

Justin hushed the colonel with a hard push of his pistol. "I want you to listen. Get up and get dressed. Be quiet and you'll live."

The colonel's eyes found Carrie. Her pistol was hovering near Li Hua's face, who was still sound asleep. Then he looked toward the window.

"Your men can't help you. But you can help yourself," Justin whispered.

Li Hua let out a low mumble as she rolled over. Her long black hair covered most of her face.

The colonel nodded.

Justin took a step back and gestured for the colonel to get up. Then Justin ushered him toward a pile of clothes thrown on the tiled floor near the foot of the bed. The man pulled out a pair of khaki pants and put them on over his black boxer shorts.

"Bathroom." Justin motioned toward the left.

Li Hua moaned and stretched on the large bed as she tried to get more comfortable. Then she opened her eyes and raised her head. "Atmaja, what are you . . ." She blinked as she tried to clear away her sleep. "And who are—"

Carrie cupped her hand in front of Li Hua's mouth and muffled her words. "Shhhh, not a sound and you'll be okay."

Li Hua fought back and tried to bite Carrie's hand.

Carrie held her grip. Her long fingers dug deep into Li Hua's neck. "Stop or die choking," Carrie said in a hushed but firm voice.

The colonel took a step forward toward Li Hua, but Justin cut him off. "To the bathroom."

Colonel Adianto sighed and shuffled his feet down the hall. Justin handcuffed him to the heavy wooden double vanity of the bathroom and stuck a facecloth into his mouth. Then he plugged the man's ears with balls made of Kleenex. Justin did not want the colonel eavesdropping on his conversation with Li Hua.

The colonel put up a small struggle, then resigned himself to his fate.

"Keep your mouth shut. We're not here for you," Justin said.

The colonel nodded but his eyes revealed his true intentions. He was plotting revenge.

"You might even thank us, once you've calmed down," Justin said.

The colonel's face flashed a look of surprise, then disbelief. He muttered something, but the gag was too tight over his mouth.

Justin returned to the room. Carrie had turned on a lamp on the nightstand on Li Hua's side of the bed. Li Hua had put on a yellow floral dress and was sitting on the bed, her hands handcuffed behind her back. Her eyes were puffy, her hair was disheveled, and she looked hung over. Carrie was standing two feet away from her.

"You know who we are?" Justin dragged up a chair and sat in front of Li Hua.

"No idea." Her voice was low, but sharp and angry.

"Let me jog your memory." Justin pulled Park's photo from his shirt pocket and held it up for Li Hua. "This was a good friend. *You* had him killed."

Li Hua glanced at the photo. A shiver raced through her body. "I killed no one. Park agreed to his—"

Justin stopped her. "No, you forced him, blackmailed him. In the same way that you're blackmailing Colonel Adianto." He dropped his voice to barely a whisper. "We know how you operate: you lure men who can't keep their pants on, record their sex escapades, and extort intelligence from them. Trapped, they have no choice."

Li Hua cranked her head to the left toward the door. "If you leave right now, I'll convince the colonel not to come after the two of you."

Justin smiled. "If you don't give us intel on Jaw-long, we'll tell the colonel about his sex tape. He would do everything to keep his wife and his children from seeing it, and in order to avoid a scandal, he'll make sure you vanish without a trace. You know he's fully capable of doing that, right?"

Justin's eyes fixed Li Hua with a stern glare.

She looked away out the window, but the right corner of her lips twitched almost involuntarily. Her left leg tapped nervously on the floor.

Justin allowed for a few moments of silence, then said, "All right, Carrie. Let's search the room. The camera should be set up for a good wide angle to clearly record their frolicking."

He looked around the room. "One of the picture frames. Or inside the top cabinet drawers. Or it could be in that lamp there in the corner. It will take us some time, but we'll find it."

Carrie turned over two framed beach landscape scenes, then moved on to the third one, a large painting of a series of temples, which had given Bali the name "island of a thousand temples." Finding nothing, she opened all the cabinet drawers, rummaged through, then shook her head.

"There are no cameras, you're mistaken," Li Hua said with much irritation in her voice.

"I don't think so," Justin said.

He pointed to a tall wooden lamp near the window across from the bed. He looked Li Hua in the eye and said, "I would put the camera right there. The angle is perfect to tape everything in one frame."

Li Hua blinked fast but showed no other sign of panic.

Carrie searched inside the lamp's round reddish shade. Finding nothing, she slid her hand along the lamp's curved wooden body. She felt around it for a few moments, then gave Justin a toothy smile. "Found it." She produced a small pinhole camera about the size of a dime. "Wireless, covert surveillance grade."

Li Hua tried to wriggle out of the handcuffs.

"It's of no use," Justin said to her. "Give us the intel we want and save yourself the embarrassment."

Li Hua shook her head. Her blue eyes had turned black with rage.

"All right, as you wish." Justin stood up and walked toward the wardrobe cabinet on the other side of the bed near the bathroom. "The camera is transmitting the video—and I'm assuming the audio as well—to an electronic recording device, most likely a laptop. What better place to hide it?" He tapped on the cabinet's door. "Your last chance, Li Hua."

She remained silent, her eyes whipping him with their dark glare.

Justin opened the wardrobe and searched through Li Hua's clothes. He found a vault at the back, but it was too small to store a laptop, even a netbook. *Perhaps she's using an iPhone or BlackBerry. We'll have to search her purse.*

He looked down near a row of flip-flops, pumps, and stilettos. Then his gaze fell on Li Hua's pink luggage bag on spinner wheels. He crouched and began to unzip the bag's compartments. Justin found bathing suits, shorts, tank tops, and, at the bottom, a small netbook. *The last place the colonel would search even if he had suspicions.*

He flipped it open and found that the netbook was still on. There was no password, so he stroked the touchpad. The netbook woke up from its hibernation and a video recording software window appeared on the screen, along with a folder in the background. Justin tapped a few keys and began to play the most recent video file. He was glad the netbook speakers were muted. The X-rated video needed no explanation.

"Would you like to have a look?" Justin asked Li Hua as he turned around. The closed netbook was in his hand.

Li Hua's face was red with embarrassment. She sighed. The discovery of the netbook had torn down her defenses. "No," she muttered in a very low, shy voice.

"Jaw-long. Tell me all you know about the man." Justin returned to his chair and handed the netbook over to Carrie.

She held it close without taking as much as a peek.

"I give you the intel, you give me back my netbook and forget everything about me." Li Hua's voice was weak and wavering, but she did her best to regain her composure.

"You're in no position to negotiate terms," Justin said with a firm headshake. "We get the intel, you get to live. But we'll keep the netbook. Our insurance policy that you'll not use any of the intel you extorted from Park. And you'll owe us one."

Li Hua grinned and shook her head. "No, after this exchange, we're even. I don't want to see you anymore."

Justin said, "We're not even. After what you did to Park, you deserve to die. But you're more useful to us as a source of intel. You'll owe us a favor and we'll come to collect one day. Or I give the netbook to the colonel. Make your choice in the next ten seconds."

Li Hua sighed, then swallowed hard. "Fine, fine," she said before three seconds had passed. "You win, you son of a—"

"The intel." Justin cut her off. "We're mostly interested in the operation where Jaw-long involved Park and the entire nuclear affair. But don't leave anything out."

Li Hua nodded and began to talk.

CHAPTER TWENTY-TWO

Klosters, Switzerland
May 6, 04:15 p.m.

The luxury hotel Nouveau Château de Chillon was truly deserving of its famous name. It was lavishly built just a few years ago, replicating some of the fabulous features of the most iconic castle in Switzerland, positioned on the edge of Lake Geneva. It had rounded turrets, sloped roofs, and grand bedrooms. Château de Chillon had always been an impregnable castle ever since it was built, back in the 11th century. The hotel, on the other hand, was accessible to anyone in the new nobility made rich and powerful by petrodollars, the information technology, or music industry.

Justin parked his rental Volkswagen in the guest parking lot to the right side of the hotel's main entrance. He made his way through the circular cobblestone driveway with a leather briefcase in his right hand and waved at the porter dressed in an immaculate maroon uniform. The porter gave him a small bow and pushed open the heavy brass-trimmed glass door, and Justin stepped inside.

The interior design of the lobby was tasteful, a fusion of the antique and the modern. Large dark furniture, wooden chests, crests, flags, and swords blended in style with flat-screen television sets, glass-top coffee tables, and computer screens. Justin glanced to the right and his eyes caught a glimpse of the Camera Domini Restaurant sign carved on a dark maroon crest hanging on the wall. He hurried in that direction.

Before he even opened the restaurant's glass door, Justin noticed the two trusted bodyguards of Prince Fouad bin al-Farhan, who never left his side. They stood near one of the corners by the floor-to-ceiling window that offered patrons a wide panorama of the Alps' majestic peaks stabbing at the fog-encased sky. Prince Al-Farhan was sitting alone at a table set up for four people, his back against the breathtaking views.

Justin entered the quiet half-empty restaurant. He nodded at the pretty redheaded hostess behind the counter and politely declined her offer of a table, informing her that his friend was already there. Justin gestured toward the prince's table, and the hostess's expression changed from one of simple courtesy to a profound interest. Perhaps she thought he was a very important person if he called the Saudi prince a "friend."

The bodyguards had noticed Justin's arrival. One of them took two steps forward, blocking the path leading to the prince's table. The other whispered something into the ear of the prince, who nodded and then dismissed the bodyguard with a wave of his hand.

Justin took in the room as he advanced with a slow gait. A few tables away, a young man perhaps in his late teens was sipping drinks in the company of a gorgeous blonde woman and a similarly striking brunette, who were or could have been high-class fashion models. A baseball cap worn sideways and a thick heavy-looking golden chain fit for a bulldog, hanging around the young man's neck, made Justin think of him as a rapper or some sort of a singer. An older man—perhaps the rapper's manager—was sitting at the table as well and was nodding and smiling at the young man's yammering.

When Justin was six steps away from the prince's table, the bodyguards nailed him with a menacing gaze and gestured for Justin to raise his arms. The obligatory pat-down. Justin placed his briefcase on the floor and allowed one of the bodyguards to go through his jacket and comb him thoroughly. The search turned up two SIG P228 pistols, which the bodyguard pocketed without any questions or comments. Then he rummaged through the briefcase, shook it, and ran his large hands along the bottom, searching for any hidden compartments. Finding nothing suspicious but a thick folder of documents, the bodyguard backtracked and stood about three feet away to the right side of the prince.

"Welcome, Mr. Hall." Prince Al-Farhan gestured at the antique-looking wood-and-metal chair across the table without making an effort to stand up or shake hands. "How are you doing?"

"I'm doing well. How about yourself?" Justin sat down.

His eyes focused on the prince's face. He had aged quite well, and although in his early sixties, he looked much younger, like a man barely forty years old. A full head of silver hair and a meticulously trimmed full beard framed his oval face. The prince wore rimless gunmetal glasses which made his fierce black eyes look a bit larger than they truly were. He had the large aquiline nose typical for the men of the House of Saud and a small wrinkle in the middle of his forehead. Prince Al-Farhan was dressed in a stylish black suit, crisp white shirt, and a black-and-white striped tie.

The prince shrugged. "Eh, can't complain too much. Busy even though I'm on holiday." He pointed at the half-empty champagne glass in front of him. "Care for a drink?"

Justin shook his head. "No, thanks."

The prince arched a bushy eyebrow. "It's non-alcoholic, Mr. Hall. Allow yourself a few simple pleasures."

Justin glanced at the gilded bottle with an emblem that resembled an ace of spades and wondered about its cost. Whatever the amount, it was probably spare change to the millionaire prince. "Sure, why not?"

He looked at the bubbles rising up to the top of the tulip-shaped glass as he poured the champagne.

"A toast." The prince raised his glass. "To good health and prosperity."

They clinked their glasses and drank their toast.

Justin found the champagne slightly sweet with a rich, full flavor. "It's fantastic."

The prince shrugged. His unimpressed face told Justin he had tasted better varieties.

"How's Sameer?" Justin asked.

The prince smiled at the mention of his nephew, whose life Justin and Carrie had saved a few months back during their mission to Tripoli, Libya. "He's fine. His chess skills have improved so much. But let's get to business, shall we?"

Justin nodded. "I'm glad you were able to meet with me on such short notice." He reached for a folder from his briefcase. "I couldn't tell you about this on the phone, you know, with the NSA always listening. But I can show it to you now." He glanced at the bodyguards to his left and right, then whispered, "It's for your eyes only."

"Leave us." Prince Al-Farhan dismissed his bodyguards.

They both nodded and left without a word.

Justin's eyes followed them until they exited the restaurant and stood on the other side of the door. Then he opened his folder and handed the prince the first document. "This is a report about a nuclear incident that occurred in Islamabad on April 6. Someone tried to buy fifteen pounds of highly enriched uranium. You know that's sufficient for a bomb."

The prince glanced at the document and skimmed through the pages. "How is this my problem?"

"The buyer was a high-level Chinese official. That deal went bad, so the official was forced to seek an alternative source for his supply. North Korea."

"Again, why do I need to know this?" Prince Al-Farhan said, a hint of irritation and impatience palpable in his voice.

"Because the final buyer of the weapons-grade uranium is a member of the Saudi royal family."

Prince Al-Farhan fell back in his seat. "You're absolutely sure about your accusation?"

"I wouldn't be here if I had even the slightest doubt." Justin tapped the folder in front of him.

The prince peered at Justin over his glasses. "Who is it?"

"Prince Ismail bin Saud. The evidence is here." He pushed the folder across the table.

The prince was silent. He lifted his glasses to the bridge of his nose and opened the folder. There were a few photographs of Prince Ismail bin Saud meeting with Jaw-long, and others of the prince in various locations in Beijing. The next document was a series of transcripts of calls between the prince or his aides with Jaw-long or his aides. Li Hua had been very devious and thorough in her intelligence gathering. She had made copies of most of Jaw-long's classified files during one of their trysts in his office.

The prince shrugged, then gave Justin a displeased look, like he was wasting his time. "I will verify the authenticity of your documents. These are some serious charges. My cousin . . . he was framed."

Justin nodded. "I wouldn't expect you to take action without a proper investigation and without being fully convinced of his complicity. But we both know this is true. And now it's up to you to decide how you want it handled."

"What are you implying?" the prince demanded in a gruff voice.

"Nothing. I'm just informing you of choices, options. But this intel is time-sensitive and has an immense value. I'm not the only one who is in the know, and soon enough other agencies, our partners, will receive the same files and even more reports. Some of them may have directives about potential solutions."

The prince peered deep into Justin's eyes. "I don't like ultimatums, Mr. Hall." His voice boomed with the same gruffness.

Justin's eyes darted for a moment to the large wall of the room adorned with a spectacular medieval mural. A knight on a white horse reared over his defeated enemies, crushed beneath his hoofs. "Far from it. Consider this a request, a polite and respectful request." He stopped and thought about whether he wanted to clarify his reply. But Prince Al-Farhan was a smart man. He could understand that if the House of Saud did not handle the rogue prince immediately and efficiently, another country would find a lethal way to resolve the problem.

The prince leaned forward. "My country has all the rights to defend itself, Mr. Hall." His voice was lower and calmer. "Our region is threatened by superpowers and we're expected to sit on the side, helpless, and ignore these looming dangers?"

Justin did not answer. He sat there and listened attentively. The prince needed to vent in order to feel better, to feel he was in control of the situation and of his actions.

"America and Iran are shaking hands and approving nuclear deals. If Iran acquires nuclear capacities, we will be defenseless.

The entire region will shake in terror, fearing the war that surely will come. Especially now that America has pretty much pulled out all of its troops from the Gulf."

Justin nodded. Prince Al-Farhan was telling the truth, albeit exaggerating it to fit his own purposes. The U.S. still had a large number of troops in Saudi Arabia and elsewhere in the Arab countries of the Persian Gulf.

The prince continued, "Israel already has the nuclear bomb and now Iran is on its way to securing it. How long do you think before they decide to prove to all who's the strongest country in the region?"

Justin was not sure if the prince expected a reply or was asking a purely rhetorical question. Saudi Arabia had a long history of sparring with Iran about influence in the region and how this influence played out in politics in the neighboring countries of Iraq, Syria, and Lebanon. And now that the relationship between the U.S. and Iran had taken a positive turn, Saudi Arabia did not want to fall behind in the arms game. They had big atomic ambitions, and there was credible intelligence that they were in negotiations to purchase nuclear weapons from Pakistan. The Saudis had funded a part of Pakistan's nuclear projects, so technically they were closer to securing the bomb than Iran. And the only Arab country in possession of a nuclear weapon would be the only Arab country to dominate the region.

The prince was silent, waiting for a reply.

Justin sighed and fell back in his seat. "Look, I'm not a politician or an expert on security matters in the Gulf or elsewhere in the world. But I know this is not the right way to go about gathering nuclear materials or related technology. And before you ask, I don't know which one is the right way. But for sure I know this isn't it."

The prince shrugged and rolled his eyes.

Justin said, "At this point, all I can say is that if this prince is not reined in by the House of Saud, someone else will do so. And they will not have in mind his best interest or the best interest of your family."

He did not need to explain to Prince Al-Farhan that Mossad would not hesitate to take action. Their agents would disrupt any plans of Saudi princes to obtain nuclear technology. Mossad might even engage and assassinate Prince Bin Saud and his close associates.

Prince Al-Farhan dropped his gaze to the folder and did not speak for a few long moments. Then he looked up. His eyes had lost some of their initial wrath. "I will take this matter under advisement," he said in a calm voice. "And . . . it is good you brought this to my attention."

Justin nodded. It was not a "thank you," but close enough. The prince would remember the favor and repay it when the right moment came, as he had done in the past.

"And just so you know, Mr. Hall, my country will demand to enrich uranium to the same extent as Iran. And if Iran makes or buys or obtains the atomic bomb in any other way, Saudi Arabia will do so as well, regardless of what the international community and America may want."

"I fully understand," Justin said.

The prince made a small gesture with his head, and Justin interpreted it as the sign their meeting was over. He stood up.

Prince Al-Farhan also got to his feet and offered Justin his hand.

"Have a safe trip," the prince said.

"Enjoy your stay." Justin pointed at the view.

"Eh, the view remains the same. After coming here twice a year for the last five years, there's nothing there I haven't seen or done."

The bodyguards materialized from thin air. The one who had given Justin a pat-down handed him back his pistols.

Justin put his weapons back in their holsters and buttoned up his jacket. He picked up his briefcase, nodded at Prince Al-Farhan, and walked out of the restaurant.

EPILOGUE

CIS Headquarters, Ottawa, Canada
May 9, 08:20 a.m.

I t had been a quick ten-minute drive for Justin from Anna's townhouse by Rockcliffe Park to the CIS headquarters. Anna's surveillance assignment had taken her to Edmonton, Alberta, and she had been tight-lipped about her operation. They had learned to share only what their secretive jobs allowed them, which was not much. In their case, it had helped their relationship. Since they could not talk about work, they conversed and communicated closely with each other about everything else.

His meeting with Carrie and McClain was taking place in the boss's office, on the fourth floor of the CIS headquarters. Justin ran up the stairs and down the hall. Then he knocked on McClain's office door.

"Come in, Justin," his boss said from inside.

Justin opened the door. "Hello, sir. Carrie."

"Hi, Justin." Carrie was sitting in a black leather chair across from McClain's large, dark oak desk, which was the centerpiece of his office.

"Take a seat," McClain said from behind his desk and pushed his tablet to the side. "How was traffic?"

"Smooth. No construction, no bottlenecks."

"Good, that's good." McClain pulled a white folder from one of his desk drawers. "I reviewed your final reports on the Korean mission, Justin and Carrie. It's very detailed and comprehensive. Good job."

Justin nodded and exchanged a quick glance with Carrie. She gave him a small smile.

McClain said, "Justin, your recommendation about greater and deeper analysis before authorizing similar operations has some very forceful language. You realize that course of action is not always available, like in this case, particularly when there is a strong need to move fast and avoid an intel leak. Still, I will present your report to the director without changing a word or a period."

"Thank you, sir. I know we operate in a muddy environment with plenty of uncertainties. I'm asking that we try harder to save our agents rather than eliminate them, especially when we don't have all the facts. I'd hate to be in the position of Park and Schultz."

McClain leaned forward and placed his elbows on his desk. "Point taken, Justin. British intelligence and the NSA were both consulted before the start of this operation. They were both duped by the Koreans' ingenious maneuvering. And we were tricked as well. But the operation ended well, albeit with partial success."

He took in a deep breath and kept silent for a long moment. It was fitting to pay respects to Park, whose funeral was taking place the next day.

McClain said, "In light of recent events, Quan has presented his resignation. The director is expected to accept it. I had a private meeting with Quan and he expressed his regrets about the false intel and its deadly consequences. It's not much, but there you have it."

Justin frowned and bit his lip. He was thinking of barging into Quan's office and giving him a piece of his mind. McClain's meeting and Quan's resignation had taken Justin by surprise and had disarmed him.

"The good news is that neither the Koreans nor the Chinese have discovered any evidence connecting us to this operation," McClain continued. "They're blaming each other for the border shooting. The North Korean media is ablaze with accusations about the involvement of one or two Western powers but they have said nothing about the prison camp. They mostly blame the CIA and Mossad."

"What about your calls to the Chinese intel about our operation? The decoy," Carrie asked.

McClain frowned for a moment, then shrugged. "It took some time to persuade them, but my Chinese counterparts are convinced we had nothing to do with this shooting. It did look very suspicious at first, and they searched the area where I pointed them but found no traces of any Canadian operatives or their activities. So I explained to them that my agents had aborted their mission at the last moment and had never crossed into the Chinese territory."

Carrie nodded. "The Chinese will have discovered the identities of Jaw-long and his men by now. They will start wondering about their business in the border area and their clash with the North Koreans."

McClain nodded. "Yes, and eventually someone may connect the dots between Jaw-long and the Saudi prince. But that's not our problem anymore."

"You mentioned CIA and Mossad as the potential villains as far as the North Koreans are concerned. Does that mean our British friends are off the hook?" Justin asked.

"Yes. No media or intel reports mention anything about them. Rex and Eve arrived safely in London and have been dispatched on other missions. I have no intel about the prisoners released from the labor camp or Jaw-long's men. If any one of them escaped during the shooting, I do not expect to receive any reports about it. But Chinese authorities are asking pointed questions about the people who boarded the Gulfstream in Yanji. We're stalling them, and soon enough, once all the paperwork and the passports have been finalized, we'll send them the flight manifest."

Justin nodded. "Perhaps the best hundred thousand dollars ever spent," he said, referring to the bribe paid to the Chinese custom officials who allowed Park, Schultz, and the North Koreans to board the plane without proper paperwork.

"Yes, very true. And once all documents are in order, the rest of the Koreans can fly to Vancouver, their preferred new home. It should only be a matter of days."

"I don't understand the delay," Justin said, with a certain amount of frustration in his voice. "It's easier to bring a dog than a human being to Canada. It should be the other way around. Laws are made for people and not people for the law."

"How does the dog like Anna's townhouse?" McClain's said.

"Okay, I think. We named him Park, and he's very unpredictable and a troublemaker. Quite hard to control him during a walk, as he growls and barks at all other dogs, no matter their size or breed. It's like he's saying, 'What are you doing here? This is my neighborhood.'"

"Should have named him Soprano or Corleone," McClain said with a chuckle.

Justin smiled. "Park's the right name and he's a sweet dog. Once he has settled down, he'll behave and keep Anna in good company when I'm away. How are Hong's wife and children doing?"

McClain shrugged. "Vancouver is a huge city, and they're finding it hard to adjust to such a big change and start a new life without Hong. We've provided them some financial support to help them get on their feet. But it will take time for them to heal from Hong's loss."

"We were so close," Justin said, the battle scene as they crossed the Tumen River flashing in front of his eyes. "If Choe had not panicked, Hong probably would still be alive."

"You can't do anything to change the past," Carrie said.

"I know." Justin sighed.

"Talking about healing, Schultz should make a full recovery. Doctors performed some quite complicated and very painful skin grafts for his burns. He'll have some permanent scars but unless there are some unexpected complications, he should be able to return to full duty."

Justin glanced over McClain's shoulders at the stunning views of the Ottawa skyline outside the two floor-to-ceiling windows of his office. His mind raced to Park and he wondered if he would have made a speedy recovery. "I have no further news from Prince Al-Farhan other than what I reported yesterday. I hope the royal family will straighten up their renegade prince."

"That's great." McClain put the white folder back in his desk drawer. He reached to the other side of the desk and picked up two green folders. "And while that mission is dwindling down, this one is heating up."

He slid the folders across the table. Justin picked them up and handed one to Carrie.

McClain said, "You'll be dispatched to Frankfurt, Germany and you'll work with their domestic and foreign intel services, respectively BfV and BND. Palestinian and Lebanese terrorist cells are becoming active in Frankfurt and elsewhere in Germany, and we're investigating potential ties to their associates in our homeland. It seems they're planning something big in the Middle East, but we don't know much more at this point."

Justin browsed through the file, containing reports, photographs, and memorandums. "Germany is not in our jurisdiction. Are we being transferred?"

"No, but after your Korean mission, the prime minister has requested your direct involvement. Our Berlin station will provide a team for this operation. Take twenty-four hours to become familiar with the details, and then take the next flight out to Germany. Questions?"

Justin shook his head.

Carrie said, "No questions, sir."

"All right, then," McClain said. "You have the files. Make initial contact with your partners and as always, be safe."

AUTHOR'S NOTE

Free Book?
Be sure to visit
www.ethanjonesbooks.com
for insider information,
new releases,
and a free spy thriller!

Books by Ethan Jones

Want to know what else I have in this or other series?
For a complete list of my books, including latest releases in each series go to:
www.ethanjonesbooks.com

Javin Pierce Spy Thriller Series

Justin Hall Spy Thriller Series

Carrie Chronicles Spy Thriller Series

Jennifer Morgan Suspense Series

And more!

Made in the USA
San Bernardino, CA
31 August 2019